# *In a Hollow Land*

# *R. P. Poe*

"Our share of night to bear,
Our share of morning,
Our blank in bliss to fill,
Our blank in scorning."

-Emily Dickinson

"Though I am old with wandering
Through hollow lands and hilly lands,
I will find out where she has gone,
And kiss her lips and take her hands"

-W. B. Yeats

To my grandparents, Mary and William Foulks,
"Bami" and "Poppie"

ها

Purify (pyŏŏrə̩fī) - to cleanse; to free from sin, guilt, or other defilement; to rid of impurities

# One

Even God had fallen out of his reach and he knew it, he could feel it. He had crossed a line, a line not entirely of his own making but his nonetheless, a line only he knew, only he saw, beyond it failure, shame, the not measuring up, the not moving past, the endless purgatory of waiting, wondering. He wished for some sort of miracle, some magic to erase all that had led him to this point, knowing well his folly, seeing no escape but what lay on the table before him.

He stared at the bulging rag then reached for it, unwrapping the gray felt, lifting a small revolver free of the cloth, surprised at the weight, the smoothness of the wood, the cool of the trigger. Light glinted off the black metal. Peering into the dark sheen, he lost himself in the reflection, the cause of his failures in work and love just out of reach, lurking in a place unknowable, beyond understanding.

He took the barrel with one hand, pointing it at his chest, placing his thumb against the trigger. He tried to imagine the blast, the recoil of the gun, the force of the bullet, and could almost feel the peace that lay beyond the moment. Shutting his eyes, he pressed the barrel into his ribs.

A knock sounded at the door. He looked up, again seeing her in his mind's eye framed by the kitchen doorway, a bag slung over one shoulder, another in her hand. She squinted at him, telling him she must leave, must escape the black despair of his presence, a rolling disgust clear in her dark eyes. He tried to speak but words escaped his mouth without a sound, vanishing into the lightless corners like bluebottle flies. A shadow of emotion crossed her face. For an instant he wondered if she might have feelings for him still, feelings even she failed to see. Taking a breath, he managed to say her name.

"Justine…"

He paused then spoke again. "Justine, we can work this out. I just need a little time, a little luck. Things will get better."

"You should've never lured me into having a fling." She squinted at him.

"I'm not sure who lured who, Justine."

"My ex, he knew how to take care of a woman proper, in the right style and all, with money, and things, and... money. I didn't need to leave just because he hit me some. At least with him I could live decent."

He rapped his finger against the table as he spoke. "I've worked as hard as anyone else to make a living. I lost count of the places I've applied since I've been out of work. I even gambled on the market with my savings. I did that for you, Justine. There's no way I could've known the economy would tank when it did."

"Don't blame your money problems on me. I didn't ask you to lose your shirt on bad investments. Besides, I know about your fling with that cute little sales rep."

He shook his head, a pained look in his eyes.

"We had one kiss at a party after I'd had a few too many. We were both embarrassed by it. It was nothing, Justine."

"Oh sure, and I guess staying out until four in the morning was just being friendly."

"She was in the middle of a breakup and upset. I was there to listen. Nothing happened."

"No, you're wrong. Something did happen but you just can't admit it. One kiss means somewhere deep down you knew we were through. You never could face the facts. You like to live in your little made-up world where the sun always shines and everything turns out fine in the end. Well, that's not the way the real world works. We were all wrong from the start. You should know that by now."

The knock came again, louder, forceful, pulling him from his dark thoughts. He stood, wrapping the cloth around the pistol as he moved through the house, still

2

caught in his dream of her, dazed, uncaring of the moment, of why someone would come to his home at such an hour.

Opening the door, he peered into the still night, the porch landing empty, no sign of the unwanted visitor. He waited, head cocked, listening but hearing no voice, no word of greeting, no sound other than his own breath. In spite of his apathy, a latent fear began to grow in his chest.

An instant later a figure appeared out of the shadows, the side of his face pale, ghost-like, highlighted by the broken light of the doorway. Black hair spilled across his forehead. He paused to survey the house, his face turned aside, his eyes revealing nothing, emotionless, reptilian.

Then the man stepped onto the porch, pulling a switchblade from his pocket and flicking it open. Light from the blade jumped about the ceiling as he scraped black grit from beneath his fingernails. After a moment he spoke, his accent odd, unidentifiable.

"I am looking for a girl."

"You're looking for a girl? Who is she?"

"She is a runaway."

"And who are you?"

"What do you mean?"

"Your name, what is your name?"

The man frowned, flustered by the question. "My name?"

"You don't have a name?"

"I am looking for a girl."

"In this country it's the custom to tell a person your name before you start asking questions."

The man squinted at him with his sideways stare then held the knife to the light, studying the blade before again looking up. "I am Zoran Jorvic. Your light is on so I thought perhaps you might have seen such a person."

"I haven't seen anyone." He glanced at the man, trying to get a better look at his face in the dim light without seeming like it, the fear growing.

"She is young and quite attractive."

3

"Why would she come here?"

"She is beautiful and knows how to use her beauty to get what she desires."

"What would she want with me?"

The man looked at him askance, unwilling to face him. "Who can know the ways of such women?"

"Like I said, I haven't seen anyone."

"She has, as they say, difficulty with the truth. She is a fraud, a liar."

"Why are you telling me this?"

"She might have convinced you she needs help."

He shook his head, trying not to show his growing irritation with the stranger, the mess of his life again crowding in. "Since I haven't seen her, how is that possible?"

"She can be persuasive."

"You should check elsewhere."

"Where would you suggest?"

"How would I know?"

"I believe she is here."

He felt the anger move up his chest and into his throat, replacing despair with something tangible, something he could act on, and for an instant he felt a surprising sense of gratitude to the stranger in spite of his fear. Then the anger swelled, sweeping him along.

"You need to leave."

"You deny you have seen her?"

"You have a hell of a nerve asking me that."

"Then you are here alone?"

"That's none of your damn business."

"You take chances with your denials. I think you hide something."

"I won't say it again. You need to leave."

"You are mistaken if…"

The man's face darkened and he took a step back, staring at him. Following the man's gaze, he looked down, spotting the pistol resting against his thigh, the felt cover fallen away. An instant later the man disappeared into the night.

Lim Specter woke with a start. Sitting up, he looked about the room, realizing he had fallen asleep at his desk. The image of the man with the switchblade flashed through his mind as he recalled the puzzle of their conversation and its effect on him. The pistol still lay before him. He wrapped the gray felt around the gun, placing it in a drawer and locking it.

Behind him a low whine of voices sounded through a half-open window, just out of hearing. Straining to make out the words, he slipped out of the chair, walking to the window and lifting a corner of the blinds with one finger, careful to move them as little as possible.

Across the street stood a bearded man and a woman, her black hair wrapped in a red scarf. They loitered beneath the streetlight, picking through a trash bin and dropping tin cans into a large burlap sack. Unable to understand their words, he watched them as he tried to clear his mind. The woman nodded toward the house before facing her companion.

"I feel a bad wind coming to this house, Merton. I feel it strong."

"You been reading those witchcraft books again, haven't you, Bruey? I thought you said you were done with that nonsense."

She waved the air with her hand. "Who says it's nonsense? You're just a bum, Merton. What do you know about witches?"

"Just because we're poor and live by the railroad tracks doesn't mean we're bums."

"I wasn't talking about myself, Merton. You're the only bum I see around here."

"I'm not a bum, Bruey. I'm a pilgrim."

"A pilgrim, is it? Then find us some turkey. I'm hungry."

5

"Not that sort of pilgrim, Bru. I'm transitory in the material world, a lost soul in search of meaning."

"From what I can see your search mostly leads to a bottle. Anyway, if your soul wasn't so lost you could see the man in that house has big trouble coming his way. He has been cursed."

He snorted, raising his head from the trash can. "What do you mean he's been cursed? You don't even know the man. How could you know if someone put a curse on him?"

"Ha! I got you on that one, Mert. I could know because I can see it." She tapped her finger against his chest. "Some witches cast a spell on him, take my word for it. Now get yourself ready to see their handiwork."

Merton leaned back into the can, his voice booming from within. "What on earth are you going on about, Bruey? You don't know a thing about spells or curses or witches neither. Help me get these cans out of here so we can cash them in and get us something to drink."

"It's true, Mert. My grandmother was a brujilda, a Mexican witch, and she taught me everything she knew about the dark arts, as they call them. She was a strong-willed woman and I was her favorite grandchild. She even picked my name. My mother wasn't too happy about that. So, I come by witching naturally."

"Why didn't you ever say so before now, Bruey? I think all those books of yours have gone to your head. I'm going to stop bringing home what I find. Or maybe you're just messing with old Mert. I'm too thirsty to be messed with. It's cruel to mess with a man as thirsty as I am." He stared into the distance, licking his lips.

"Okay, Mert, be your old stubborn self and don't believe me. But some witch or witches put a spell on the man. He's a man of science but he crossed someone and now he's about to have a taste of the other side of this world, the side of magic and miracles."

"Now why would he get a taste of that, Bru?"

6

"He probably did his woman wrong somewhere along the line. Or maybe one of his ancestors did and now it's finally catching up with the family. That's what spells are used for, to make things right, to get justice. I'd do it if I was asked and there was reason enough."

"I don't buy it, Bruey." He dismissed her with a wave of his hand. "Even if you did learn about curses, why hex somebody you don't hardly know? Why not spell someone that deserves it, like that lying Thurman Stiles? He still hasn't paid me for running those squirrels out of his attic even though he's said he would more than once."

"Thurman is my cousin. I won't go so low as to put a curse on my own family."

"But you'd put one on some feller you don't even know?"

"Are you calling me a liar? I don't tolerate disrespect, Merton, even from you. A man could get a spell put on him for that or even less."

"I'm not disrespecting you, Bruey. Besides, I got me enough curses to last a lifetime. I don't need any more. What's going to happen to the man, anyway?"

"He's about to get bad news in spades, that's what. And then his past is going to... Wait! There's somebody coming, Mert." She cocked her head to listen.

"Put on your sad look, Bruey. Maybe they'll drop some cash on us if we look real pitiful."

She frowned at him. "I'm not looking pitiful for you or anyone else. Besides, I don't want to get run out of here just when this story is about to get good."

"But Bruey, last night you put on the best pitiful act I ever did see."

"That wasn't an act, Merton. I was having a bad night. I need to find a spell that gets rid of hot flashes. Anyway, hurry up. Here they come."

"I got just one more can to fish out..." Merton bent over the trash can.

She grabbed the back of his shirt. "Lordy, Mert, one of them has a badge. We're not supposed to be out here, remember? The law has warned us twice already."

A voice called from down the street. "Hey you! What are you doing over there?"

"Run for it, Bruey!"

"Head for the alley behind the cursed man's house, Mert! I know a place we can hide back there."

Lim watched as the man and woman scurried into the darkness, leaving vacant the pool of light across from his house. A moment later, two men appeared, one in uniform, the other wearing a wrinkled suit. They ambled along the street together, staring at Lim's house. For a moment he wondered if they knew he knelt behind the blinds watching them. Then the man in uniform pulled a paper from his shirt pocket, studying it before turning to his companion.

"Hold it right there, Run. Now, let's see here. According to these papers, that house over there is the one we're looking for."

"Of course it is. The bank owns the house and I work for the bank. Don't you think I've been by here before?"

"There's not a single light on so I don't believe anyone is at home. I reckon we'll just have to wait for him to show."

"How long do we have to wait, Constable? I got no time to dillydally while this criminal is off carousing."

"The man is no criminal, Run. He just can't pay his mortgage. Besides, Judge Hackett likes me to serve the papers in person."

The man in the rumpled suit took a step back. "You mean old Mace in the Face Hackett signed those eviction papers?"

"He did and I know better than to cross The Hatchet."

"I went to grade school with Mace Hackett. If you ask me, he's just a washed up judge that's been on the bench too long."

8

"How about if I pass that along to the Judge, Run? I'll bet he'd like to know what you think of him."

"What?" He took another step back. "Don't even say that! It's bad luck to even kid about such a thing."

"I believe you're scared of him, Run."

"I got my job to think of, Constable. The bank won't like it if I get on the wrong side of The Hatchet."

"If you say so, Run."

"Here's a neighbor coming up the street. Order him over here and find out what you can about this feller."

"I can't order people around like I was their boss."

"I'll do it, then." Run stepped into the pool of light. "Hey you! Sheriff Cherrybark here needs to see you right away about a crime. You can get yourself thrown into the pen if you don't cooperate."

The Constable frowned at him. "I'm no sheriff and there's been no crime, Run. Don't be causing any trouble or you'll be the one that gets locked up."

"The man reneged on his loan."

"Run, you spend too much time harassing people. Last time I checked there's no law against being poor."

"Sheriff Cherrybark is a busy man." Run waved at the man. "Snap to it, mister... what's your name?"

A short, round man, nervous and agitated, stepped beneath the streetlight, looking to each of them in turn. "The name's Carson Philbank. What's happened? Was my house robbed?"

"You sure your name's not Specter?"

"Of course I'm sure."

"What does the man look like, then?"

"He's average height and medium build with brown hair, not short but not long."

"That's real helpful, Mr. Philbank. The man you describe sounds like ten thousand other miscreants walking the streets."

"I guess so... except for his eyes. They're brown almost to black and when he looks at you a certain way,

9

you know to give him your attention, your complete attention. There's a hardness there, a determination. What's this all about?"

"My name's Run Settles and I work for the bank. Where do you live, Mr. Philbank?" Run peered at him.

"Well, I…"

"It's against the law to withhold information from the Sheriff, you know."

The Constable moved next to Run. "I'm not the Sheriff, Run. Don't lie to the man."

"I live right over… what did you say?"

"I'm Constable Dub Cherrybark not the Sheriff himself."

Run waved off the explanation. "You're still a lawman. Give him the fifth degree, Constable."

"It's the third degree, Run, and this is no interrogation."

"Constable, am I in trouble or something?"

"No sir, Mr. Philbank, you're not. Run here has got his self a little worked up is all. He gets that way when he's about to evict somebody."

"But I paid last month's mortgage."

"Philbank, if that's your real name, you live in that house?" Run pointed at Lim's house.

"Why no, Mr. Settles. I live a few houses down."

"What do you know about the man who lives here? I believe he goes by the name of Limerick Specter but that could be an alias. These sorts have usually done this kind of thing before."

"What kinds of things are you talking about?"

Constable Cherrybark stepped between Run and the little man. "Run, do you want me to do the asking or not?"

'Right you are, Constable. Put him on the hot seat. Sweat it out of him."

"Ignore him, Mr. Philbank. What can you tell us about your neighbor?"

"I know he lost his contract job some months back, maybe even a year now, and has been struggling to make ends meet. He had been without a job for a year or two before that. He does something scientific, computers I think. Lots of people are having trouble in these hard times. I didn't know he was about to be evicted."

"I don't believe the man is aware of the situation either. What else do you know about him?"

"Well, Lim seems nice enough in a quiet sort of way. He's not much of a talker but he's always willing to help out if something comes up. He's been under a particularly black cloud the last few days."

The Constable cocked his head. "I don't catch your meaning, Mr. Philbank."

"Well Constable, first it's the threatening calls, then his truck catches fire and he barely makes it out in time, and to top it off someone breaks into his house."

"I didn't hear anything about a break-in."

"He said nothing was taken so he didn't bother to report it."

"Did he say anything about leaving town, Mr. P.?" Run squinted at Philbank. "The bank has had a rash of these types skipping out on their loans."

Philbank kept his eyes on the Constable. "He's really going to lose his house, Constable?"

"Yes sir, it appears so. Does anyone else live in the house?"

"He had a girlfriend."

"Do I take that to mean she no longer lives there?"

"She left. She said she couldn't stand living with a loser anymore. I know because after she told him she came over to my place to use the phone."

"That might drive a man to do something foolish." The Constable pulled at his ear.

Philbank shook his head. "He believes she'll come back."

11

"What makes you think that, Mr. P.?" Run peered into his face.

"He said so to my face, Mr. Settles. He said he if he can just get some things straightened out, she'll come back. He said it might take a couple of days and he asked me to keep an eye on the house while he's gone."

The Constable grabbed Run by the shoulder, pulling him away. "Are you sure about that, Mr. Philbank?"

"That's what he said, Constable."

"Well, I'm done here." Run threw up his hands. "There's no sense in standing around in the dark if the man won't be back anytime soon, even if he does plan to return. My money's on him skipping out. Just the same, go ahead and slap that foreclosure notice on the door, Constable. I'll call the locksmith to come change the locks."

"I don't need you to tell me how to do my job, Run."

Philbank held up a hand. "There's something else. When Lim's girlfriend came over to my place, she called the Sheriff to come get her."

"She called the Sheriff?" Run leaned toward him, squinting. "What the hell for?"

"It was not official business, I can tell you that. She tried to hide it but I could see clear as day they're having an affair."

Run jumped backwards. "She's cavorting with Catfish Hamm? Well, that puts a kink in the old weeter, don't it, Constable?"

"You got that right, Run. We best tread carefully." He nodded. "You go ahead and call your locksmith. I'm going to do some checking around before I post this notice."

As Lim watched, the two men turned to leave just as another figure in uniform appeared at the edge of light, waving a handful of papers over his head. Lim's curiosity finally took control. Leaving the window, he crept through the kitchen and out the back door, hurrying down the alleyway and around the corner. He stopped before a thick hedge, crouching within earshot of the men. Constable

Cherrybark and Run pivoted at the sound of the man's voice.

"Stand aside you men. I got me some certificated papers here that I need to serve on a dangerous criminal. Why, hello Constable. What are you doing here?"

Run leaned toward Philbank, whispering to him. "Mr. P., are you going let on you know about the Sheriff and the man's girlfriend having them a fling? This could get dicey, you know."

"Are you crazy? I don't want to get on the Sheriff's bad side anymore than you do."

"You men forget how to talk?" The man in uniform surveyed the group. "You look like you just saw a ghost."

Run grinned at him. "Well, if it isn't Deputy Lindheimer. I knew the law would show up sooner or later. We got us a real crime scene here, Mr. P."

"The house across the street is being foreclosed upon, Deputy." The Constable held up his papers. "I have my own set of papers. What might yours be for?"

"Well, Constable, I'm looking for a Limerick Specter, last known to be cohabitating with that address directly across the street. His former employer has sworn out a warrant for his arrest. He says the man did some temporary contacting with the firm and transponded with company funds."

Philbank held up a finger. "I don't know that I'd believe that. Lim told me the business has been struggling for months and he suspects his boss is doing some funny financing."

"We have relatable coronation of the crime from other employees. This man violated the law and will be held equitable, just like it says under the Constitution."

"The Constitution doesn't say anything about absconding company funds."

"And who might you be?"

"Carson Philbank, Lim's neighbor."

"Don't let yourself be fooled, mister. It's a short step from fraud to rape and murder. We've got ourselves a desperated man here. Beware, gentlemen, these criminal types will confabricate anything to get people's sympathetics going."

Philbank shook his head. "I don't believe he's done what they say."

"Think what you want, mister, but he's still going to have to make a formal apparition before the judge."

"That may take awhile, Deputy. We have it from a reliable source that Mr. Specter won't be back for a couple of days. Might as well save yourself the trouble and go home."

"I don't know that I trust that testamentation. Who is this reliable source of yours, Constable?"

"I'm the source, Deputy." Philbank raised his hand. "Lim told me to my face."

"And you believed a known prefabricator of falsies, Mr. Philbank?"

"What did you say?"

"The man is not to be trusted."

"I've known Lim for years and he's never lied to me before. Why would he start now? You sound like you've already decided he's guilty."

"I know of the criminal elegants and they'll lie to save their skins without lamentation." He tapped the papers with his finger. "But since I got a whole raft of warrants to serve, I best come back later. I'll bid you men a salacious night."

The Deputy turned, disappearing the way he had come. Run threw up his hands.

"I'm done wasting my time on this case. I got other fish to fry and the night is young, gentlemen, not to mention salacious. I'll get the boys out to change the locks in the morning."

The Constable faced Philbank. "I'd better do that checking around before we have some real trouble on our

14

hands. Mr. Philbank, I thank you for your time. You best not speak about this to anyone. If you see Mr. Specter, call me right away."

He handed Philbank a card. Run followed by pulling a business card from his shirt pocket.

"You won't forget to call me too, will you Mr. P.? You know I can be of assistance if you ever have bank troubles."

Philbank held up both hands and stepped away. "You mean the way you're helping Lim?"

"No need to get testy, Mr. P. I have a job to do just like the Constable here."

As he returned the card to his pocket, the Constable pointed a finger in his face. "I'd appreciate it if you'd not compare me to yourself, Run. I believe I'd be dogcatcher before I'd do your job."

Run looked from one to the other. "Well, I can see my expertise is no longer appreciated around here so I'll be on my way."

-He disappeared into the darkness. The Constable nodded at Philbank.

"You take care, Mr. Philbank. You have yourself one touchy situation next door. Goodnight, then."

## Two

Lim watched as Philbank paced the middle of the sidewalk, muttering to himself as the Constable's footsteps echoed into the distance. A streetlamp buffeted by the coursing wind cast a vibrating pool of light at his feet. Surveying the street in both directions, Lim struggled with whether to call out to him. The Constable's car disappeared around the corner and he again heard Carson talking to himself, louder than before.

"Poor Lim, what did he do to deserve this? It's almost like he's been cursed." He stopped pacing and turned to face Lim's house. "What a strange thing to say. Why would I think that?"

As he turned to leave, Lim called from behind the hedge.

"Carson, wait!"

-Startled, he jumped back onto the curb.

"Who's there?"

"I'm over here, Carson." Lim emerged from the bushes.

"Lord Almighty, Lim!"

"Are the lawmen are gone for good?"

"You took the breath right out of me, stepping out of the dark like some sort of a ghost.'

"You mean a specter don't you, Carson?"

"How can you joke at a time like this?"

"My entire life is a joke."

"What are you doing here, Lim? I thought you were off somewhere trying to fix things with your girlfriend."

"I was. I spent all last night and today searching for her. I think she must be having an affair."

"I wouldn't know about that." Carson peered down the street, avoiding his gaze. "So, how did you end up back here?"

"I needed to think so I came home but was so exhausted I fell asleep at my desk. Then voices outside the house woke me."

He faced Lim again. "I told the Constable you were away and would be for a couple of days."

"Will you turn me in now?"

"Of course not, Lim." He waved off the question. "I was just trying to act agreeable so they'd leave. How much of their talk did you hear?"

"I know the bank plans to take my house."

"Is that all?"

"And I know my ex-boss has accused me of stealing funds from the company."

"Did you do it?"

"Not exactly."

"What did happen then?"

"I borrowed money from the company without telling him and then lost it to the stock market."

"That sounds bad, Lim."

"I paid it back."

"So that's why he reported you."

"The company is bankrupt, Carson." Lim paced as he spoke. "My guess is he's trying to blame me so he can make off with whatever money is left instead of letting the bank have it. It's a clever plan if you think about it. I'm left fighting the charges while he skips out to who knows where."

"Revenge is an ugly thing, Lim. What will you do?"

"I don't know. That three month contract was the only work I've had in the last two years. And I used the last of my savings to pay back the money I borrowed."

"You're broke?"

"I'm beginning to think I'll never have a real job again. I've gotten myself into dire straights, haven't I?"

"It'll get worse if they find you. Maybe you should go away for awhile."

"I don't have anywhere else to go."

"You can't stay here. They're going to change the locks soon."

"I heard."

"I almost forgot. I came to check on your house this morning and I found this on the doorstep."

Carson pulled a letter from his pocket and handed it to him. Lim tore open the envelope, lifting out the paper and reading it aloud.

"Someone you think of as kin
The one who this letter did send
Is seeking your aid
In keeping a maid
From finding an untimely end"

"It's a poem. What does it mean, Lim?"

"Who knows? It's actually a limerick, and not a very good one."

"A limerick as in your name? Is that a coincidence?"

"I doubt it. Did you see anyone around that might have left it?"

"Some guy has been picking through the trash but he doesn't seem like the poet type. He usually has a strange-looking woman with him. She gives me the creeps. I told her to stop hanging around in the alley behind my house and she acted like she was putting a hex on me. She did a sort of ritual and recited some mumbo-jumbo. She even drew a weird symbol on my sidewalk."

"I've seen her hanging around too. She does seem a little odd."

"That's an understatement. I get the willies just thinking about her. Have you talked to her? Maybe she got us mixed up and put a curse on you instead of me."

"That's just what I need."

"I haven't seen anyone else."

"You didn't see a guy with pale skin and black hair?"

"No, who is he?"

"I don't know. He came by earlier asking about a girl. My guess is he has something to do with this but I can't see how."

"The limerick mentions your kin. Do you have any family around here?"

"I lost my parents when I was a kid."

"Both of them?"

"My father committed suicide and a month later my mother disappeared."

"She just vanished?"

"She had gone off sailing by herself, something she would never let me do. They found the boat but not her."

"Good lord, Lim, I'm sorry."

"It was a long time ago."

"That must've been hard for you."

"I don't like to talk about it, Carson."

"Okay. So, we should get back to the letter. There's something in there about an untimely end. What could it mean?"

"I have no idea."

"I think I see some writing on the back."

Lim turned over the paper, studying it for a moment. "It's a drawing of my house and yard. There's a star where the back porch should be."

"That must mean there's something more. Shouldn't you go check?"

"I suppose that's the only way we're going to solve this riddle."

They turned toward the house, the windows standing dark, the porch deep in shadow. Above the roof, black silhouettes of trees groaned before the wind.

"Uh... well, sorry, Lim but I have someplace I have to go. It's, uh... work. I have something to see to, uh... at the office... someone I have to meet. In fact, I'm already late. I'd better get moving."

"You have a meeting at this hour?"

"You know how important work is. Oh, uh… sorry, Lim. That was an unfortunate way to put it."

"But Carson, what if…"

"I'd better be on my way then."

Carson hurried down the street, quickly disappearing inside his house.

Lim squinted at his porch, looking for some clue that might explain the odd letter. Who could have written it and why now, of all times? He knew he should be tending to the important matters pressing in on his life, yet the problems he faced seemed to fade as he pondered the strange note. He peered into the shadows as he crossed the empty street and climbed the porch steps.

Pushing past the front door, he lifted a baseball bat from the hat rack and moved across the living room and down the hall, angling toward the kitchen and the back porch beyond. The house lay silent around him. As he stepped onto the kitchen tiles, the back door swung open in a wide arc, its hinges singing.

He stopped and stood still, peering into the dimly lit doorway, imagining the man with the pale face just beyond. Then a shadow appeared on the floor before him. An instant later the front doorbell rang. Out of habit, he turned toward the sound just as a voice sounded from the back doorway.

"Don't answer that, Limerick Specter."

He pivoted, raising the bat above his head as a man stepped through the doorway. Wearing a gray beard and black collarless shirt, he resembled a priest except for the mischievous, almost sinister, gleam to his blue eyes. Lim stared at his ruddy face, feeling a dim recognition just beneath his consciousness. He blinked, squinting as the man cocked his head, the hint of a smile passing across his lips.

"You don't recognize me, then?"

"Am I supposed to?"

"Has it really been that long?"

Lim lowered the bat and leaned forward, peering at the man. "You do look like someone I once knew."

"Once knew but no more?"

"I can't say for certain."

"It's true. There's nothing certain in this life."

"Wait a second... Uncle Luster? Is it you?"

"You do remember after all."

"What are you doing here?"

"I've come to find you. I need your help."

"You need my help? What with?"

"First we must leave here without delay."

The doorbell rang again, followed by a pounding knock."

"But there's someone at the door."

"That's why we need to leave."

"But why are you here? Where have you been for so long?"

"There'll be time for that later. For now, you must trust your uncle and follow."

He disappeared through the door. Lim stood frozen in place, unsure of what to do, whether or not to answer the door, whether or not he would be arrested if he did. He glanced back into the house, thinking he might never see it again.

Then he moved past the doorway, down the porch steps and into the darkness beyond. In the dim light of the yard he caught sight of Luster stepping through the wooden fence that opened onto the alley. Voices sounded from the front of the house and Lim hurried across the yard, pushing through the gate and nearly running into a small green sedan idling in the middle of the alleyway.

Luster waved him inside. An instant later they were speeding along the alley, past gap-toothed fences and the backs of houses. Emerging from the alley and onto a cross street, they turned south and then west along the main highway, the city lights racing by Lim's window in a blur before dimming as the outskirts of town thinned to darkness.

Before him, a blood-red moon perched on the black horizon like a glowing eye. As he stared into the distance, an image of the woman in the red scarf came to him and he suddenly felt as if his life might be cursed after all. He turned to face Luster.

"Why did you come back?"

"How old are you, Lim?"

"What?"

"Do you know how old you are?"

"Of course I do."

"Well then?"

"I turned thirty-two last month."

"Could you really be that old?"

"I'd have thought you of all people would remember my age. You were always the birthday man, baking the cake, making me dance with my mother, leading the badly done birthday song."

"Badly done song, you say? The song was my favorite part, although your father could never hold a tune. But time has a way of collapsing in on itself when you reach a certain age, Lim. Things you hardly noticed suddenly become very important."

"Is that why you came back? Have you reached a certain age?"

"I came to you because I need your help. Didn't you read my limerick?"

"I should've known it was you. You're the only person on earth who would leave a limerick instead of an ordinary note."

"Never settle for ordinary, Lim. Life is far too short. Each day should be extraordinary."

"Still philosophizing, I see. Some things never change. But enough of your words of wisdom. I'm sitting in some beater car in the middle of the night heading who knows where and I'd like to hear why."

"Harriet is not some beater car. She's a vintage 1968 Renault."

"You call your car Harriet?"

"Don't you remember?" He patted the steering wheel. "I named her after the tortoise Charles Darwin brought back from the Galapagos Islands. Harriet lived to the ripe age of one hundred seventy-five and I'm hoping my Harriet will last as long."

"Stop stalling, Luster. Why are we speeding down the highway in your vintage beater?"

A voice spoke out of the darkness behind him, the accent hanging in the air like a scent. "It is because of me."

Lim turned, squinting into the dim light until the profile of a woman emerged. Silhouetted by the gray horizon, she stared out the window, the auburn sheen of her hair iridescent in the swirling wind.

"Luster is helping me find my sister, Mirela. My name is Ileana."

"Your sister disappeared?"

"She was kidnapped by people in Romania, my father's country, people who knew him, people that he owed money."

"They're making your father pay to get her back?"

"My father is dead."

"I'm sorry to hear it."

"Be sorry for my sister. These men will make her work to pay the money back."

"Why doesn't she just leave?"

"She is their captive, their slave."

"What sort of work?"

"They will keep her as a prostitute and take the money she earns. If she tries to leave, they will kill her. But Luster will get her back. I know he will. He is a magician, you know."

"He's a magician?"

"Yes, he is."

"Well, he did pull quite a disappearing act once, a long time ago. Isn't that right, Luster?"

"Lim, many events lay in the past, events you know little of. But now we have a young woman who needs our help."

She leaned toward him, suddenly becoming visible in the dashboard light. "You will help us, won't you, Lim? I can't stand to think what will become of my sister if we don't find her." Lim stared into her luminous gray eyes, her beauty taking all thought, all words from his mind. With difficulty, he turned back to Luster.

"I don't know if I'll be much good to you. I may even be the opposite with the sort of luck I've been having. I mean, not much else could go wrong with my life. In fact, I was just wondering if someone put a curse on me."

"Why would you say that, Lim? Did something strange happen?"

"Well Luster, do you mean something other than losing my house, my truck and my girlfriend, not to mention having the law after me for something I didn't do?"

"I know all about that."

"How could you know?"

"Don't waste your time worrying about such worldly matters, Lim. They hold little of importance."

"You wouldn't say that if they happened to you."

"But you did see something odd, something you can't explain?"

"Not exactly."

"What do you mean by 'not exactly'?"

"There was something but it's hardly worth mentioning."

"Sometimes the smallest happenings are the ones most worth mentioning. What did you see?"

"It was probably only my mind trying to make me feel like less of a screw-up."

"Tell it to me exactly."

"There's not much to tell. A strange woman has been hanging around my house, or what used to be my house. She threatened to put a hex on my neighbor after he did something to offend her. He said she drew some symbol on his sidewalk and did some sort of ritual."

"What did she draw?"

"He didn't say."

"Do you believe in the supernatural, in the magical, Lim?"

"If you can make me wake up from this bad dream, I'll believe anything."

"Don't you know that there's more to this life than what we can see with our eyes or hear with our ears?"

"I'm having enough trouble believing all I *can* see. Why would I want to believe in what I can't, especially if it's likely to bring more bad news?"

"What an unnecessary and bleak view of life, Lim. I'm saddened to hear it, and from you of all people, with your history."

"What history?"

"There's so much that's magical all around you, Lim, so much that makes life worth living, that opens up avenues, new possibilities. But you've taken on such a pedestrian outlook. I can't understand how it could happen. I fear you'll miss out on all that really matters."

"What does this have to do with the woman?"

"The woman?"

"The woman you asked about."

"Was she wearing a red scarf?"

"How did you know? Did you see her?"

"I had a sense of her."

"What do you mean?"

"Never mind and answer Ileana's question. Are you willing to help or not?"

Lim turned toward her, seeing her form outlined in the window, imagining the curve of her face, the sheen of her hair, the luminous glow of her gray eyes. He shifted his gaze to Luster, feeling rootless, adrift. Then he nodded into the darkness.

"I don't see that I have much choice."

Three

They lapsed into the awkward silence of near-strangers. The narrow highway, crowded by blonde grass and scrub, appeared out of the thickening night before slipping past. Beyond the roadside, dim shapes of cattle emerged from the blackness, hovering above the featureless earth like moonlit clouds.

Road cuts of roughhewn limestone, layered in hues of yellow and orange, flashed between the headlights. Racing past the windows, they seemed the architecture of some undiscovered race. Above the highway, clusters of stars vanished then reappeared then vanished again, tracing the distant hilltops in silhouette.

Lim thought of his lost home and a plan for the future that now seemed little more than a fool's errand. Staring into the darkness, he felt it all fading from memory like a pipedream. He looked over at Luster, trying to shake off his grim mood.

"You never did say where we're headed."

"You never asked."

"Sure I did."

"You asked why, not where."

"So, I'm asking now."

"I know someone in Syracuse."

"We're driving to New York?" Lim leaned toward him. "That'll take days."

"Of course it would, Lim. That's why we're going to the town of Syracuse, not far from where we are now. I'm surprised you don't know of it."

"I've been too busy looking for work to get out much. I guess I don't have to worry about that anymore."

Lim turned toward the back seat, grateful for a chance to speak to Ileana. "Is that where your sister is, Ileana, in Syracuse?"

"My friends call me Ili."

"Is that where she is, Ili?"

"We don't know where she is. Not yet, anyway. But I know Luster's magic will find her."

"Why do you keep talking about Luster as if he's some sort of sorcerer?"

"I say it because I believe it, because it's true."

"What would make you think that?"

"Luster can tell you."

He faced Luster. "What's all this talk about magic?"

"Never mind about that, Lim. What we need I hope to find in Syracuse."

"Why a town in the middle of nowhere?"

"The people of Syracuse would be offended to hear you say it's the middle of nowhere."

"Okay, it's somewhere but why go there?"

"We're going because we need a place to stay for the night, and I want to take a look at a portrait that might help us in our search."

"What sort of portrait?"

"It's actually a plate out of a book, an engraving, but it's also a well-known portrait in its own right."

"What's a famous piece of art doing way out here?"

"You'll see."

"It seems like a lot of time and effort just to look at a picture."

Luster's face seemed to light up in the dashboard glow. "I also have my own reasons for going."

"You're sounding mysterious again, Luster. Is this more of your so-called magic?"

"Like I said, Lim, mystery and magic are all around you if you're open to them."

"Speaking of mystery, who was at the front door when you showed up? You acted like you knew."

Ili's voice came from behind him and he turned as she emerged from the darkness, her eyes luminous, compelling. "Those were the men Luster saved me from, Lim, the same men who took my sister."

"They kidnapped both you and your sister?"

"Yes, but they separated us and lucky for me Luster came along. I don't know how but suddenly he appeared and I was able to slip away. It was like magic."

"It sounds like luck."

"It was not luck, Lim. It was magic. Why won't you believe me?"

He looked away, unable to face her, his failures again invading his thoughts. "The only magic I believe in is the kind that comes from hard work, and sometimes not even then."

"But we need magic to keep our hope alive, Lim. Tell him, Luster."

"Do you really believe what you say, Lim?

Lim shrugged. "Why wouldn't I?"

"I suppose you'll think what you like regardless of what I say but that's a grim view of this amazing world we live in."

"I call it realistic, Luster."

A dim glow appeared above the highway, brightening as they rounded a gradual curve that followed a low, scrub-covered bluff. All at once the distant sky filled with yellow light as the road widened, passing beyond the cliff and opening onto the outskirts of town. Small homes and one-story buildings appeared out of the blackness before vanishing again into the night. The road climbed to the top of a low rise and Lim caught sight of the courthouse clock tower stretching above the treetops, its black face and white hands showing a quarter to ten, a good deal earlier than he thought.

Luster drove alongside the town square, past eighteenth-century brick buildings and whitewashed churches, and then turned onto a side street. Before them, a two-story stone building stood next to a brick warehouse. Pulling to the curb, he cut the engine and turned to Ili.

"Ever seen the inside of a Romanian jail, Ili?"

"No, thank God. I've heard stories."

"The stone building on the right was the county jail back when Syracuse sat on the edge of the frontier, the limit of what people considered civilization." Luster pointed through the windshield. "The jail played an important role at a time when some men, not a few, believed the law was something they could take or leave."

She nodded. "That sounds like home."

"The old jail is now a world class art museum with priceless work from around the world. They have an especially extensive collection of eighteenth century engravings. Are you familiar with that period, Lim?"

"I don't know anything about art, Luster." He waved off the question. "What happens now?"

"Lim, you must learn some patience. But first, I have an old friend to see."

"It's late. The museum is bound to be closed."

"I hope to find my friend next door."

"In that old warehouse?" Lim peered through the windshield.

"That building is a sculpture studio and if luck is with me I'll find her there at work. We must approach her gingerly. She may not be all that glad to see me."

"Why do you say that?"

"I'm afraid I'm here to atone for a wrong I did her long ago, Lim."

"I thought we were looking for Ili's sister."

"I thought the same, Luster." Ili leaned toward them. "Will this help?"

"I need to locate an engraving that may help us find your sister. In order to gain something I must give something up."

"And so you give up your pride and apologize to this woman? You try to make up for what you did?"

"As a woman, you can understand how important that is."

She shook her head. "But sometimes an apology is not enough."

"That's what worries me, Ili."

"You can do only what you can, Luster. The past we cannot change."

Lim squinted at him. "What on earth did you do, Luster?"

"That's for another time, Lim. We must not delay. Follow me."

Lim climbed out of the car, walking alongside Ili and stealing an occasional glance at the side of her face as they followed Luster toward the warehouse entrance. Light flickering from between two metal doors sliced the steps of the loading dock into odd shapes. Streaks of rust lined the narrow walkway below.

Beyond the doors the whine of a circular grinder sounded against metal, lighting the space beneath the doors in flashes of white and orange. Luster stepped up to the entrance, pounding the door with his fist. An instant later the noise inside stopped, followed by footsteps on concrete. Luster turned to Ili, flashing a weak smile.

"Wish me luck, Ili. I could use some just now."

"We Romanians have no luck to give. Just look at our history."

"It's just an expression, Ili."

Lim leaned toward him. "Maybe you should try some of that magic I keep hearing about."

"You're not helping, Lim."

Luster took a step back, pulling a necklace from his pocket and holding it up to the light. The shining pendant held the iridescent green of a fire opal. Ili grabbed his arm.

"Are you giving that to her?"

"Yes, for the second time. She gave it back the last time I saw her. To be honest, she threw it."

"You must not hand it to her until you are through the door."

"What do you mean?"

"In Romania it is bad luck to give someone a gift while on a threshold."

He took a breath. "I knew I could count on you, Ili."

A latch clicked and one of the doors began sliding to one side, its metal wheels chirping. A moment later a woman stepped into the opening. Slight and attractive, her short hair half to gray, she peered at them with a distracted look, as if she had just returned from some distant place. An instant later she emerged from the daze, giving them a quick look before pointing toward the stone building next door.

"The museum is over there but I'm afraid it's not open. Small towns like ours have a tendency to shut down early, even on a Saturday night. Unfortunately, the museum is closed on Sundays and Mondays so you'll have to come back Tuesday. They open at noon."

Luster stood as if frozen while an awkward silence followed the woman's voice. Moments later Ili stepped past her, pulling Luster behind.

"We are not here for the museum. May we come in?"

"I believe you already have." The woman followed Ili with her gaze. "I don't mean to be unfriendly but this is a private studio and I have work to do."

Luster stepped toward her without a word, holding out his hand, the necklace stretching across it. She stared at the stone before raising her eyes to him, squinting as she studied his ruddy face. A gradual look of recognition appeared in her eyes, her expression shifting from surprise to anger to sad resignation.

"You came back. Why? What do you want?"

"I don't want anything, Sam, at least not for myself."

"People don't come all the way out here for no reason."

"I didn't say I had no reason."

"What is your reason, then?"

"We're trying to find someone, a young woman, and we need your help."

"You've got to be kidding. You want my help after all this time, after all that happened?"

32

She turned to Lim, her face flushed with anger. "Do you know what he did?"

Lim shook his head.

"He ran out on me, that's what. We get engaged and a week later he just picks up and leaves without a word of where or why. I had to break the news to everyone. Do you know how humiliating that is?"

Lim looked at the floor and again shook his head, unable to face her.

"You have a lot of damn gall showing up after all these years, Luster. What's this really about? Why did you come find me?"

"You know more about eighteenth century art than anyone I know, Sam."

"What does that have to do with…?" She took a step back, squinting at him. "Wait a minute. I get it. You want forgiveness, don't you? I've read about this. You think you're going to die and you want to make up for all the harm you've done, all the people you've wronged, all the lies you've told. Well, it's not that easy, Luster."

"I do want to make up for the things I've done, Sam. Don't you? Doesn't everyone? That's why I need your help. I can't turn back the clock. I can't change the past. But with your knowledge, your expertise, I can do some good. I can find a young woman."

"Why would I want to help you do anything?"

Ili stepped past Luster. "You would help us if you understood. You would help my sister."

"And who are you?"

"I am Ileana and this is Lim, Luster's nephew. Please help us."

She glanced at her watch. "You have two minutes to explain. What's this about?"

"My sister was kidnapped and taken into forced prostitution by Romanian gangsters to pay for my late father's debts. But with your help and a bit of magic, Luster might find her.

"Your sister was kidnapped? How can I possibly help with that?"

Lim moved next to Ili. "Both Ili and her sister were taken. Luster found Ili and she was able to escape. Now we need your help so we can do the same for her sister."

Sam looked from one to the other. "I've heard stories of forced prostitution but never thought it could happen here."

"Crime can come even to a quiet place like this, Sam."

"I know, Luster. Just yesterday the newspaper reported that the Mexican gangs are spreading into the rural areas. And last month a town not far from here had a triple murder. They think it was gang-related."

"Sam, I know you have no reason to help me. But if what I'm looking for is where I think it is we might be able to find Ili's sister."

"I still don't see how I can help. I'm only an artist."

"Exactly, and you've studied eighteenth century art, particularly engravings."

"But a lot of people know more about that period than I do. Why come to me?"

Luster pointed out the door. "You live next to one of the most extensive collections of eighteenth century engravings in the country."

"I don't like the direction this conversation is going." Sam held up a hand. "Tell me what you're thinking, Luster."

"All you need to do is take a look at an engraving and tell me about it."

"The museum is closed, remember?"

"Is it, Sam?"

"You want me to break in?" She stared at him, her eyes wide.

"I was thinking more along the lines of a private tour. Your studio is right next door. I'm sure you must know a way to get us in. All we need is a quick look."

"Alright, suppose I could get you in. I still don't see how it will help some poor girl."

"You're so right, Sam. I haven't told you that part yet. When I was helping Ili escape, I heard the kidnappers say their boss is laundering money though stolen books, *eighteenth century* books."

She shook her head in confusion. "But what does an art museum have to do with stolen books?"

"I got a look at a book they plan to sell. It looked very old and had an engraving next to the title page, a portrait of someone, a man. I know I've seen the portrait before."

"Let me guess. You think they have it next door."

"I'm almost sure of it, Sam."

"What's the title of this book?"

"If I knew the title I wouldn't be here."

Sam stared at him. "I don't get it, Luster. How does knowing the title of a book help you find the girl?"

"The book is bound to be valuable and probably rare, right?"

"It wouldn't be much good for laundering money if it wasn't worth something."

"Exactly, and it seems likely if it contains an authentic eighteenth century engraving it might be worth a great deal. I'm no book expert but I know someone who is. Once I know the title, he may be able to help us figure out where the kidnappers would go to sell it."

Sam ran a hand across her brow. "But, Luster, I thought you said you saw the title page.

"I did see it, Sam. Unfortunately, the book was written in French."

"I read French."

"I know you do, Sam. And you know eighteenth century engravings."

"So, come back on Tuesday and we'll go see if it's the engraving you think it is."

"Sam, we can't wait that long when a young woman's safety is at stake. Think if you were in her position. Every hour is important."

"I suppose you're right."

"I knew you'd see it my way, Sam."

"Oh, you're as sneaky as ever, Luster Lester." She waved her finger at him. "Alright, I'll get you in to see your engraving. But don't forget that I live here. These are my friends. You have to promise me to be careful."

They passed through the metal doors, moving back down the stairs and into a night now moonless, dense and forbidding beyond the town glow. Edging along a yellow pool of light between the studio and museum, Sam led them down a narrow alley to the rear of the building. Before them a low, recessed entrance sat midway along the stone wall.

She put a finger to her lips and leaned toward the door, cocking her head to listen. Then she turned and reached for the wall, moving a small stone aside and pulling a key from the opening. A moment later she stood before the open door, motioning them through.

They moved along a wide hallway crowded with wooden crates and boxes, some half open, and through a set of double doors, emerging into a large room scattered with paintings and glass-topped display cases. Sam punched a code into a security panel and turned to Luster.

"Lucky for you I know the security guard is off tonight. You don't want to get on the wrong side of his dog." She flipped the light switch and pointed to a case in the center of the room. "That case has several book-sized engravings. Let's see if one of them is the one you're looking for."

Luster moved to the case, peering through the glass in silence as the others gathered around him.

"What do you think, Luster?"

Luster pointed to a portrait of a man standing next to a stack of books, a curling white wig falling to his shoulders. "That's the one, Sam."

"The middle one?"

"Yes, I'm sure of it."

"The timeframe fits. That's Dimitrie Cantemir, an eighteenth century scientist and historian. He was prince of Moldova and an advisor to Peter the Great."

Ili moved next to her. "Sam, did you say he was prince of Moldova?"

"That's right, Ili."

"Yes, I thought I recognized the name. He tried to gain Moldovan independence from Turkey."

Lim leaned over the case. "Wasn't Moldova a part of Romania at one time?"

"How do you know that, Lim?"

"I haven't forgotten all the history I learned in school, Ili. So, the Romanian kidnappers that have your sister are trying to sell a book written by a Romanian prince?"

"That's how it seems. Strange, isn't it?"

Lim nodded. "That's an understatement, Ili."

"At least we have a name to go with the portrait. That will help my sister, won't it Luster?"

"Yes, but we need to match a book to that name."

"Luster, there's something written at the bottom of the engraving." Lim tapped the glass top.

"Sam, come have a look." Luster leaned closer to the case. "The print is tiny and ornate but you may be able to tell what it says."

She peered into the cabinet. "If this engraving was made specifically to face the title page, the title of the book could be listed. Let me study it for a moment."

"I can just make it out, Luster." Luster moved behind Sam, peering over her shoulder." It looks as though the artist included a footnote to the engraving. I can see the Prince's name and I believe it says something about the Ottoman Empire."

"That could be helpful, Sam. Since he was a historian, he might have written a book about the Ottomans. I believe my bookish friend might be able to tell us something more. That is, if he will see me."

"What do you mean, Luster?"

"Not now, Lim. We have more pressing matters. Sam, could we impose on you for a bit of sustenance? I'm famished and I know Ili must be as well."

She faced him, hands on her hips. "You expect me to break you into a museum *and* feed you?"

"We're asking, Sam, not expecting."

"I'll fix up something for Ili and Lim. You can have whatever's left."

"You're still angry with me, aren't you?"

"Making up for what you did isn't that easy, Luster."

"But it happened so long ago, Sam."

"It may seem long ago to you, Luster but it seems like yesterday to me. Anyway, you look like you could stand to skip a meal."

"No need to get personal, Sam." He put a hand on his belly.

"This is as personal as it gets, Mr. Lester."

"You're right, Sam. Thank you for helping. You're a good person, even to people you don't care for."

"Don't patronize me, Luster. That makes me madder than anything. Come on Ili. Let's see what we can find for dinner."

Sam took Ili by the arm, leading her back down the hallway. Lim glanced at Luster, shaking his head."

"You handled that well."

"I don't know what else I should say to convince her I'm sorry."

"Nothing is what else you should say. Let's go."

Lim followed Luster through the rusted doors of Sam's studio, past the foyer and into an open room framed by brick walls and a scarred wooden floor. Two broken down couches sat at one end. Overhead, intricate squares of pressed tin stamped with fleur de lies stretched across the ceiling in varying shades of blue.

In the center of the room a forest of steel tubes pocked with holes stood amid piles of metal scrap and shavings. A small kitchen and dining area filled one corner below a loft hidden from view by a dark curtain. Ili and Sam had already started setting plates and bowls on the table when Lim walked in. Sam waved him to a chair.

"Come and sit, Lim. I want to hear how you and Ili got mixed up in this mess. Lucky for us we had a studio tour last night, so we have plenty to eat and drink as long as you don't mind leftovers."

Luster held up a finger. "Did you say drink, Sam?"

"You can join us, Luster, but only if you agree to pour the wine."

"Why, thank you, Sam."

"And keep pouring it as long as I tell you to."

"I will make like Ganymede himself, bringer of wine to the gods."

She handed him a bottle. "Just pour and keep your literary mumbo-jumbo to yourself."

"But Sam, literary mumbo-jumbo, as you call it, is going to help us find Ili's sister."

"Alright, Luster, we get it. Now let Lim tell me about himself."

Lim's face paled and he glanced around the room as if looking for escape. The last thing he wanted was Ili feeling sorry for him. After some quick thinking, he pointed to the middle of the room."

"I'd rather hear about those metal tubes. They look like giant flutes. What are they for, Sam?"

"Oh, that's just a project I'm working on, Lim. You're right about them seeming like flutes. They're sound sculptures. I put them in a windy spot, like between downtown buildings or beside a lakeshore and they make music. They add a bit of magic to a place. But I spent all last night talking about my sculpture and right now it bores

39

me. On the other hand, you look like you have an interesting story to tell."

"And a very sad tale it is, Sam. The winds of fate have been against our Lim."

"Be quiet and drink your wine, Luster. Go ahead, Lim, tell us about your fate."

He sat on the edge of the chair, trying to sound like he felt the least bit of control over his life, trying to forget the failure, the directionless feeling again gnawing at him.

"I don't believe in fate. There's a logical explanation for everything that happens, even what happens to me. I'll reason through it sooner or later. It's just that I've been having trouble thinking straight since my girlfriend left."

"Do you miss her, Lim?" Ili reached out, lightly touching his arm. His face flushed as he stared at her hand.

"What?"

"Your girlfriend, do you miss her?"

He peered at her for a moment before answering, unable to think of anything but the truth. "It may sound strange but I haven't thought much about her. Somehow, it all seems so long ago. I know it isn't but it feels that way."

Luster drained his glass and refilled it. "That's because you've entered into another world, Lim, a world where time doesn't follow the usual order, where wonder outranks logic."

Sam slapped a plate on the table and squinted at Luster. "What on earth are you talking about, Luster?"

"You said it yourself, Sam. A change, the right change, can add magic to a place or even to a life."

"I was talking about sculpture, not Lim."

Lim shook his head. "I plan to rely on reason, Luster. If I can reason it out, I can understand it."

"I have nothing against reason, Lim. Reason can fix an engine or solve a math problem. But there's more to the world around you than what you can reason through. Your intuition can serve you well if you'll let it. My intuition tells me our book expert will know where to find what we're looking for."

"But you said he might refuse to see you."

"That's right, Ili, he might."

"Why wouldn't he want to see you?"

"Do we really need to discuss this?"

All three of them nodded at once.

"The last time I saw him he had a gun in his hand."

An image of the small revolver sitting on the kitchen table flashed through Lim's mind. "He had a gun?"

"A pistol to be precise, Lim."

Sam leaned her elbows on the table. "Good lord, was he threatening to shoot you?"

"Not exactly, Sam. He was threatening to shoot himself."

"Why would he want to do that?"

"It was because of me, something I did."

"Why am I not surprised? What did you do, Luster?"

"You don't really want to hear this sad and sordid tale."

"Yes we do. Come on, out with it."

"If I must. Just keep in mind it was a long time ago. Well, I got this idea I could make some badly needed money by posing as his agent without telling him. I sold a book as a rare first edition when it was actually a common copy worth about ten dollars. I just forged the key pages. I'm no rare book expert but I did a fine job if I must say so and the buyer never knew the difference."

"There's something familiar here." Sam leaned across the table. "Who is this person, Luster?"

Luster ignored the question. Lim looked at him askance.

"If you got away with it, why did your friend want to kill himself?"

"When he found out what I'd done he was terrified his reputation would be ruined once the ruse was discovered, and he was convinced it would be. Bookselling was his life and he couldn't stand the thought of losing his store or the humiliation he was sure would follow."

"Why didn't he go through with it?"

"Fortunately, he came to his senses."

"What changed his mind?"

"When I realized what he was about to do, I agreed to tell the buyer what I'd done, give the money back and sell him a different rare book at a substantial discount. The buyer agreed that nothing would ever be said or done to discredit my, by then, ex-friend."

Sam nodded. "That's plenty reason to never want to see you again."

"I had a feeling you'd say that, Sam. Unfortunately, the buyer was not so generous toward me. He went straight to the police and as a result I had to leave rather suddenly."

Sam sat back and stared at him, her mouth agape. Then her face clouded with anger. "You're talking about Orvis! That's the reason you left me the way you did?"

"I had no choice, Sam."

"You could have told me. At least I would have known you weren't running from me."

"My shame wouldn't allow it, Sam."

"If you ask me, you got off too easy. I can see why he wouldn't want to see you, now or ever."

Ili sat up. "But we're going to go anyway, aren't we, Luster? We must soon find my sister."

"Try not to worry, Ili. Like I said, my intuition tells me he'll see us."

Lim snorted. "My reason tells me he won't."

"Hush, Lim. Such talk will bring bad luck to my sister. Luster's friend must see us."

"Well, if Sam will let us camp out in her studio we'll find out first thing tomorrow." Luster drained his glass.

"We don't go now, Luster? I fear for Mirela."

"Ili, if we want a friendly response from our bookseller we should wait until a decent hour to make contact."

"If we must, we must, but I worry so for her."

Retort (ri'tôrt) - a sharp, angry, or wittily incisive reply to a remark; a container or furnace for carrying out a chemical process.

## Four

Sam stepped onto the loading dock and surveyed a morning sky that stood clear and featureless above the black silhouettes of trees. Thin shadows stretched between the trees, crossing the gravel roadway below her. A dry wind coursing along the empty street carried with it the hint of the latent heat she knew would soon fill the air in shimmering waves.

She stood alone, watching as Luster climbed behind the steering wheel and slammed the door of the rattling car. He raised his palm toward her, the sorrowful expression in his eyes clear even from a distance. She squinted back, unwilling to show her ambivalence toward his unexpected reappearance. Behind her, slivers of sunlight cut the studio doors into quarters. As the car drifted down the street and around the corner, Luster managed to catch one last glimpse of her before she disappeared from sight.

Her image haunted him as they drove north past open pastures scattered with rusted oil pumps and bald-faced cattle, the climbing road now and then dipping into tree-choked washes and dry creeks. Live oaks stood against the horizon in dense clusters, their shadows indigo beneath the growing daylight. The car crested a steep rise and the land seemed to change all at once, the rolling hills replaced by a vast treeless plain broken only by fence post and windmill. Blonde grass stretched into the distance. To the east the white tip of a church steeple rose above the flat horizon.

Luster pointed through the windshield as a cluster of trees and low buildings appeared on either side of the road. A moment later a town square not unlike the one they had just left came into view. Brilliant sunlight cast the stone courthouse into relief, the three arches marking the entrance lost in shadow. He rounded the corner, pulling to a stop in front of a one story brick building fronted by two large windows and a single blue door. A hand-painted sign overhead read 'Bowman Books'.

Beneath one of the windows, a bearded man in a wheelchair thumbed through a tattered book, an empty bottle of beer next to him. Luster climbed out of the car and paused, staring into the distance and tapping the hood with his fingers. Then he stepped onto the sidewalk. The man in the wheelchair tossed the book aside and swiveled toward Luster, squinting with one eye while the other rolled about like a loose marble.

"I can tell your fortune for a dollar."

"Not today, old man." Lim stepped past Luster. "We've got business here."

"Who're you calling old, junior?"

Luster moved Lim aside. "Lim, I believe this man directed his offer to me."

"You're not going to waste your time on some wino's nonsense, are you Luster? I thought we were in a hurry."

"But Lim, what if he can help us?" Ili approached the man."

"You don't really believe in fortunetellers, do you, Ili?"

"I do if it will help Mirela. We must let him tell Luster what he can."

"I would like to do that, miss." The man pointed a finger at her. "For a dollar, that is. Besides, junior, I'm no wino. I have the second sight for real."

Lim snorted. "I don't believe you or anyone else can see into the future."

"Ah, but I do, Lim." Luster nodded at the man. "Clairvoyance is as real as any other so-called reality."

"I don't buy it, Luster. Time moves in one direction only. The past we know and the future we don't. It's that simple."

"Time is no straight line, Lim. Luster traced a circle in Lim's face with his hand. "It's more of a circle. Look in one direction and you see the past. Face the other and you see what's going to happen, or at least some of it. Take a look at Einstein's theories if you don't believe me."

46

The man slapped the side of his chair. "I don't know a hoot about all that. I just know what's likely to happen. It's a damn gift, not no science."

Luster reached into his pocket and pulled out a large coin, handing it to the man. He whistled, turning it over in his hands.

"Dang, I haven't seen a silver dollar in a dog's age. I'll have to give you a good tell then. Let me take a look at your hand real quick-like. A long look can confuse the gift."

The man spread Luster's palm before him and studied it with his good eye before looking up into his face. "You are from somewhere a fair piece away."

Lim snorted again. "Hell, Luster, anyone in a town this size would know that."

"Lim, please be quiet and let this man tell us what he sees. It could help my sister."

The man winked at Ili with his good eye before returning to Luster's palm.

"Thank you, miss. Like I said before junior sounded off, you've come a long way but you have a good ways to go yet. You will soon see snow."

"Snow is it?" Lim glared at Luster. "It's heading toward a hundred degrees out here in case you haven't noticed."

Ili touched Lim's arm. "Please hush, Lim."

"The snow is where someone important to your journey lives." The man released Luster's hand. "And there's music. At least I think that's what it is. It has a rattling sound like those gourds the Mexican fellers down in Cuba or somewhere thereabouts play."

"You mean maracas?"

"I believe that's what they call them. You'll have to be real careful when you hear that music."

"Can you tell what we'll need to be careful of?"

"When I looked at your hand I saw fire and water close together, too close. That's never good."

47

"Did you see anything else?"

"I saw a girl, a real good-looker with dark hair. She was walking into a white castle. Her name sounds like miracle or something close."

"It must be Mirela." Ili leaned toward him. "Is she safe?"

"She appeared so for the time being, miss. And there's one more thing, mister. You're hunting someone but someone's after you too, someone who would do you harm. Now, I got to get myself out of this damned heat. Junior, you take care of this sweet young thing and get her something cold to drink." The man pushed passed them, disappearing around the corner.

Lim and Ili followed Luster through the bookstore's blue door and into a small room crammed with hardback books, some locked in glass cases, others left open on narrow tables. A single air conditioner rattled over the window. Novels lining the odd-sized shelves spilled onto the floor in places, looking as if a stream of books might soon follow and fill the room completely.

Curled up in one corner, a gray-faced Dachshund raised its head, studying them for a moment before losing interest. Otherwise, the room appeared empty. Luster put his finger to his lips, waving Lim and Ili over to a wooden door tucked behind a free-standing bookshelf. They followed him through the creaking door and into another room.

Once Lim left the cool of the entryway a dense wall of heat surrounded him, for a moment taking his breath. Before him a cavernous room stretched into the distance, its long rows of bookshelves reaching toward a high ceiling, the odor of books so strong he imagined he could almost taste them. A huge box fan humming off to one side threw the hot air at them in waves.

Lim stole a glance of Ili's graceful profile, wondering if she would notice the sweat already forming on his brow. He looked back down the aisle, catching sight of Luster as he disappeared behind a wall of books. Lim took Ili's hand, pulling her along.

They rounded a corner and spotted an old man in horn-rimmed glasses stooping over a pile of books, checking the spine of each before tossing it onto a nearby pile. Wearing jeans and red suspenders, the skin of his hands parchment-like next to the white of his shirt sleeves, he took no notice as they stood by. His white hair fluttered in the fan-whipped air.

Wondering where Luster had disappeared to, Lim turned to Ili before realizing he still had hold of her. She smiled as she slipped her hand from his. An instant later Luster moved past them, walking toward the man as he continued sorting through the books. Lim motioned Ili to remain where she stood, then followed Luster down the aisle. A moment later the man looked up, squinting at Luster, his blue eyes large behind the thick lenses.

"Has the goddamned devil finally come to carry me off, then?"

"What do you mean?"

"When you get to be old as me the devil's always just a step behind. I figure you could be him, showing up out of thin air like that. You've got that evil look about you."

"So, it's the devil I'm to be now?"

"Of course, it could be my mind playing tricks again."

"Am I as bad as all that, Orvis?"

He jumped, squinting at Luster. "How do you know my name?"

"It's me, Orvis. It's Luster. Don't you recognize me?"

"If you mean Luster Lester, he's long dead."

"Why would you say that?"

"He passed from this world long ago."

"Are you blind?" Lim waved his hand in front of the man's eyes. "He's right in front of you. He's not dead."

He faced Lim, frowning. "Who the hell are you?"

"The name is Lim Specter and I'm telling you Luster is not dead."

"He is to me, not that it's any of your damn business."

"How can you say that when he's standing right here?"

"I'll tell you how, sonny. The day he betrayed his best friend he ceased to exist. The moment he ran from this place like a coward he was dead to me."

"But I tried to make amends, Orvis. I tried to make it right."

The man continued facing Lim. "If he thought he made it right, why did he run off like he did? He just disappeared from the face of the earth. No letters or phone calls, nothing. What's not dead about that?"

"But he would have been arrested."

"That's a damn lame excuse. The charges wouldn't have amounted to much of anything."

Luster faced the floor and sighed. "I suppose there's some truth to what you say."

"Of course there is. I may be old but I'm not daft."

He shifted his gaze toward Luster and peered at him. Then he stood, stretching out a finger and poking him in the chest.

"My mind isn't too reliable but I believe you might be real after all. I suppose you could be him. There is a resemblance."

Luster looked up at him. "Of course it's me, Orvis."

"Could be those left over French fries I had for dinner last night. They looked a little suspect.

"Stop being Dickensian, Orvis. I'm here in the flesh and you know it.

"That doesn't change what happened or the way you just vanished, never a word where or why.

"I didn't think you'd want to see or hear from me after what I did.

"Leaving without a goodbye or single word of explanation was as bad as what you did, maybe worse. You see me at my lowest and then you take off to God knows where like I don't still need a friend. What kind of person does that?

"I didn't know where to begin or what to say.

"You didn't even try, did you?

"Would you have listened?"

"Hell no." He frowned at Luster, his watery eyes blinking behind the lenses.

"I didn't think so.

"I might have been willing to after awhile, if I'd ever had a chance.

"Well, you do now. If you'll stop torturing me, that is.

"So, why have you come back, why after all this time?

Lim squinted at Luster. "This is starting to sound familiar.

"Stay out of this, Lim. The reason I'm here is because I need your help, Orvis.

"I need a drink.

"Will you help?

"You want my help, Luster, just like that? You think you can show up out of the blue and I'll be glad to see you, much less help you?

"I meant to say *she* needs your help.

Luster pointed down the aisle to where Ili stood. He motioned her toward them. As she approached, Orvis' eyes grew wide behind his bifocals.

"Now I know my mind has gone. There's a beautiful woman in my bookstore.

"Your mind is working just fine. Her name is Ili.

"This young woman is with you?

"Is that so hard to believe?"

"Of course it isn't." Ili stopped next to Luster, smiling at Orvis. "Luster is charming and kind, and he has a way with women. You should have seen how Sam looked at him when we left her studio this morning."

Luster turned to her, his face hopeful."How did she look, Ili? I think she despises me."

Orvis grabbed his arm. "Luster, you went to see Sam after what you did? I think you're the one that has lost his mind."

"I had a good reason, Orvis. Ili's sister has been kidnapped and we went to see Sam because I thought she could tell us something useful. Now we've come to you."

"Will you please help us?" Ili took Orvis' hand in hers. "We need to find my sister as soon as possible."

"I suppose I have no choice." He shrugged. "I could never say no to a beautiful woman."

"Please call me Ili."

Orvis again faced Luster. "What the hell can an old bookseller do?"

"The kidnappers are laundering money by buying and selling rare editions. They have a book that they may try to sell, a book by an eighteenth century Moldovan prince named Dimitrie Cantemir. Have you ever heard of him?"

"I knew those two hombres were up to no good."

"The men we're looking for were here?"

"They came in yesterday."

"Did they have a woman with them?"

"No, it was just the two of them. They told me they were looking to sell a book by Cantemir. They asked a few questions but they were so vague and evasive I didn't learn much. Unfortunately, they didn't have the book with them. Which of his works are they trying to sell?"

"We're not sure of the title but it has to do with the Ottoman Empire."

"He wrote a history of the Ottomans that was a well-known and influential work. He was one of the first historians to believe that the rise and fall of a culture is a pattern all civilizations go through."

"That must be it. I caught a glimpse of it but the text was in French."

He peered into Luster's face. "Are you sure it was in French, Luster?"

"I'm sure. I can't read French but I can recognize it. Is the book valuable?"

"If it's the book it seems to be it would be priceless. But more important, it would be impossible."

"What do you mean?"

"The only copies known to exist are in libraries and those libraries would never sell them."

"Could they have stolen one of the copies?"

"If one was stolen I would've heard about it."

"So, how would a Romanian gang get hold of a book that doesn't exist?"

"There is one possibility, although it's so unlikely I hesitate to even mention it."

"At this point it's all we've got to go on, Orvis."

"Alright, it's quite a story but very few people outside the book world have heard it. The story goes back a ways, all the way to the early nineteenth century. During the War of 1812 the British burned a good portion of Washington, including the Library of Congress. Thomas Jefferson was so distraught by the loss of such an important national resource that he sold his personal library to the country as a foundation for a rebuilt Library of Congress. Jefferson's library contained a copy of the book we're talking about, Cantemir's Ottoman history, a French copy."

"You mean the kidnappers have a book that belongs to the Library of Congress?"

"That's the puzzle, Luster. The Library of Congress burned again on Christmas Eve some years later and most of Jefferson's books were lost, including that one."

"I don't understand. How could they have a book that was lost in a fire two hundred years ago?"

"Luster, do you realize what it would mean if they do have it?" Orvis paced the aisle. "A book owned by one of the Founding Fathers of this country, one of the most famous personalities in history, seemingly appears out of nowhere when some gangsters decide to sell it."

"But, Orvis…"

"Hold on, Ili, there's a problem with this theory. The book we're talking about is beyond price. I can't believe they know quite what they have, if they have it at all."

"But Orvis…"

"Think of it, Ili." He gestured wildly. "The appearance of one book means there could be other books from Jefferson's lost library out there, a thrilling prospect for any bookseller."

"But did you see where these men went, Orvis? Do you know where they might stay, where they might be keeping my sister?"

He stopped and stared at her for a moment, running a hand across his face. "My apologies, Ili. I've been so caught up in the idea of finding a lost book I forgot that finding a lost girl is what's of real importance just now. I'm sorry to say I know very little. The men said only what was necessary, stayed a short while and avoided my questions. They left in a black sedan with windows so dark I could see nothing inside. They could have had your sister in there for all I know."

"Can you remember anything else that might help?"

"I'm afraid not, Ili. They were here and then they left."

She sighed and faced Luster. "Luster, what will we do now? We must find her but still we have nothing."

"Perhaps, Ili, but we may yet discover a hidden gem with a bit of luck. Orvis, will you do something for me, something a little odd?"

"I don't like the sound of that, Luster. I believe you're asking me to trust you."

"I don't have any other ideas. Will you do as I ask?"

"Oh, alright, I'll do it if it will help Ili find her sister."

Luster pulled a folding chair from the wall, directing Orvis to sit. "Now, close your eyes. Imagine I'm standing next to you."

"You are standing next to me."

"I mean imagine we're standing together exactly where you stood when the two men came into the shop. Where were you?"

"I was looking for a book on the shelf just inside the front door."

"So you and I are standing there and the men come through the door. Can you imagine them coming in? Can you see them?"

"I can see them."

"Describe them for me."

"One is dark and muscular with a tattoo of a griffin on his neck."

"And the other?"

"He's thin and has long black hair and a scar running from his forehead down his left cheek.

Ili put her hand to her mouth. "It is Jorvic, the man who kidnapped me."

"What?"

Orvis' eyelids fluttered. Luster leaned toward him, speaking in low tones. "Try to concentrate, Orvis. Can you still see them?"

"I can see them."

"Tell me about them."

"Although the dark one looks like he could break your neck without trying, the slender one is scary. It's his eyes. I try to keep a distance from him."

"Now, tell us what happens, what the two of them do."

"They wander about the room asking about the value of works by Cantemir and occasionally pulling books from the shelves. But they're doing that for effect, with little real interest in the books. They're trying to see what information they can get out of me without letting me know what they're after."

"So, we're following them about the room. I'm beside you and we're listening to what they have to say."

"Their accents make them hard to understand."

"Try to listen. Do they ask about anything other than the book, even something that seems trivial or unrelated?"

"Not that I can remember. Wait! When they're about to leave, the dark one turns and asks about books on herbs, books about herbal remedies. He says he has been sick with a stomach bug but he won't take medicine, only herbal cures. He asks if I have a book for him."

"And do you sell him a book?"

"I try to but he doesn't like what I show him and says what he really needs is an herbalist, someone to make up a cure for him. As it happens, I know of someone, not exactly an herbalist but close enough. So, I give him her card and they leave in the black sedan."

Luster stepped away. "Very good, Orvis. You can open your eyes now."

He sat back blinking at them, his eyes dancing behind the thick lenses. Ili leaned toward him.

"Orvis, how could you send those thugs to some unsuspecting woman? What might they do to her?"

He waved off her question. "She can take care of herself, Ili."

"But you don't know these gangsters as I do. They are ruthless."

"Cyril is no ordinary woman, Ili. She knows about things few have heard of and even fewer understand, things having to do with cures and potions and rituals. And she has this strange power over people. It's as if she can make them do anything she likes. I can't explain it but I believe it. She'll be able to handle those two."

"I hope you are right."

Luster turned to her. "You can go see for yourself, Ili. All we need is one of her cards."

"We are going to see this woman?" Ili stared at him with a confused look on her face.

"We are thanks to Orvis."

He stood. "You mean I was able to help?"

56

"And we thank you and your memory, Orvis. We would have been lost without your observations."

Lim pointed a finger at Luster. "Are you telling me we're going to waste our time going to see some quack?"

"We are, Lim."

"What the hell for, Luster?"

"Isn't it obvious? She's clearly in tune with the unseen and unknown, and there is plenty we don't know."

"I can't stand all this mystical nonsense. We need to stick with facts, what we know for sure, not what some nut-ball dreams up."

"When it comes to understanding, dreams can be as real as what you see and touch, Lim."

"But we can't go running around chasing after every dream or visionary that comes along. We'll never get anywhere. We need to work with what we're sure of, what's real."

Ili peered at Luster. "What if he is right, Luster? We could run in circles and never find my sister."

"If we're lucky she will have seen the kidnappers, Ili. She may even have taken some herbal something-or-other to wherever they're staying. Is that real enough for you?"

"Of course, Luster. I wasn't thinking. I just want to find Mirela."

"No, no, there's something wrong here, Luster." Orvis shook his head. "What the hell will you do if you find out where the girl is? Those two hombres aren't likely to just hand her over because you ask."

"I was wondering when you would bring that up, Orvis."

Luster reached into his pants pocket, pulling out a thin metal flask, unscrewing the top and handing it to him.

"Now that's what I call real. It's about time we had a drink. All this talk is making me thirsty. On the other hand, when you pull out a flask it usually means bad news."

"I have a plan that requires one more favor."

Orvis took a long pull on the flask and then held up a finger. "What did I tell you? I knew it couldn't be so easy."

"We need a book to sell to the kidnappers, one that's worth a good bit."

"Oh, no. You're not getting your hands on any of my books, Luster. I've learned my lesson."

"But Orvis, we know they're interested in buying and selling rare books. If we can pose as sellers we may be able to get close enough to free Mirela."

"Why not call the cops if you find out where they are?"

Ili took a step back, shaking her head. "No, no, we must not contact the police, Orvis."

"Why not, Ili? That's what people here do when someone commits a crime."

"Don't you see? My sister will have no chance of escaping the mob if she is deported back to Romania."

"Your sister won't be deported just because the Sheriff arrests those thugs."

"But she will be. We are not allowed to be here. We were brought to America illegally and have no papers, no passports.

"Let me get this straight, Luster." Orvis faced Luster, squinting over his bifocals. "I'm just supposed to fork over a valuable book, a book that I'll probably never see again?

"We won't actually sell the book.

"How're you going to manage that?

"We'll price it so high they'll pass. Offering to sell it is just a deception so we can get Mirela out."

"Well, I know from experience you're a master at the art of deception. Why don't you just forge another book? You haven't forgotten how, have you?"

Luster raised a hand. "I most certainly have, thank you. Besides, we can't take that kind of chance when a girl's safety is at stake. Surely you understand that."

Ili moved next to Orvis, again taking his hand. "Please let us have the book. We came to you for help and you have been wonderful but we still need you, my sister needs you."

"Now how can I say no to a face like that?" He sighed. "We best have another drink, Luster. You'll need it if you're going to hobnob with those banditos."

Orvis took another swig and then reached out, tapping Luster's chest with the flask. "I want to hear about your meeting with Sam. I can imagine the fireworks."

"If I must, but first we need to choose the book I'll use. It has to be one they're likely to want."

Orvis nodded. "I know just the one."

Seeing his chance to be alone with Ili, Lim turned to Luster. "Ili and I will wait for you out front. I can see you and Orvis need a word in private."

Orvis slapped Lim on the back. "You don't want to get on the bad side of a woman like Sam, Lim. You young people go play so I can hear the whole gory story. Hold nothing back, Mr. Lester."

Lim followed Ili through the creaking door and back into the cool of the air conditioned rare book room. Sunlight filtering through the plate glass windows played across the tips of her auburn hair in ruby streaks. A sudden urge to reach up and run his fingers through it caught Lim by surprise, stopping him where he stood. She turned to face him.

"Lim, are you feeling well? You are looking a little pale."

"What? Oh, no... I'm alright, Ili. I'm just tired is all."

"We have both been visited by bad luck, I think."

"That's an understatement."

"I am sorry you lost your home, Lim."

"I'm sorry too. At least I didn't have to leave the country like you did. Do you miss your home, Ili?"

"I miss some of my things but not my dingy flat nor the town where my sister and I lived. The gangs had taken over and were demanding money from the shopkeepers and business owners. There was nothing to stop them, not the police, not the courts."

"There are places in Mexico like that, out of control and very dangerous."

Her face darkened. "The stress of it killed my father."

"How long ago was it, Ili?"

"It has been almost one year since we buried him. I can scarcely believe it though I am still angry with him for leaving my sister and me with such a mess. He came into debt gambling away all his savings and then collapsed pleading with the bank for a loan. The next thing I knew the kidnappers broke down the door, threw us in a van and we woke up in America."

Lim felt a nagging at the back of his thoughts. "You called the pale one Jorvic. That name seems familiar."

"He is a Serbian."

"I thought you said they're Romanians."

"He is not like the rest. They say he executed many Bosnians. When he looked at me, I knew he would kill me without hesitation."

"That must have been a nightmare."

"It still seems so. And what of your family, Lim?"

"My parents died a long time ago."

"Luster is your only family?"

"Not exactly. He's not really my uncle."

"I don't understand, Lim."

"Luster and my parents were good friends so I grew up calling him uncle."

"He is like a godfather, then?"

"I'd say he's more like someone you think you know until you find out he's really someone else, someone selfish, someone you can never rely on."

"Why are you angry with him?"

"I'm not angry with him. It's the truth."

"You sound angry. Luster is a good man, Lim."

"You think he's good? I'll tell you how good he is. He acts like a friend, like part of the family. Then he decides to disappear, not for a little while but for years. One day he shows up again acting like he never left, like he's always been there for you, like leaving was no big deal. You heard Sam and Orvis. He does it to everyone."

"I'm sure he had his reasons."

"He doesn't believe in reason, Ili. Instead he talks some nonsense about dreams and predicting the future as if he really believes he's some sort of magician."

"He *is* a magician, Lim. He found me and soon he will find Mirela."

"But how did he find you, Ili? It had to be something other than magic."

Before she could answer the door opened and Luster stepped through, a small book in his hand. He walked past them and out of the store without a word. Lim glanced at Ili as they hurried after.

## Five

Thin clouds scratched the blue dome of sky as Luster drove west on the barren highway, winding between rusted pump jacks and abandoned farmhouses. The tops of church steeples, brilliant under the noonday sun, passed in and out of view behind hills of crumbling sandstone. Scattered Longhorn cattle grazed lean patches of scrub.

Turning south toward Browerton, and then east, they followed the rough blacktop as it left the high plain, dropping into hills scattered with mesquite and salt cedar. Occasional stands of oak and pecan appeared along the edges of dry creeks and arroyos. From his seat in the back, Lim watched Ili's profile, wondering what she must think of him, his failures in love and work so apparent. An image of his ex-girlfriend came to him and he again wondered at how he had scarcely thought of her since Luster's appearance the night before.

Puzzling over how easily she had faded from memory, he stared out the window at waves of heat vibrating below the distant horizon. A restless breeze moved through the dry grass, coursing between pools of tree-cast shade. Turkey vultures tilted against rising thermals like black checkmarks, circling the broken hills in a column that stretched into the sky.

The sunlight dimmed as they rounded a sharp curve, the road dipping into a wooded hollow heavy with undergrowth. White frame houses and buildings emerged from the dense foliage and then vanished, their images caught in memory like dim specters. The roadway then climbed an abrupt rise to the top of a narrow ridge.

Luster slowed the car, turning onto a gravel road that edged an abandoned church and overgrown graveyard. Angling the car through a metal gate and into a clearing, he stopped and cut the engine. Before them, the way disappeared into mass of brush browned by the summer heat.

"We must walk from here."

"But Luster, to where do we walk?" Ili looked to either side of the car. "I see nothing but trees."

"The path starts just beyond that thicket, Ili." He pointed through the windshield.

"But how do we get past the bushes? There are so many."

"Orvis said we would have to pick our way through the underbrush to find the trail."

"We go into that?" She peered into the dark mass.

"I believe we must, Ili."

Lim threw open his door. "We won't find anything just sitting here and talking about it."

He bolted from the car, heading for the wall of brush and disappearing into it before Luster could say another word. He shook his head and sighed.

"I understand why Lim might be testy after all he's been through but I must say I've grown tired of his moodiness."

"He has failed in love, Luster. He fears no woman will ever again want him. That is a very hard place to be."

"How can you know that, Ili?"

"I was once there myself."

"Ah, the voice of experience."

"One I remember too well."

Ili climbed out of the car, wandering along the edge of the thicket as Luster ambled toward the brush line, poking about the spot where he had last seen Lim. Hot air stirred the dry leaves into a rustling murmur. In the distance a dust devil stretched toward the sky, pulling the clay-colored earth into a twisting column of red. A moment later, Lim burst into the clearing twenty yards away. He turned one way then the other, mumbling to himself as he paced the thicket. Luster called to him.

"So, you found the path?"

"Hell no."

"You didn't find it?"

"If I did I would've said so, wouldn't I?"

"Why did you come back, then?"

Lim stopped and glared at Luster."

"Oh, I see. You got lost and ended up where you started."

"At least I did something other than sit around wasting time."

"I was waiting for luck to pay me a visit."

"You'd have a long wait, then."

"You must believe in what's possible, Lim. We're near someone who can help us and with a bit of luck we'll find her."

"Where's Ili?"

"I last saw her over there."

Luster pivoted, pointing along the edge of thicket just as Ili appeared and waved them to her.

"Luster, the path it is this way. Come and I will show you."

"Damn!" Lim slapped his thigh. "I looked all through that underbrush. How in the hell did she find it?"

"You see, Lim, a bit of luck is always waiting if you allow yourself to believe."

Lim led the way, trying to recover some of his lost dignity. Ili and Luster followed. They wound down a narrow trail that twisted through the dense thicket, thin sunlight breaking about them in shards of green and brown, fading with every turn. Dead leaves crackled beneath their feet. Pushing aside a tree limb, Lim glanced at Ili hoping he might catch her eye but she scarcely seemed to notice him as she dodged the branch.

He turned around and took a step before realizing the path had all but vanished beneath the wall of brush ahead. A wave of panic passed through him but he said nothing and instead scanned the thicket for anything that might help him know where to go. Through the maze of twigs and branches a tiny flash glimmered for an instant and then vanished. He stared into the trees. A moment later the light flashed again.

Marking the spot in memory he pushed ahead, Ili close behind, the sharp branches grabbing at their clothes, slapping their faces. He held up his forearm trying to shield his face before reaching back and taking Ili's hand in his, her soft skin melting into his palm. Then he lowered his head, crashing through the shrubs, using his body to protect her.

Just at the moment he thought they could go no further, the branches before him gave way and he burst through the thicket, Ili still in tow as they tumbled to the ground. He landed with a grunt. Turning to where he thought she would be, he instead found Luster peering down at him, a wry smile on his lips.

"What are *you* laughing at?"

"Lim, do you always prefer the shortcut?"

He sat up, finding Ili next to him. "How did you get here before us?"

"That's a little secret between me and the sprites and fairies, not to mention my gnome friends."

Ili glanced back toward the brush. "I thought you followed close behind me, Luster."

"I prefer the road less traveled, Ili. Now, let me help you to your feet." He bent over, taking her hand.

"Where did you go to then?"

"Why, the trail of course. Lim just took the scenic route so he could have some time alone with you."

She blushed as Lim scrambled to his feet. "If you're so smart, where do we go from here?"

"The path begins again at that patch of thistles, Lim." Luster pointed across the meadow.

"Oh dear, Luster." Ili put a hand to her forehead. "Please tell me we are through with getting scraped and scratched.

"Don't worry, Ili. The trail is open and clearly marked there and in the forest beyond. It should pose no problems for such intrepid explorers as you and Lim. I suggest we keep moving. It's a bit warm out here in the open."

They hurried across the meadow and entered the field of thistles, knee-high at first but soon stretching above their heads. Butterflies floated among the few remaining blossoms, the majority of blooms having gone white with feathery seeds. A hot wind rustled through the dry stalks.

All at once, seeds took flight by the dozens, moving on the heated air in swirling spirals, rising toward the blue dome of sky like a swarm of tiny creatures. Lim stopped and followed the delicate seeds with his gaze, awed by their beauty. A small cloud of them moved about him before sailing above the nearby tree line and vanishing from sight.

Then as quickly as it started the wind died, the warm air falling around them in a heavy stillness. Lim turned to Ili as curtains of downy seeds floated past them, falling down through the towering plants, winding their way among the stalks and to the dry grass below, gathering in small drifts at their feet. Ili reached for him, grabbing his arm as she pointed to them.

"Do you see, Lim? What do they look like?"

"Like thistle seeds."

"No, they look like snow! It is snowing just like the fortuneteller said it would, but we have seeds instead of flakes. Isn't it magical?"

Though it seemed the fortuneteller might be right, Lim resisted the idea. He wanted certainty, predictability in his uprooted life.

"It's just the heat, Ili. The air gets hot and rises. Then all it takes is a breeze and the seeds take off."

"But don't you see the magic in them, Lim? Tell him, Luster."

"Lim, is there no poetry, no romance, in your young heart?" Luster spread his arms to the sky.

Lim glanced at Ili but was in no mood to humor him. "The truth is good enough for me, Luster."

"But Lim, look at the way they move, their grace, their beauty. They're like fairies dancing on the wind. Can't you see it?"

"I see floating seeds."

"I see a ballet of sprites, a dance of wood spirits. Can you see them, Ili?"

"Do you think they mean to greet us?"

"I do, Ili. They welcome us into the forest ahead. We must continue on, then."

The trail passed beneath thick-trunked oaks, their black branches stretching to the ground in gnarled arcs, and through breaks of cedar, windless and silent. Dropping down a gentle slope, they rounded a grove of persimmon trees. The purple fruit littered the ground.

Once they had cleared the grove, the trail again seemed to end abruptly in a wall of brush. Luster turned to Lim and shrugged. An instant later, footsteps sounded ahead. Luster raised a finger to his lips, cocking his head as he tried to listen. Then a woman's voice called from beyond the thicket.

"You believe you are lost but you can find your way. Just close your eyes and follow the blue light."

Lim frowned at Luster. "How in the hell are we supposed to see a light with our eyes closed?"

The voice again called from beyond the bushes. "You must trust your intuition."

Lim snorted. "I bet you feel right at home, Luster."

"Stop talking and close your eyes, Lim. We must try to concentrate."

"Why the hell not? I'll try anything at this point."

A brilliant azure beam shot through the trees, fracturing the forest into slivers of dark and light. Lim squinted, turning away from the painful glare. Then he took a breath, closed his eyes and again faced the light, at once surprised to find the blue beam clear but no longer painful. He took a step, and then another. The underbrush he expected to tear at his clothes seemed mere twigs and hardly worth notice.

A moment later Ili's hand found his, squeezing as she pulled him toward the blue glow, the warmth of her skin rising up his arm and through his chest as if her blood mingled with his. He could almost see her walking before him, her auburn hair tinged with blue. Suddenly, a breeze smelling of rain rushed past them as a roll of thunder shook the treetops overhead. In the silence that followed the woman's voice, close and somehow calming, spoke again.

"You can open your eyes now."

## Six

They stood on a limestone ledge above a broad glen. Before them, a rocky path wound down the gentle slope, passing through a stand of cedar elm and disappearing behind a line of post oaks. Grass-covered hills ranged along the ragged horizon in sets of diminishing blue while the distant thunderstorm rolled out its dull thump of thunder at short but regular intervals. The woman was nowhere in sight. Lim turned to find Luster staring at him.

"I see you had some help getting here, Lim."

"What?"

Luster nodded toward Lim's hand, still clasped by Ili. He looked at her and released his grip, although less than willingly. A shy smile passed across her lips as she wondered what might be going through his mind. Lim looked to his left and right, feeling a bit perturbed by Luster's comment.

"Where's the person who was talking to us? Where's the blue light?"

"Who can say?" Luster shrugged. "You heard what Orvis said, Lim. She's no ordinary herbalist."

"You mean she can throw her voice?"

"Not necessarily."

"How else do you explain it?"

"There are times when no explanation is required."

Lim squinted at him. "Just give me a straight answer for once, Luster."

"Oh, Lim of little faith, what will become of you?"

"Where is she then?"

"I believe this path may take us to her. Shall we go see?"

Lim threw up his hands and started down the path. "Anything is better than talking nonsense with you."

They followed the gravel trail, rounding a tree line where the path leveled out before opening onto a broad grass-filled meadow, blonde beneath the clearing sky. Red tips topping the thick grass stirred in the noonday heat.

Beyond the field, a grove of massive live oaks stretched their black branches over a small house, its stone walls the color of honey. Wooden chairs and benches, watermarked and grayed by the sun, sat scattered along a deep porch and stone patio. Beyond the house, a lily pond marked the center of an herb garden arranged in rows of limestone boxes. Their raised beds, some flowering, others going to seed, seemed to glow beneath the mottled sunlight.

An ancient oak crowded the stone walkway leading to the house. The hollowed-out trunk of the massive tree seemed the size of a small cave. As Lim stepped onto the sidewalk, the plucked notes of a guitar and a wavering tenor rose from the tree, stopping him where he stood.

> "There was a young man from the east
> Who found it quite hard to believe
> In anything much
> That he could not touch
> Thus leaving him quite ill at ease"

Lim glanced at the others, putting his finger to his lips. Then he turned back to the tree, searching the huge trunk for the singer, walking around one side and then the other before turning to Ili and shaking his head. They stood together listening as the music drifted about them, lyrical, mesmerizing. The song ended and a moment later the voice spoke.

"Well, not so much as a thank you or single how-de-do? What is the poor world coming to?

"That was a very beautiful song." Luster leaned toward the tree.

"Only a part of a song it was, to tell the truth."

"And the words were quite true."

"And why wouldn't they be? Is that all you have to say?"

"Perhaps it would help if we could see you." Luster glanced back at Ili and Lim.

"Is that so important?"

Luster nodded. "I'm afraid it is."

"I don't see anything." Lim circled the tree, searching the upper branches. "Where is he?"

Luster leaned closer to the tree, whispering. "Do you see what I mean?"

"Oh, alright then. I'll show myself if I must."

Out from the hollow trunk climbed an old man carrying a gnarled cane, red hair rising from the top of his head like flame. Clearly blind, his cloudy eyes darted about as if searching some unseen world. He turned and looked down the walkway, scratching his thin beard and mumbling to himself. After a moment he again faced them.

"Welcome to Isadora, home to Cyril. She's the owner of this peaceful garden and kind enough to let an old soul like me make his camp in this blessed tree."

"You live in there?" Lim leaned into the dark opening.

"I do and you will kindly keep your nose out until invited, just like you would anyone else's home, Mister... What would your name be then, son? Have you no manners?"

"My name is Lim Specter."

"Well, that's quite a name you have there." He scratched at his beard. "Lim is short for Limerick then, is it?"

"You know the answer, hence your little song."

In a flash he raised his cane like a rapier, pressing the end to Lim's chest. "A work of art it is, a little song it is not. And quite old too, not having a thing to do with Your Grumpiness."

Lim raised his hands. "I meant no offense."

"I suppose you'll call my noble tree a little house as well, though it is a grand abode if I do say so."

71

"No, I…"

"Just because I'm a wayward soul in Cyril's good graces doesn't mean I have no right to any bit of privacy whatsoever."

Luster cleared his throat. Lowering the cane, the little man faced him.

"And you would be… ?"

"My name is Luster. He means no disrespect. He's just a curious sort, Mister…"

"Yes, yes, of course. Here, I've gotten myself so worked up that I'm the one forgot his manners. The name is John Doe."

Lim stifled a laugh.

"Be careful there, sonny. You won't be the first that's made light of my name and them that did fared poorly. But you can make up for it by introducing your lady friend, and pretty as a flower she is too."

"How do you know that?"

"I may be blind but I'm not so old I don't know when a pretty lady is near. She is pretty then, wouldn't you say?"

"Yes, she is." Lim managed a nod as he felt the blood rise to his face.

"So, get on with it then."

"This is Ileana but she goes by Ili, Mr. Doe."

He bowed to her and then stood leaning on his cane, a mischievous look on his face.

"You can call me Buck, Ili. I'll not have a pretty lady calling me a doe."

She stared at him, mouth open. He held up both hands grinning at her and shaking his head.

"No, no, I'm only fooling with you, Ili. Call me Jonny, if you please."

She eyed him for a moment and then smiled. "You are a funny one, Jonny. You have lived here long?"

"No, Ili, a mere trifle of time. Let's see, it's just shy of twenty year since Cyril took me on. As long as I welcome in good people and run off those that aren't, I hope to stay a short while more."

"Twenty years seems a long time to me."

"That's because you're such a young thing, pretty as a flower but still young. You'll see what I mean when you get a bit older, say in forty or fifty a year."

Luster peered at him. "How old are you then, Jonny?"

"Well, Luster, I lost count around eighty year or so but it must be a good deal more by now."

"You don't look a day over seventy."

A frown crossed his face. "In truth, I'm only fifty-three."

Then he let out a laugh, again raising his hands. "No, no, Luster, I'm fooling with you as well. I'm ninety if I'm a day. It's the tree, you see. Long ago a bolt of lightning stuck this tree, splitting the trunk but giving it something in return, a spirit, a soul you might say. Over many a year the tree became a wonder, a force of nature, of life. I suppose a bit rubs off on me. Now what do you make of that, Mister Limerick Specter?"

"I'd rather not say." Lim avoided facing him.

"Well that's an improvement over what I've heard so far. But you're not here to listen to the likes of me then, are you? It's Cyril you'll want to see."

"Is she here, Jonny?" -Ili leaned toward him. "We do need to see her as soon as we can. Will you take us to her?"

"I'd sneak you in to see the Queen of England herself if you asked me to, Ili. Taking you to see Cyril is a sight easier. Truth is you don't need me at all. Just follow the rock path past the house and there you are. She's in her shop helping out a young woman, and a poor thing she is too."

"Thank you, Jonny."

"There's one more thing I should tell you." He held up a finger. "Cyril has been hanging her herbs up to dry and some of them are quite powerful. Be careful not to touch or you might start seeing gnomes and sprites instead of funny old men."

Dragonflies swarmed the stone walkway as they made their way past the house. Seeming to move in concert, the creatures swirled around Ili and Lim, dipping toward the foot-worn path one after the other, their wings crinkling like wax paper. After circling them three times, they disappeared all at once.

Lim blinked, unsure of what he had just seen. They continued beyond the garden, approaching a small wooden cabin draped with flowering vines. Clusters of grapes hanging from a nearby pergola swayed before the breeze. Behind the cabin, a half a dozen tables held plants of various sizes drying in the emerald light. A murmur of voices drifted out the open door. Then someone called through the nearby window.

"I'm so pleased the blue light proved helpful to you, Limerick Specter. Come join us."

Lim looked at Luster and shrugged as they passed under the arbor. Stepping through the doorway into the small space, they found a woman perched on the edge of a chair. She looked up and smoothed back her golden hair, checking the loose braid as she studied each of them in turn. Her smooth skin glowed in peach-colored hues.

On the floor in front of her lay a young woman with her arms and legs outstretched in the shape of a cross, her palms and tops of her feet smeared with a green paste. Black hair spread about her coffee-colored face in curling strands. She seemed not to notice them as the golden-haired woman nodded at her.

"Maria must stay still for a moment more. Please find a chair and make yourselves comfortable."

She stood and took Lim's hand. "Your questions will have to wait for an answer, Limerick Specter. I'm Cyril."

"My mother was the only person who called me by my full name. I go by Lim now."

"A difficult loss at a young age, it's true. That can make a person mistrust the world around him."

Lim turned to Luster. "What have you told her?"

"I'm only just meeting Cyril myself, Lim."

"And your pretty companion must be Ili."

Ili leaned toward her. "You will help me find my sister, won't you Cyril?"

Cyril turned to face the woman on the floor. "Alright, Maria, that's long enough."

The woman lifted herself and stood staring at her hands.

"You can wash off the salve whenever you like."

She raised her palm toward Cyril. "Bless you my child."

"Promise me you won't burn yourself anymore, Maria."

The woman nodded before facing Ili and making the sign of a cross. "With my body, I have atoned for your sins and the sins of your family. May you now find peace."

"Do you mean my sister?" Ili peered at her. "Do you know something of her, of where she is?"

The woman turned and stepped past her, moving across the room and out the door without another word. Ili looked at Luster.

"What did she mean, Luster? What does she know?"

"I couldn't say, Ili."

She faced Cyril. "Cyril, does she know something of my sister?"

"Maria sometimes forgets who she is, instead believing she is the Christ. She lays herself out and burns candles on her palms and the tops of her feet as a sort of symbolic crucifixion, a penance. She was badly burned when she first came to me."

"You mean she's crazy?" Lim stared out the door.

Try to be understanding of her, Lim. She has what's called a fixed delusion. Other than being unusually devout she's like anyone else most of the time.

"Have you been able to help her, Cyril?"

"For the time being I have, Ili. Now I'd like to help you if I can."

She turned to Luster.

"Orvis has told me some but it might help to hear the story from you, Luster."

"We're hoping that two men have been to see you, men that could lead us to Ili's sister. One of them is called Jorvic, a Serb with a scar down the side of his face. He seems to be in charge. The other has a tattoo of a griffin on his neck."

She nodded. "Yes, they were here yesterday. I made up an herbal tea for the one with the tattoo and sent them on their way."

"Might they have told you where they are staying, Cyril?"

"They told Jonny. He sensed they might be trouble and refused to let them pass until they answered his questions. It's an old trick he uses to stall visitors until I can come round to see for myself."

Lim snorted. "That old man couldn't stop the two of them by himself."

"You'd be surprised what he can do with that cane if he has a mind to, Lim."

Luster cast a frown toward Lim before continuing.

"And what did Jonny find out, Cyril?"

"They're staying at a ranch house a half mile from town, back the way you came. You can't see it from the road but you shouldn't have any trouble finding it."

She scribbled the address on a scrap of paper, handing it to him. Lim and Ili stood, preparing to leave as Luster crammed the note in his shirt pocket.

"We'll be off then."

"May I give you something that might help? I have a special brandy that can make your dealings with these men a good deal easier."

Luster stroked his chin. "Yes, a toast could be good way to break the ice."

"This is no ordinary liquor, Luster. Drinking even a small amount will knock them out, but only for a short while."

"Surely they'll suspect something if we don't drink with them."

"I'm afraid so. But I'll give you an elixir to drink beforehand that should protect you."

"That's brilliant! I still had yet to work out how we'd free Mirela if we found her. This should do the trick."

She rummaged through a nearby cabinet, pulling out a flask filled with a golden liquid along with a small glass vial. "You must take care to be quick, Luster. The herb in the liquor may cause hallucinations that can make a person quite violent. And each person responds to the sedative differently. Some of them may not be out for long."

She walked to where the three of them stood together, giving Luster the flask and vial before turning to Ili.

"I'll wish you the best then, Ili."

"Cyril, you are so kind to us. Thank you for helping me to find my sister."

Ili kissed her cheek. The warm glow of Cyril's face seemed to brighten as she turned to Lim, taking his hand in hers, studying his eyes. She reached into her pocket with her free hand, pulling out a small glass frame containing a single pressed flower, the oval petals pink against the green of the leaves. She handed it to him.

"What is it?"

"The flower of the almond tree symbolizes promise. I see promise in you, Lim, in your loyalty, in your potential. But you must find it for yourself."

Precipitate (pri'sipəˌtāt) - to hasten the occurrence of; bring about prematurely, hastily, or suddenly; a substance precipitated from a solution.

## Seven

They pulled up to a broad entrance flanked by limestone posts, the driveway beyond blocked by a black metal gate and high fence that stretched in both directions before disappearing into the trees. Waves of heat vibrated above the road. Though a new lock securing the gate gleamed beneath the midday light, there was little evidence a house lay somewhere down the steep grade. Sweat beaded on Lim's brow as searched the fence line for a way inside.

Ili studied his profile, the anxiety and self-doubt clear on his face. He seemed a good man beneath the anger that masked his shaken confidence, a man she might like to know better if he would allow it, if he could set aside his mistrust, his past, and she hers. As if sensing her thoughts, Lim turned to her.

"This place is a fortress. There's no way we can get past the fence.

"But we must find a way, Lim. We are so close.

"Just give me a moment to think.

"The grass, it grows on this road. Is this right?" Ili walked toward the gate.

"What do you mean?"

"Could there be another way in?"

Lim moved to where she stood and studied the tufts of grass sprouting undisturbed along the wheel ruts. "Of course there could, Ili."

They hurried to where Luster paced along the drive as if in a trance. Staring into the distance, he silently counted off the many ways his plan could go wrong. Yet try as he might, he could see no alternative. Lim stopped and stood before him.

"Ili thinks there's another entrance. I believe she's right."

Luster squinted at her. "Do you now, Ili?"

"I hope I am correct, Luster."

Luster stepped to the gate, bending toward it for a moment.

"Yes, of course. These hinges are rusty. It has been some time since anyone passed through. There has to be another entrance."

"I saw a road that turns off the highway a short distance back."

"Good eye, Lim. That must be the way." Luster held up his hand. "You must be the only one to go in, Lim. Ili can't, of course. And they may have seen me when I found her. I can't be sure."

"Luster, must it be so?" Ili looked from one to the other.

"I don't see any other way, Ili."

She placed a hand on Lim's arm. "I worry for you. These men, they are killers."

"We can do this." He waved off her concern. "Tell me the plan, Luster."

They returned to the car and Luster bent inside, lifting a brown paper bag from beneath the seat and pulling a small book from it. He cradled the leather cover in both hands as if blessing it, then handed it to Lim. Ili reached out, running her fingers across the cover.

"This is the book, Luster? It is also in French."

"Yes it is, Ili. It's Charles Baudelaire's *Les Fleurs Du Mal* or *The Flowers of Evil,* a collection of poems. In view of the other book, the Cantemir, Orvis thought French might be an advantage."

"It's poetry?" Lim frowned at the book. "Poems are the last thing these people are going to want, Luster."

"This is no ordinary book of poems. Baudelaire was charged with offending public morals and prosecuted because of six poems in this book. Besides, it's worth fourteen thousand dollars."

"This little book is worth that much?" Lim stepped back, his eyes wide.

"A first edition can go for thirty thousand or more."

"What price do I tell them?"

"Orvis priced this copy at twenty-five thousand but I'm changing the plan."

"What do you mean?"

"I want you to listen to me very carefully, Lim." Luster tapped his finger on the cover. "Act as if you have a book to sell but once you're inside offer to trade it for the Cantemir."

"But Orvis won't like it if we lose his book."

"Don't worry about Orvis. I'll deal with him when the time comes."

Luster pulled the vial and flask from his pocket, handing them to him. "Here is the brandy. You should drink a bit of the small one now."

Lim lifted the vial, taking a gulp and nearly retching. "Oh, that tastes awful."

"I hope it works like Cyril said. Otherwise, you'll be taking a trip to the Land of Oz."

"Someplace you've been before, no doubt."

"Remember, Lim, you haven't much time. Just focus on finding the girl. And do your best to get the book by Cantemir."

Ili took Lim's hand in hers, staring into his eyes. "Thank you, Lim, for what you do here. Find Mirela, but make a safe return for yourself also."

A short while later Lim turned onto a rutted gravel drive, stopping long enough to let Ili and Luster slip from the car and duck behind a clump of underbrush. Continuing along the driveway, he angled the car up to a gate all but hidden behind a tall break of juniper that stretched past the fence line. A small camera sat perched atop the closest gatepost, an intercom just below. As he cut the engine a voice sounded from the speaker, the accent vaguely familiar.

"You trespass on private property. You must leave."

"But I'm here on business."

"You must leave."

"I hear you're in the market for rare books."

"Why do you say this?"

"I have a book that might interest you, a very unusual and rare copy. I heard you might want a chance at it before I go elsewhere."

"How do you know this place?"

"The book world is small. Word gets around."

The speaker became silent before again crackling to life.

"One moment."

Lim glanced back at the thicket, hoping Ili and Luster could hear what was said. A moment later a small metal gate next to the drive buzzed before popping open with a loud click. He hesitated, the fear of yet another failure gripping him. Then he took a breath and stepped past, following a stone pathway that wound through the junipers and up a rocky incline. A dog barked in the distance. He quickened his pace, sunlight and shadow falling in broken shapes about him, slicing the uneven trail ahead.

After what seemed a long way, the trees thinned and then fell away as the path spilled onto a cobblestone plaza fronting a low brick house. Other than a black metal door, a narrow line of windows stretching just below the eaves offered the only variation to the stark exterior. The place resembled a fortress. He made his way toward the shaded doorway as a dry heat radiated from the plaza.

Before he had a chance to knock, the figure of a man appeared in the doorway, a griffin tattoo circling his thick neck. He motioned Lim inside with a flick of his shaved head, following him through a narrow hallway and into a broad room floored with Mexican tiles of glazed azure and gold. Walnut shelves filled with books stretched from corner to corner, rising to the ceiling. In the middle of the room a leather couch and chair shone dully in the dim light.

The tattooed man disappeared and a moment later footsteps sounded from the hallway as a woman stepped into the room, the click of her high heels echoing off the tiles. Wearing a turquoise-hued dress that seemed to vibrate next to her clay-colored skin, she looked about the room before turning to Lim and studying him without a word. Her dark hair glistened in the half-light. He started to speak but checked himself, surprised by her striking appearance. He had expected to deal with one of the men.

As she moved toward him, a slight smile crossed her lips. She stopped and held out her hand, her low-cut dress scarcely covering the smooth curve of her breasts, her eyes so dark they appeared almost without color. For an instant, Lim felt captured by her intense beauty. He blinked, taking his eyes from her with difficulty. Then he held up the book, trying to gather his thoughts. She stepped back, her hands on her hips, appraising both him and the book.

"So, you have a book to sell? Will I like it as much as I like you?"

Embarrassed by the comment, he studied the book, trying concentrate, the familiar fear of failure again gripping him. He took a breath and tapped the cover with his finger, looking up at her.

"I hope you'll find it worth taking a look at, but shouldn't we introduce ourselves first?"

"I find names make for unpleasant complications in such business."

"That is a point. What do I call you then?"

"You may call me Magdalena."

"Ah, the fallen woman of the Bible."

"Only a myth, I think. She was a patroness of wayward women. And what shall I call you?"

"My name is John Doe."

"An unusual name, I think."

"You can call me Jonny."

"Yes, a suitable name for a handsome man."

And are any of your wayward women here now?"

If you are interested in a woman, I am here."

He felt the blood rush to his face but managed to focus on what he wanted to say. "You and no more?"

"Only Bogdan is here with me, the one with the tattoo. As you could see, he is no woman. And our cook, an old man, is here also." She cocked her head, squinting at him. "So, you came here for business or for women?"

"I was trying to make a joke. Please forgive me but I find it difficult to think clearly in the presence of a beautiful woman."

Smiling, she stepped toward him as he handed her the book. "Ah, the poetry of Baudelaire."

They sat. As she leafed through the pages, Lim listened for any sign of Mirela but heard nothing except dishes clinking in the nearby kitchen. A moment later she stood.

"I must have Bogdan do some checking."

"Actually, I'd like to trade the book rather than sell it."

"Trade it for what?"

"I understand you have a book by Dimitrie Cantemir."

She stepped back, frowning. "Why do you say this?"

"Like I told your assistant, the book business is a small world."

"You would trade this book for the Cantemir, if we have it?"

"If you have it."

"Like I said, we must do some checking. I will ask Clavo to bring out some wine while you wait."

"Let's have brandy instead." Lim pulled the flask from his pocket.

"I never drink brandy before dinner but I thank you for your gift."

Before he realized what was happening she had lifted the bottle from his hand. She turned and disappeared down the hallway, her footsteps still echoing as a gray-haired man in a white apron emerged from the kitchen carrying a bottle of wine and two glasses. Studying him as he filled the glasses, Lim decided to take a chance and speak.

"Buenos tardes. Como esta?"

"Muy bien. And you?"

"I'm alright. My name is Lim. Do you mind if I ask you something?"

"I am Clavo Ortiz, an old man with nothing to hide. You may ask what you like."

"Are you from around here?"

"I have lived in this place all of my life."

"Have you worked here long?"

"No, I work here a short time only. I own a café in town. I come here just to cook the lunch."

"What do you know of these people?"

"There is the woman and two men. The bald one is a thug from Albania. The other, the one with dark hair, is a Serb. It is said he is hunted for war crimes. Do you look for these men?"

"No, I'm looking for a girl. Her name is Mirela. Have you heard anything of her?"

The man glanced back toward the hallway, speaking beneath his breath. "It is dangerous to ask such questions."

"But you know her?"

"Yes, I know of her."

"I must find her. Is she here?"

Footsteps echoed from the hallway and the man again glanced behind him before whispering to the side of Lim's face.

"There are no girls here but I can tell you what I know. Meet me at St. Mary's Church in Wilder tonight at eight."

He jerked upright and hurried back to the kitchen as Magdalena strode into the room carrying two books, one large and leather-bound, the other the thin volume by Baudelaire. She held out the larger book.

"I have here a history of the Ottoman Empire by Dimitrie Cantemir. It is very old and, as you can see, in excellent condition. It is also written in French. We will sell it to you, if you like, but we will not trade."

"If you're willing to sell, why won't you trade for it?"

"I am sorry to say we have no interest in this book." She held up the book of poetry, pursing her lips. "As it turns out, we also have a copy. I thought as much but I wanted to be sure."

"Well, it was worth a try."

"We are willing to sell our copy of the Baudelaire to you, if you are interested. It is rare because it has a dedication to Ernest Hemingway in Baudelaire's own hand. Aren't you impressed?"

"Yes, that's very impressive. But I came here to trade or sell, not buy."

She set the books on the side table, drawing close to him and taking his hand. He found himself again mesmerized by her dark eyes, alluring but impossible to read.

"What a pity. Do you mind if I ask how you came to have the book?"

"I represent a bookseller who wishes to remain anonymous."

"You are unable to tell me the name of this person?"

"That's his wish."

"You have represented this bookseller before?"

"Why do you ask?"

She released his hand and stood, her eyes dark with anger."

"What is the real reason you are here?"

"What do you mean?"

"Baudelaire made no such dedication. He died thirty years before Hemingway was even born. You should know this. Do you work for the authorities?"

"No. Don't you think you'd know by now if I did?"

"Who are you, then?"

"I thought we said no names." Lim searched for some way around her questions.

"Yes, of course but you must explain. If I think you deceive me I will call Bogdan. It would be a shame to make a mess of such a handsome face."

"Alright, I'll tell you. I'm doing a favor for a friend who needs the money."

"Your friend is a bookseller?"

"Yes, and I do represent him. So, I was telling you the truth. Unfortunately, I don't know a thing about rare books."

"Ah, so you only want to help your friend?"

"He's in poor health and needs the money to pay medical expenses. He couldn't come himself so I agreed to come for him. I apologize if I seemed to deceive you."

"I believe you. But you would do your friend a favor by learning about the books you sell. You must understand there are thieves and forgers who can cause us trouble we wish to avoid."

"That I do understand. My friend once had a very bad experience with a forger."

"So, you will let me apologize by sharing a glass of wine?"

"I would but I have an appointment."

"That is a pity. It is sad to bid farewell such a handsome man. Will you take a moment for just a small toast so I may make amends?"

"Alright, but I can stay a minute only."

She sat and had raised her glass just as a phone sounded from down the hall. Setting down the glass, she sighed and again stood.

"Please excuse me. I must take this call."

Lim watched her disappear around the corner before downing most of his glass, hoping for a quick exit. A moment later a flash of light thrown by a small mirror hanging in the corner caught his eye. In the reflection the woman stood facing a pale man with dark hair, the same man that had shown up at Lim's door two nights before. Lim stared at the man, trying to puzzle out why he was there until the man turned, showing a scar down his face just as Orvis described, the man Ili called Jorvic.

Lim peered at the mirror, a wave of panic gripping his chest. If Jorvic recognized him he would surely tell the woman. Lim glanced toward the exit just as she reappeared, passing the chair and instead sitting on the couch next to him. She held another leather-bound book in her hand.

"This is a book of poems by Pablo Neruda, the poet of Chile. His poems to his wife are sensuous, very sexy. It is not for sale but someday I would like to read them to you if you will let me."

She leaned into him as she held up the open book, the heat of her arm burning his skin, her breath hot against his cheek. He looked into her face, mesmerized by the depth of her eyes. Shifting his gaze to the book, he studied the page but the words seemed to move about, vibrating against the cream-colored paper. He looked up to find her standing over him. Then she set the book by the others and drifted away. He sat wondering where she had gone when a voice echoed through the house, followed by a scream and the sound of breaking glass.

He shook his head, staring at his glass, the realization of his mistake coming to him in pieces. He reached for Orvis' book. Unable to tell it from the others, he grabbed all three and forced himself to stand, moving toward the door as the room tilted about like a ship at sea.

Fumbling with the latch, he managed to open it and stumble out the door, weaving across the rock plaza and into the junipers, the stone path swimming before him. Sunlight splintered through the treetops, fracturing the way ahead. An instant later the scene faded to white, then to black. He felt himself falling into a deep well. He tried to call out and for a moment believed he heard Ili's voice in answer. Then a dense silence swallowed him.

Lim struggled to open his eyes, for an instant fearing they had been sewn shut. A moment later a blurred image of Ili's face appeared, then vanished, then reappeared before him. He thought he must be dreaming. A voice spoke from somewhere though no words seemed to pass her lips. Above her, dried stalks of lavender rustled before a warm breeze, the fragrance wafting about his head in waves, leaving him queasy. He blinked, wiping his eyes with the back of his hand. When he looked at Ili again she peered down at him and spoke, the voice now clearly hers.

"You have decided to come back to us, Lim Specter?"

"Where are we?" He struggled to sit up. "We need to get away from here."

"You must go slowly, Lim." Ili placed her hand on his shoulder, steadying him. "We are back in Cyril's home. You have been sleeping."

"How did I get here?"

"You owe Ili your safety and possibly your life, Lim." Luster's voice came from behind him. "She went to find you. She claims to have heard you calling her name but I heard nothing. That's a bit odd, isn't it?"

"Where did you find me?

"You were nearly to the gate but you had fallen."

He flinched as she ran her fingers across his forehead. "That explains my headache."

Orvis appeared before him, two books in hand. He bent toward Lim, concern in his eyes.

"How're you holding up, son?"

"Orvis, what are you doing here?"

He peered at Lim, his voice warm, kindly. "You were on a risky venture and I wanted to be sure you got through it in one piece. I also wanted my Baudelaire book back. I'm glad to see you kept hold of it in spite of your mishap. And you managed to come away with this other jewel by Neruda. It should fetch a nice price.

Lim squinted at the book. "You're going to sell it?"

"Why not? They're not likely to report it the police, now are they?"

"Where's the other book?"

"What other book?"

Lim blinked again, looking about the room. "It's a bit blurry but I remember grabbing three books when I left. At least, I think I had three."

"These are the only two he had with him, right Luster?" Orvis held up the books.

"That's right."

Luster faced Ili.

"You didn't see a third book, did you Ili?"

"I saw no books at all, Luster. I worried so for Lim I could see nothing else."

Luster patted Lim's shoulder. "If you did have another book, you must have dropped it somewhere along the path."

"You were damn lucky, Lim." Orvis shook his head in disbelief. "It sounds like you barely made it out. How in the hell did those hombres figure out you were a fake?"

"I'm not sure but I have an idea."

"You weren't able to follow our plan?" Luster moved around to face him.

"It was my fault. I was stupid and lost the brandy. Then I let myself get talked into drinking a toast."

"I wondered how they managed to drug you."

Lim lowered his head. "I should've known better, Luster."

"It could have been worse, Lim. Cyril's elixir kept you from passing out until you were able to get away."

"They didn't follow us, did they?" He glanced out the window.

"I believe they were otherwise engaged."

"What do you mean?"

"Cyril heard that a man with a shaved head was found wandering the highway and ranting incoherently. A man and woman were in similar condition inside the house."

"They drank the brandy?"

"It appears so."

Cyril walked through the doorway carrying a glass filled with a blue liquid. She paused, reaching up and picking a few petals of dried lavender, then sprinkling them over the glass before handing it to Ili. She held it to Lim's lips. After a couple of swallows, his head seemed to clear and he took the glass in hand, finishing it at once. He looked up at Cyril.

"What is this?"

"Just something I made up to help you feel better."

"I don't just feel better, I feel great. I think I can get up now."

Ili took his hand, helping him to his feet. As he stood, he gazed into her dark eyes, suddenly overwhelmed with the urge to kiss her. As if she could read his thoughts, she blushed before turning away. Cyril took him by the arm.

"Even though you're feeling better, you must give yourself some time, Lim."

"Alright Cyril, I'll try to… wait, the time, what time is it?"

"It's seven-thirty."

"We have to leave! We need to go now! How do I get to St. Mary's?"

Luster peered into his eyes. "Have you suddenly found religion, Lim?"

"Luster, this is serious. When I was in the house I managed to talk to the cook. He knows something about Mirela."

"My sister is there?"

"No, Ili." Lim shook his head. "He said she wasn't and I believed him. We got interrupted so he didn't have time to tell me anything more except to meet him at St. Mary's. He'll be there at eight o'clock."

Luster angled the car up the steep hill leading to St. Mary's Catholic Church, cutting the engine a short distance from a wide set of stairs. They climbed from the car and approached the steps, the tile-roofed bell tower looming above them, its reddish-orange bricks framing several floors of arched windows.

At the top of the stairs a sign reading "Sanctu Maria Ora Pro Nobis" stood suspended between white metal filigree. A small cross topped the sign. Beyond the sign, two broad doors set below a circular stained glass window of Mary marked the church entrance.

Noticing a sidewalk to the right of the stairs, Lim followed the short path to a rock grotto carved into the hill, the concrete archway and interior studded with stones, shells and bits of broken glass. In the center of the room, shriveled bouquets and potted plants surrounded a small granite altar fronted by a table of votive candles, some flickering against the damp walls. The dark space seemed a cool respite to the fuming heat beyond.

He stepped back into the evening light, walking to where Ili and Luster stood at the base of the stairs. A dry breeze swirled about them, stirring the leaves at their feet. Lim glanced up the stairway.

"If we go in together we're likely to spook him and miss our chance. You wait here and I'll ask if you can join us.

Ili took his arm. "Lim, is this best? It could be a trap."

I was the one that asked him for help, Ili. I believe he wants to tell us what he can.

Luster watched Lim disappear up the stairs but sensed a need to follow, if only at a distance. He waited a moment before turning to Ili.

"I am less certain of Lim's plan than he is. I'm going to follow and try to keep out of sight. Wait here and I'll call to you if Lim says we can join him."

Luster climbed the double set of stairs, careful to stay off to one side as he passed beneath the metal sign. Glancing back at Ili, still waiting at the bottom of the steps, he slipped into the small foyer. A gust of cool air rushed past him. He inched up to the massive doors and peered between them into the glowing interior.

At the far end of the room, Lim stood in front of a flower-covered altar backed by a triptych of the patron saint. The ceiling rose above him in soaring arches, their stained glass windows lit by a low western sun that filled the space with hues of crimson, fuchsia and turquoise as if tinting the air itself. Seeing no one else inside, Luster crept through the door, making his way along one side while keeping to the shadows.

Lim paced the front of the sanctuary, peering into the dim corners for any sign of Clavo. Pausing, he thought back to their conversation, wondering if he had somehow misunderstood the plan. Just as he was about to give up, he stopped as if frozen in place, staring at his feet. Luster moved to him.

"What is it, Lim?"

He bent and then turned to Luster, holding up two fingers stained red. "It looks like blood."

Luster scanned the aisle behind him, pointing toward a side door. "There's a trail of drops leading that way."

"What's happened here, Luster?" Lim looked about the room.

It doesn't look good. Someone was badly hurt.

Lim's mind raced as they followed the drops to the door.

"Who could it have…? Luster, where's Ili?"

"She's still waiting down the stairs."

"She's alone, Luster! What if…?"

Lim rushed down the aisle and through the door, leaping down the steps to the bottom landing and scanning the area, hoping for some sign of Ili. To his right the street and parking lot stood empty. Remembering the grotto, he turned left and moved around the side of the hill toward the half-circle opening. A hot wind roared up the steep slope, making it all but impossible to hear anything, even the sound of his own footsteps. An image of the man with the pale skin flashed through his mind.

He leaned around the corner, peering into the shadows. At first the small space seemed empty. Then his eyes adjusted and he spotted a shoe behind the altar. He crept toward it, listening for any clue to what lay beyond. An instant later Ili's voice sounded against the walls.

"Try not to move."

Lim stood upright, spotting her where she leaned over Clavo, her hands pressed against his chest. Blood pooled beneath him. She turned to face Lim, her eyes wet with tears.

"I wished for you to come. I've only just found him but I could not leave when he bled so. He has been trying to speak."

Lim pulled out his phone and called for help before leaning toward the old man, cocking his head to listen. His eyes closed, Clavo whispered between breaths.

"The girl was sold. She would not prostitute herself."

Lim bent closer to him.

"They sold her?"

He managed a weak nod.

"Who did they sell her to, Clavo?"

"You must find her." He opened his eyes, raising a hand toward Lim. "The religious ones, they pay well, take them for wives. No good."

"Where, Clavo? Where did they take her?"

The old man managed to raise his head, coughing deeply before he could again speak. "Near El Consuelo, far to the southwest."

Then he fell back, his eyes closed.

## Eight

They watched the ambulance disappear over a distant rise before heading back to the car. Luster leaned against the hood, staring into the evening half-light, lost in his thoughts as Ili and Lim lingered near the grotto. A single star punctured the fading horizon. Up the wide staircase people approached the church for a late evening mass, their restrained voices rising as news of Clavo's assault spread among them.

Luster mulled over how the kidnappers could have known Clavo and Lim planned to meet. Discovering a fraud as inexperienced as Lim seemed plausible given his limited knowledge of rare books. But Luster could see no way they could have guessed the time and place of his meeting with Clavo. Hearing footsteps behind him, he turned as Lim and Ili rounded the bumper. Ili looked at him, cocking her head to one side and frowning.

"Something troubles you, Luster?"

"Yes, Ili, something troubles me. I'm unable to explain what's happened here. How did the kidnappers know of the meeting?"

"I have wondered so too."

Luster turned to Lim. "Could you have said anything after you drank the tainted wine?"

"I don't see how. Once I realized they had slipped me something I went for the door right away. No one else was anywhere in sight. After that it gets a little hazy but I still remember everything until I was up the hill. I didn't see or talk to anyone. Then I heard Ili's voice."

"Yes, it is a puzzle." Luster pulled at his beard. "But one thing we do know is that it's no longer safe here. We must leave."

"But what of my sister, Luster? Where do we go to find her now?

"I wish I could tell you, Ili. El Consuelo is a small town with nothing of consequence nearby. And it's located in the middle of a vast, rugged area, mostly uninhabited. She could be anywhere.

"What will we do then? We cannot give up on her."

-He stood silent for a moment then faced her."

"I have a plan but I must go alone."

"But why must you, Luster?"

"The people I need to see live near El Consuelo and may know something that will help us. But they are very private and suspicious of others. I hope they will talk to me if I go alone."

Lim frowned at him. "What are we supposed to do while you're off to see these people? It's not like Ili and I have a home we can go to."

"There is a place you can stay but I need to make a stop before we go there. Besides, I could use a drink."

They slid into the creaking car, turning onto the highway as lights flickered across an empty horizon silhouetted by the slate-colored sky. A dry wind buffeted the small car. They followed the road south and east, dipping into and out of road cuts, the narrow blacktop disappearing before them into the blackness. High clouds drifted overhead, starlit, ethereal, stretching across the broken plain and into the indigo east as the still-fuming heat of day spilled through the windows.

Sitting in the back seat, Lim watched Ili's profile, her hair swirling about her face like smoke. A vision of her looking down at him as he awoke flashed through his mind and he wondered what he had seen in her eyes or if he had seen anything at all. He shook his head, silently wishing he had the courage to ask her. She turned toward him as if about to speak, then the car slowed and Luster held up his hand, looking at Lim in the rearview mirror.

"We are approaching our first stop. We must be careful. This can be a rough place. Ili, you may want to stay in the car."

"No, Luster." She shook off the idea. "I know about such places. I will come with you."

Luster pulled the car up to a low building of yellow brick surrounded by a gravel parking lot filled with pick-ups and flatbed trucks. A single light burned over a mottled doorway and sign reading "Muleshoe Lounge". Pushing through the heavy door, they entered a squat room hazy with cigarette smoke and scattered with mismatched tables and chairs. A group of men crowded the bar, talking among themselves.

Luster pointed toward a table in the far corner. As they crossed the room, one of the men whistled at Ili, ogling her as she glanced toward the sound. The other men turned to watch. An instant later, she split off from Lim and Luster, making directly for the bar. Unsure whether to follow, Lim paused and watched as she stopped before the man, her hands on her hips.

"In my country it is an insult to stare at a woman so."

A gap-toothed man turned to the chair next to him. "Why, she's a pistol, Eli."

The man frowned. "You're lucky I don't take you across my knee and tan your hide, Red."

"Hey, that's a good one, Eli." The gap-toothed man slapped his thigh. "I'd like to see that. I sure would."

He waved off his gap-toothed friend and nodded toward Lim. "You going to call your friend over to bail you out, Red?"

Ili smirked at him. "Your mother, she taught you no manners?"

"My mother is long passed. She's no concern of yours."

"You forget she also was a woman."

"I'm telling you to leave her out."

She leaned toward him. "You disrespect her memory."

"But I… "

"You should have shame for such a thing."

The other men turned back to the bar, talking among themselves in low tones. She stepped closer to the man, speaking beneath her breath.

"You see, I need no help. You heard about the man stabbed in the church?"

He nodded, leaning back in his chair.

"I was there. I sat with him, watching him bleed. Do you understand me?"

He swallowed, nodding again before she turned and walked away, Lim close behind. They sat across from Luster and a moment later a waitress appeared, in her hand a frayed notepad. Her blond hair glowed beneath neon beer signs as she bent toward Lim, her half-open blouse stretching tight.

"What do you all want, handsome?"

Lim nodded toward Ili and Luster. "We'll have three of whatever's on special."

"That'd be the draft beer, hon'."

Luster raised his hand. "And I'd like to ask a favor of you, if I might."

"Would you now? Well ask away, then."

"I'm looking for Hanley Ledbetter. I believe he once worked here."

"Hon', you just got lucky, if you know what I mean." She glanced at Lim before giving Luster a wink. "Did I?"

"Hanley still works here. He's in the kitchen right now. You want me to tell him something for you?"

"It's important that I talk to him. Will you tell him Luster needs to see him?"

"Hello, Luster. They call me Kit. You just sit tight and I'll get Hanley out here straightaway."

She disappeared and a moment later a man in a red apron emerged from behind the bar carrying three mugs of beer. A thick mustache stretched past his bottom lip. Making his way across the room in a bowlegged amble, he set the mugs on the table and squinted at Luster and Lim before settling his gaze on Ili.

"Kit said some hombre wants to parlay but I'm hoping she got it wrong and you're the one, senorita."

Ili gestured toward a chair. "Please sit, Mr. Ledbetter. I will be glad to parlay, as you say."

"Well, good then. You can call me Hanley. You're not from around here, are you?"

"I am Ili and this is Lim. I believe you know Luster."

Hanley started in his chair, tugging on his mustache and peering at Luster. After a moment, he leaned across the table.

"Holy hell, I didn't recognize you behind that beard. You look more like a preacher than the Luster Lester I remember. Is it really you?"

"It is me, Hanley."

"Speaking of holy rollers, didn't you go off to a nunnery or some such place and become one of them friars?"

"It was a monastery, Hanley."

"Luster, you are a monk?" Ili stared at him, her eyes wide.

He sighed, running a hand across his face. "I have tried many paths, Ili."

"I can't believe this." Lim leaned across the table. "You really became a monk?"

"I'm afraid that's the truth of it, Lim."

"What sort of monk are you?"

"I belonged to the Gyrovagi, wanderers who follow their passions."

"You don't much act like a monk."

"I had to leave the order."

"Who did you do wrong this time?"

"I slept with the Mayor's wife."

Lim squinted at him. "You're not serious."

"I know. Not such a good idea if you're living in a small town. The Brothers had to sneak me out in the middle of the night."

Lim looked at him askance, skeptical of the story. "But aren't monks supposed to be celibate?"

"As I said, Gyrovagi follow their passions."

"So you claim. And when did this supposed story take place?"

"It was a long time ago, Lim. But don't worry yourself with my past. We have more important things to talk of just now."

Luster tapped the table with his finger, eying Hanley. "I sought you out because we have a problem and need your help."

"I can't be getting into anything shady, Luster. I sure as hell don't want to go back to jail."

"You needn't worry, Hanley."

"What sort of problem is it?"

"It has to do with forced prostitution.

"I heard there was some of that going on around these parts. Not firsthand knowledge, mind you."

"Will you help us?"

"I don't know, Luster. I've got enough problems of my own just now."

"It's especially important to Ili."

He pulled on his mustache, squinting at her before turning back to Luster."

"Oh, alright then. But why come to me? I know next to nothing about whores."

Ili slapped the table with her palm. "My sister is not a whore! She is a victim, kidnapped against her will."

Hanley jumped backwards and held up both hands. "I didn't mean anything by it, miss."

"Men, they are pigs."

He whispered across the table. "Help me out here, Luster."

"So you'll work with us, Hanley?"

100

He nodded and glanced at Ili.

"No promises but I'll do what I can."

"I'm guessing you're still in touch with some of your fellow inmates.

"Who else is willing to hobnob with an ex-jailbird?"

"Just as I thought. Do you know anything about a mob out of Eastern Europe operating in the area?"

He leaned back. "I've been through this already, Luster."

"What do you mean?"

"Your friend Orvis was in here last night asking about the same thing."

"Orvis was *here*?"

"You didn't know? He was asking about you too."

"Was he, now?"

"I never imagined you'd show up out of the blue a day later. That Orvis is a cagey old codger. He wouldn't let on what he was after."

"So, you know something?"

"I know some guys with funny accents have been buying and selling antique stuff like jewelry and art, even old books. The word is they aim to stake out territory around here and get into whatever will make the most money, maybe running whores… I mean, victims. From what I hear, they're a rough crowd. You'd best steer clear of them."

"I'm afraid it's too late for that."

"I don't know much else to tell you. If I were you I'd get as far from those bandoleros as I could."

"That's good advice, Hanley. We're leaving straightaway for someplace I hope we can stay."

Hanley smoothed his mustache and winked at Ili.

"Is there anything else I can do for this pretty lady, Luster?"

"There is. We need to get a story to the foreigners, but in such a way they don't suspect it's a smokescreen."

He nodded. "I know some boys who can float a story that'll get back to them but quick."

"I thought as much."

"What's the tale?"

"We want them to think we've gone to northeastern Oklahoma in search of a girl."

"That's it?"

"I hope that's all we'll need."

"Consider it done, Luster. I still owe you for keeping this place running while I was in the hoosegow."

"That was long ago, Hanley." Luster waved off the comment. "You don't owe me anything."

"Us ex-cons don't often hear those words."

"You are a good man, Hanley." Ili reached out, touching his hand. "Forgive my anger. Thank you for helping us."

He looked up at her, his face flushed, his eyes wide. "Why… I… uh… I… now listen up. From what I hear, these foreigners don't give in easy. You had best get moving."

# Nine

The road crested a rise before beginning a slow descent out of the scrub-covered plain and into dense breaks of cedar scattered with post oak and mesquite. Although seeing little past the headlight glow, Luster recalled the look of the place as if he had only just left. Above the road, limestone bluffs jutted from the hillside, marking brush-choked creeks and dry washes that crisscrossed a broken landscape. Somewhere in the distance the wind-whipped lake reflected a thin sliver of moon. Luster followed the narrow road, saying little, his thoughts filled with his errant past and the path he must now take.

An image came to him of a young woman standing on the porch of a two-story house, the fading hues of sunset caught in her dark hair as she turns to leave. He watches her move down the long driveway, passing through the metal gate before vanishing from sight. Staring into the darkness, he is unable to move.

A narrow intersection appeared in the headlights and the image faded to a blur of broken vows and missed chances. He blinked, trying to clear his mind of the memory as Lim sat up. Leaning toward the windshield, he peered into the dense night.

"Where are we, Luster?

"I know someone who lives near here. It's a place we can stay, I hope. I believe we have traveled far enough to be safe, at least for a time."

Ili stirred in the back seat. "Who is it we go to, Luster?"

"Someone I'm sure will be glad to see me."

"You mean there's a person still alive you didn't do wrong?"

Ili leaned toward the front seat. "Lim, you are unfair to Luster."

Luster raised a hand. "It's alright, Ili. I have been inconstant in my past and now face the consequence."

"You must have had your reasons."

"I thought I did, Ili, but now I'm not so sure."

"This person we go to see, you have known a long time?"

"He's my uncle."

"Is this a real uncle or a fake one?"

She slapped the seatback. "Lim! You must stop."

He glanced at her and nodded, wondering what lay behind his sharp tongue. Luster angled the car past a rusted gate, following an unpaved road that wound up a steep slope. Even in the dark the land looked just as he remembered, though the trees seemed thicker, the grass higher than when he had last visited the place. Ashe juniper crowded the drive, their striped limbs scratching against the car in pitched squeals.

Then the thicket fell away. Up the hill, a small ranch house came into view, the porch lights casting trees into shadow. He pulled up to the stairs, cutting the engine as a thin figure of a man stepped through the doorway. Silhouetted by the yellow glow, his hands in the back pockets of his faded jeans, he stood waiting. Luster turned, speaking in a whisper.

"Now I don't quite know what to expect. It has been some years since I paid Uncle Vix a visit. He's lived out here for a long time and some think he's a bit eccentric as a result."

Luster climbed from the car, Lim and Ili following. The old man studied them over his reading glasses, saying nothing, his eyes without expression. As they reached the top step, a hint of recognition passed across his lined face and he shifted on his feet, leaning toward Luster.

"How'd you get so old?"

Luster paused, trying to catch his breath. "Time passes, uncle, whether we like it or not."

"Has it been that long since you were here last or you been living hard?"

"It has been long and I'm sorry for it."

"Not so long you forgot your manners, I hope."

He took off his glasses and nodded toward Lim and Ili.

"Lim, Ili, this is my uncle, Van Zandt Lester."

He shook Lim's hand before stepping aside and opening the door for Ili.

"Welcome to my house, miss. It has been a long spell since a woman passed through this door."

"Please call me Ili, Mr. Lester."

"Most folks call me Vix. Make yourself at home while I get us something cold to drink. It's still hot out in spite of the dark."

He ambled across the room with a noticeable limp, disappearing through a doorway. A moment later he reappeared carrying several cans of beer. Setting them on the coffee table, he eased into a chair, popped open a can and leaned back.

"You all help yourselves and tell me what brings you way out here."

Luster opened a beer and sat. "We've run into a bit of trouble, Vix, and we need a place we can stay for a while."

"You know you're welcome here as long as you like, Luster. Lord knows there's plenty of room now that I have the house to myself."

"You have lived here long, Vix?" Ili sat next to him.

Running a hand through his silver hair, he glanced about the room as if searching for something lost. Then he faced Ili, his blue eyes studying her from beneath heavy lids.

"My wife of forty-seven years passed on two years ago next month. She and I moved in right after the honeymoon. You'd be surprised how quiet it can get without the talker of the family around."

"You must miss her."

"Some nights when I'm out on the porch I almost believe I can hear her. But it's just the night critters and wind fooling with me. Still, I do like to sit for a moment and imagine she's somewhere down the drive taking her evening walk. She always did love that time of day." He looked at them each in turn, shaking his head. "If you don't watch out I'll end up doing all the talking to make up for so much quiet. You were about to tell me what brought you here, Luster."

"We've been trying to locate Ili's sister. We believe she's with a religious group of some sort, a ways southwest of here. Unfortunately, we ran into trouble and need to lay low for a while."

"You mean the law is after you?" Vix squinted at him.

"We've had a close call with a gang from Eastern Europe, Romania and Serbia, maybe elsewhere."

"Europeans, you say? I'm surprised the Mexican cartels allow them around here."

"It seems they're trying to establish a territory for themselves up near Syracuse."

"That may be far enough north to avoid the Mexicans. From what I hear, gangs these days are nothing to fool with no matter where they come from. They'd just as soon shoot you as look at you."

"That's what we'd like to avoid."

Vix nodded. "Well, you should be safe enough way out here. Say, you folks must be hungry. I'm trading cooking duty for the use of my bunkhouse to an old vaquero. Rogelio may be past his riding days but he can sure cook. Let's go see what he's got in store for dinner."

They followed him down a short hall and through the kitchen to a back stoop opening onto a square patch of lawn and small vegetable garden. Beyond the yard, a low-roofed cabin stood next to a stable and circular corral where three horses milled about in a restless bunch. Vix called through the open door of the cabin as they made their way past the garden.

"Rogelio, we've got company. Are you decent?"

A man appeared in the doorway wearing a grease-stained apron over an undershirt and jeans. His clay-colored face and white hair glowed beneath the yellow porch light. He pointed a large fork at Vix.

"I'm going to cook your chickens if I find them in my house again."

"Well, don't leave your windows open."

He looked up at the sky and took in a breath. "An old man used to outdoor work likes the fresh air."

"Now that I think about it, those yard birds are too damned much trouble." Vix pulled at his ear. "It's time we got rid of them."

"I will feed them to the pigs."

"Let's eat one or two ourselves. Speaking of eats, what're you burning for dinner tonight? We're going to need more than the usual plates."

"You are in luck. I cooked all the skirt steak so we have plenty of fajitas. I got a pot of beans going too."

Vix turned to Luster. "Pinto beans and fajitas sound alright for a late dinner?"

"We're grateful for anything you can spare, Vix."

"Old men like Rogelio and me don't eat enough to choke a bird so we have trouble getting rid of food more often than not. Besides, I'm glad to have the company. I've heard about all the cowboy stories I can tolerate."

He turned to Rogelio. "This here is my nephew, Luster, and his compadres, Lim and Ili."

Rogelio nodded to Lim and Luster before taking Ili's hand. "My name is Rogelio Garza and I am honored to meet you, senorita. Please excuse the mess. I hope the fajitas will make up for it."

"I have never had the fajita." Ili sniffed the air. "It smells wonderful."

"I soak them in beer all day before I grill them so they are tender as cabrito. Of course, I have to drink beer also if

I am to cook them right. You will do an old man honor if you sit and drink with me. Todos, all of you, sit por favor."

He pulled an ice chest from beneath the cupboard and lifted out several bottles, setting them on the table. Lim finished his can, tossing it aside before grabbing a bottle and twisting it open. The golden hues of the wood-paneled walls seemed to settle around him like a warm day. He took a swig and sat next to Ili, grateful for a chance to be near her. Vix took a long pull on his beer before facing Luster.

"How do you plan to find this girl you're looking for?"

"I know a family that may be willing to help. I'll go see them tomorrow.

"Where are these folks?"

"They live in a remote area southwest of here, near the town of El Consuelo. I helped one of them once so I hope they'll talk to me."

Vix turned to Rogelio. "Now I don't want you to start in on stories from your riding days but didn't you cowboy down that way?"

"I worked a big ranch down there until the old man died and the family sold the land to some rich men from San Antonio. After that I had to shear goats until I could find another ranch to take me on. I have no use for goats. That mohair wool, it smells bad. But the shepherd dogs I liked. Those sheep dogs, they are smarter than most people. They could tell I was going to cook even before I myself knew. I would find them at the pit waiting for me."

Vix nodded. "We can visit later. When can we eat?"

"Vix, he thinks I start to talk about riding again so he sets me to work. But I am hungry too. We will eat now."

After dinner, Lim followed Ili onto the porch as the pitched calls of shorebirds drifted up from the lake, mixing with the bell-like trill of crickets. He reached back into the house, switching off the light. Down the hill, the night sky stretched above a distant tree line standing ink-black against the gray horizon. Stars glowed behind a late-summer haze, gas-like, ethereal. Ili leaned against the porch rail. Somewhere in the blackness a blue heron passed overhead, twice calling out its hoarse croak. Lim moved next to her.

"The sky, it is more beautiful than at home. Yet I cannot enjoy such beauty when my sister is still lost."

"We'll find her, Ili."

She turned to face him. "But what terrible things happen to her, Lim?"

"She's a fighter. Clavo said they couldn't make her become a prostitute. Don't forget that.

"What does it mean they sold her?"

"I don't know." He searched for an answer. "It sounds like some religious group is buying wives for its members. It may not be as bad as it sounds."

"Is a wife treated better than a prostitute?

"Try not to think too much about it. We're doing what we can. Luster will talk to those people and then we'll go find her.

"The night, it is beautiful but so dark." She took his hand in hers, facing the darkness beyond the porch. "I feel afraid when I look out into it, as if the evil in the world comes close and I face it alone."

"I'm here with you, Ili." Lim studied her dim features.

"You must feel alone too, your parents both gone. She turned to face him, her eyes glistening.

"I'm alright."

"I wish you would say the truth to me. You don't have to be always strong, Lim."

He looked away and then back at her. "But I do, Ili. It's the only way I know."

"But this must keep you from the truth?"

"You want me to tell the truth?"

He peered into her eyes. She nodded.

109

"The truth is you're a beautiful woman, so beautiful I never know what to say to you. I never know what to say because I think whatever I do say will sound stupid or you won't like it or you won't like me."

"But I do like you, Lim."

"You do?"

"Of course I do. You are so good to help me with my sister. If not for her, I…"

The porch light flashed on and without thinking they stepped apart, blinking into the brightness as Vix stepped out the door. Spotting them, he took a step back.

"My apologies. I didn't think anyone was out here."

"The stars, they are so many and beautiful here, Vix."

He walked to the stairs and stood for a moment, staring into the restless night. "My wife and me would sit out here in the dark and look at the stars. I should've remembered that before I came barging out. Just the same, Luster is looking for you, Lim. He says he needs to talk. I believe I'll stay here and keep this pretty lady company if it's alright."

Ili smiled and nodded at Lim before moving to the porch swing. He disappeared through the door. Vix pulled out a chair and sat, taking a penknife from his pocket and reaching behind the chair. Lifting out a fat piece of wood, he studied the shape while turning it over in his hands. Ili waited without a word. A moment later, he looked up at her and held out the half-carved form.

"I'm working on a Bufflehead, a kind of sea duck. I have a whole room full of these things, not all Buffleheads, of course. If I remember right, Linnaeus first identified this bird sometime during the sixteenth century. He was a Swede, a scientist, and one of the first to put plants and animals into some sort of order."

"Do you hunt these birds, Vix?"

"It's been a long while since I hunted much of anything but I always did love it. Some folks think it's a cruel practice but hunters care more about wildlife than most folks, and they believe in conservation and taking care of the natural world. Once you see a doe and her fawn starving to death because there's not enough to eat, you don't need anyone to tell you a quick end is more merciful than slowly wasting away."

"Did your wife hunt also?"

"No, she never had the taste for it. She'd rather watch ducks than shoot them. I suppose that's why I quit. I never decided to outright but when I hear geese flying overhead on a cold night or I catch sight of an Oriole passing through on its way south, I think of her."

"She sounds like a person I would have liked to meet."

"She was the finest kind, that's a fact. The best thing I ever did was to talk her into taking up with me."

"And you have children?"

"I have a son who works for a company based in China. He never had any use for this place and couldn't wait to leave so I don't much see him. I reckon it's better that way. Enough talk about me. What about you, Ili? Do you plan on marrying and raising a family?

She sighed, realizing how seldom such thoughts had come to her. "It is hard for me to think of a future when my sister is missing and I don't know what might happen to us."

"Luster told me what all you have been through and I'm sorry to hear it. You're too young to have such difficulties. I want you to know you're welcome in my home as long as it suits you. I hope you'll find it a place of rest."

"You are too kind, Vix. It is true I am exhausted."

"Well, I've fixed you up in a nice room that Elna used for her reading. She did love her books. The room looks out onto the porch through that window right next to you. It's the first door on the left once you're inside. You're likely to hear the crickets chirping."

"Then they will sing me to sleep."

He stood and nodded to her. "I'll say goodnight, then. I'm not used to staying up so late and it sounded to me like Luster was just getting started. I'll tell them to keep it down so we can get some sleep."

"I will stay a moment longer. Will you again switch the light, Vix?"

He nodded and stepped through the door, leaving her to the restless night, the sky now studded with low clouds, silvered, starlit, drifting over a blackened horizon barely visible above the gate. Wind rattled the nearby trees. In the distance, coyotes called to one another out of the low hills that sloped from the house to the lake.

Ili stirred at the sound, at once both joyful and threatening, and thought of Lim's kind face, his eyes troubled yet hopeful. She stood and moved toward the door, wondering where time might lead them, together or apart, knowing either way she would do whatever it took to find her sister.

## Ten

A brisk wind coursed above the sloping hill that sat between the house and gate, rippling through trees and splaying bone-dry grass that shone yellow beneath the cloudless sky. Beyond the road, a rusted pump jack tilted up, then down, then up again in ceaseless motion. Lim stood at the top of the stairs, watching Luster's car cross the cattle guard and turn onto the narrow blacktop, soon vanishing behind the hill.

He had stayed up well past midnight listening to Rogelio describe the area near El Consuelo. Something he had mentioned now lurked in the back of his mind, inaccessible but bothersome. The more he tried to recall the words the further they seemed from his grasp. He turned as the door opened and Vix stepped through.

"Ili asked me to tell you she and Rogelio have gone down to check the vineyard."

"I thought you raised cattle."

"I used to. But after an old bull pinned me against the fence and broke my leg in two places, Elna made me promise I'd get out of the cattle business. She had reason to want me out after having to tend to me every day for two months. I might have been stubborn about it, even after having pins and all put in my leg, but I was ready for a change. Besides, I never could go against her wishes if it was something she cared about."

Lim leaned against the rail, thinking of Ili. "You were lucky you had her to take care of you."

"I knew my luck the day I met her and I never thought any different. Good fortune has to smile on a man to find a partner like Elna."

"It seems like the only fortune I've had is the bad sort."

"Don't lose heart, son. You're still young and have plenty of time. You'll find your way."

Vix put on his cap and pulled the door shut. "I'm going into town to pick up some stakes and wire for the vines and I thought you might like to come along."

"You're good enough to put us up, Vix. I'd like to lend a hand wherever I can."

"Alright, I reckon I could use the company." Vix started down the stairs. "I try to make a trip into town more than just another chore. Living out here is not real exciting but we find ways to enjoy ourselves."

They followed the road as it turned away from the lake, rising between limestone cliffs dotted with fossil and quartz, honey-colored against the heat-scrubbed sky. Lim leaned toward the windshield, following a hawk as it rode an updraft along the rock wall before disappearing over the top. A moment later the truck crested a rise, rounding a tight curve that brought the town into view.

Trim houses stretched along a main boulevard like a photo from an old magazine. Edging the street, a row of pecan trees cast the well-kept lawns into deep shade, dense, ink-like. Lim stared out the window, his lost home coming to mind, and he again wondered where fortune would next take him. Wherever it was, he hoped Ili would be there.

Vix veered onto a gravel side street and the truck bounced along, kicking up a smoke-like cloud of dust soon ripped by the gusting wind. On their left, a corrugated tin building rose above a line of dying cottonwood trees like a monolith. A sign near the street read "Riddell Feed and Hardware". He pulled into the parking lot and cut the engine, waiting to open the door as another gust rocked the truck, sending a wall of dust whistling past. He turned to Lim.

"This damn gale worries me. If a wind gets up enough it can wreak havoc on your vines."

"At least it helps cut the heat a little."

"It's true we could use some help in that department as hot as it's been. I keep telling myself fall will be here soon. Still, I'd suffer the heat to be rid of a wind this big. One spark could mean real trouble."

They climbed from the truck and walked through a wide doorway, a wall of hot air greeting them in the stillness beyond. Wisps of dust drifted through slim shafts of light. As they waited for their eyes to adjust, a voice echoed above the shelves. A moment later a squat man in a sweat-stained cap and overalls rounded the corner and hobbled toward them.

"Son of a biscuit, there's Vix standing there and blinking like a scared owl. I was wondering when you'd show up. You planning to stop in at the Dog House?"

"Well, it was time for lunch some ways back. Now that I think about it, I'm about due for a burger."

"A burger, is it? So, is this here young feller your designated driver in case you have too many fries?"

"This is my grand-nephew, Lim."

The man's hand felt like sandpaper against Lim's palm.

"I'm Bunk Riddell. If I were you I wouldn't admit being related to this old buzzard.

"But Vix, I'm not…"

Vix put a hand on Lim's shoulder. "Don't pay him any mind, Lim. Half the time Bunk has no idea what he's going on about. I believe his memory went south years ago."

"I can still remember well enough to know I bought the round last time we were at the House."

"That's what you say every time."

"I do what?"

"Never you mind, Bunk. We need to get a move on or Rogelio will be standing around with nothing to do."

"I'll get Blanket over here to help out. I've got to finish a big order so I'll have to catch up with you later."

He yelled across the open room and a young woman in jeans and a sleeveless gingham shirt appeared from behind a wall of shelves. Brushing the stray hair from her face, she took a step toward them then stopped and stood still, staring at Lim. An instant later, she turned her eyes to the floor and waited there, tugging at the braids framing her strawberry-hued cheeks. Bunk looked from her to Lim and back.

"Don't stand there like you just got struck by lightning, niece. Come on over here and help Vix get what he needs."

He turned, whispering to Vix. "She's real smart and good with numbers but people are another matter. She's no good at small-talk. I don't know why I ever told her mother I'd take her on. On the other hand, she's awful swift at keeping the books, and if a customer happens to bring up something she's interested in she'll talk their ear off."

He turned back to Blanket.

"You remember Vix, don't you?"

She gave Lim a quick look and nodded. As awkward as she seemed, Lim couldn't take his eyes off her sun-streaked hair and blue eyes.

"This is his nephew, Lim, and they're in a hurry. I'm tied up so you'll need to take care of them, alright?"

She nodded again.

"You can still talk, can't you?"

She looked up at him with a pained expression. "I'm nearly thirty years old, Uncle Bunk, not some child."

"Alright, alright, I was just joshing with you, Blanket. What can she get you, Vix?"

"We need some wire and stakes for the new vines we're putting in."

She glanced at Lim and then turned to Vix, managing a weak smile as she spoke, her voice a slow drawl.

"You have yourself a vineyard now?"

"It's a fairly new project for me, Blanket. I'm determined to do it right."

116

"We just received an order of stakes that are real solid and should last a good while."

"That sounds fine."

She set off down the aisle, talking over her shoulder. "Did you know that staking vines rather than trailing them is still practiced in places like France, Italy and California? Some growers believe it results in healthier grapes and better wine. Staking can also protect against wind damage."

"I sure as hell hope that's true as windy as it's been. But I use stakes because I like the tradition of it."

Lim hurried behind them, trying to think of something to say.

"The practice goes all the way back to ancient Greek and Roman cultures."

"How did you get to know so much about grape vines, Blanket?"

She glanced back at Lim again before answering. "I just like wine. I like the way it brings together geography, geology, chemistry and culture. There's so much variety, so much to learn. It never bores me. I even went to a school for it."

Vix nodded. "Is that right? Why don't you come out and see the vineyard? You might have some ideas for improving things. No doubt I could use the help."

"It's nice of you to invite me, Mr. Lester."

"I'm not real big on formality, Blanket. Please call me Vix."

"See what you think of these."

She stopped and pulled a wooden stake from a bin, handing it to Vix. She again glanced at Lim but held his gaze for a moment longer than before. He leaned toward her, trying to get her to face him.

"You have an unusual name, Blanket. How'd you come by it?

She looked up at him, worry in her eyes. "You think there's something odd about it?"

"No, I mean… it's just… I like your name. I've never met anyone called Blanket and was wondering where it came from. Is it a family name?"

Her eyes relaxed a bit, making her even prettier. "My mother named me after the little town near where I was born."

"There's a town called Blanket?"

She squinted at him, still unsure of his intent. "Yes, there is. It's located south of here, not too far. My mama is called May, for the town near where she grew up. She decided to do the same for me."

"Will you come out to see the vineyard, Blanket?" He took a step closer. "Vix isn't the only one who'd like to hear what you think."

She blushed and tucked a strand of sun-streaked hair behind her ear. "I'll have to check and see when Uncle Bunk can spare me but I'll try to."

Vix pulled an armful of stakes from the bin and tossed them at Lim, knocking him back a step.

"We'll look forward to your visit, Blanket. We best get a move on."

Vix pulled into a dirt parking lot fronting a windowless building set on short piers. On one end a faded blue stairway climbed to the entrance. Clouds of dust streamed off the rutted ground as Lim followed him out of the truck, up the steps and beneath a sign reading "Riley's Dog House". They hurried through the entryway, the wind pulling at their shirts before a gust slammed the door behind them.

Across the room, an antique marble bar sat perched atop a line of fifty gallon oil drums lashed together with wire cable, the names of bankrupt oil companies stenciled across their sides. Lim followed Vix past the single pool table. Men in dingy coveralls and caps took no notice as they made their way to the bar and sat.

118

Vix held up two fingers and nodded to the bartender while Lim looked about the place, his eyes adjusting to the dim light of neon beer signs and a single barred window near the back exit. A moment later, the bottles appeared as if by magic. Vix took a long pull on one before he spoke.

"Back when oil was big there were boomtowns all around here. The towns grew up fast and there was plenty of money to spend. Then the easy fields played out and the price of oil sank so the jobs dried up. You can still see the effects here and there in empty buildings and abandoned yards of rusted equipment, leaving a town with a sad, rundown look."

Lim nodded as he tipped back the bottle. "We passed through a few on our way down here that seemed pretty rough."

"Some towns, like this one, pulled together and decided to make the best of it. They cleaned up the eyesores and made it a place people like to visit. Other towns did nothing but complain and let the weeds grow. There are beautiful buildings all over this area literally falling apart. It's a sad thing to witness such change, but it happens."

"I don't guess you can escape it."

"When the situation changes you have to adjust or get left behind, sit dead in the water or try something new. That's why I planted the vineyard, or part of the reason anyway. The other was I could never say no to Elna. Nothing was ever as important to me as her happiness. I don't know if you can understand that, Lim, but that's how it always was for me."

"I think I understand, at least some."

"Bunk's niece sure got your attention back there." Vix looked at him and smiled. "I had an idea you were sweet on Ili."

"She's just pretty, is all. Blanket, I mean." Lim felt his face burn at the thought, all too aware of his unpredictable nature.

"I know what you mean."

"Besides, she's probably not my type."

"Are you trying to convince me or yourself?"

"I don't need to convince myself."

"Are you sure about that?"

"You're right, Vix." Lim sighed and leaned his elbows on the bar. "I don't know what's wrong with me. One minute I'm trying to get Ili to notice me and the next I'm can't take my eyes off Blanket."

"Don't be too hard on yourself, son. She is a pretty one, and smart too. Besides, Luster told me a little of what's happened. I think I have an idea of what it's like for you."

"You do?"

"There was a time when I didn't know up from down. I'd made a lot of bad decisions and couldn't seem to get out from under them. Then I met Elna and that righted me pretty quick."

"I've been out of work most of the last three years. I don't know if I'll ever work again."

"You'll find your stride, Lim. Just keep your head up and you'll see your chance when it comes along."

The door swung open, filling the room with light. Lim turned to see Bunk hobbling toward them, followed by Cyril, Jonny at her elbow. Lim blinked and looked again, trying to reason out why Cyril and Jonny would show up at that bar, and with Bunk of all people. They seemed an odd threesome. But the concern on Cyril's face snapped him out of his musings. While Cyril settled Jonny into a chair, Bunk pointed into the air.

"Now, there's a time for drinking and a time for talking. I'm sorry to say this here is the second. Cyril came to the store looking for you two so I brought her here straightaway. She has something important to tell you."

"Hello, Cyril." Vix leaned toward her. "It's been a long time since I've seen you over to the lake."

120

"It has been and I'm sorry for it, Vix. I wish I was here under better circumstances but I'm afraid I've made a terrible mistake."

"What is it, Cyril?"

She faced Lim. "Orvis came to me asking where you and Luster had gone. He said he had sold the book you brought back from the kidnappers and wanted you to have the money. So, I told him you had gone to stay with Vix. I didn't think much of it at the time but Jonny came to me shortly after. You can tell them what you told me, Jonny."

"Well, I was surprised to find Orvis back so soon." The little man shifted in his chair, scratching his thin beard while his eyes darted about. "We don't see much of him, you know. So, we got to talking and right away I could see he was laying it on thick, as they say. I know, I know, I'm blind but I can see plenty, especially when someone is trying to pull one over on me.

"Old Orvis kept on and on about how much he wanted to help you in your search and how the funds might come in handy. I tried to find out what he was truly up to but he caught on and claimed he needed to get back to his books or some such nonsense so I sent him on to Cyril. As soon as he left, I went to check in with her."

She nodded. "I had an uneasy feeling too but I couldn't figure out why. Once Jonny came to me, I knew Orvis was up to no good so I followed him back to the bookstore. Since I know he uses the back entrance, I went one street past, to a spot where I'd have a clear view. Sure enough, there he stood talking to a thin man with dark hair and a scar down his face."

Lim frowned, trying to make sense of her story. "He's working with the kidnappers?"

"It does look that way, Lim.

"And you think Orvis told him we'd gone to stay with Vix?"

"Why else would he meet him right after finding out?"

"I don't know but we can't take that chance."

121

She looked about the room as if she'd lost something. "Vix, where's Luster?"

"Why, he didn't come with us."

"But if he's at your place alone, he could be in danger."

Lim hopped off the stool, calling over his shoulder as he headed for the door. "He's not there but Ili is."

Fire (fī(ə)r) - a fervent or passionate emotion; Combustion or burning, in which substances combine chemically with oxygen from the air and typically give out light, heat, and smoke.

## Eleven

Rogelio followed a narrow dirt road edging the vineyard, a thicket of scrub cedar and mesquite rising just beyond. The open-topped jeep jostled between wheel ruts and tufts of grass whipped by the relentless wind. Sitting in the seat next to him, a pair of binoculars hanging from her neck, Ili scanned the sky for birds. Vix had told her of several types she might spot near the lake. To the southwest, a sky scrubbed free of cloud rose above the jagged horizon.

Stopping the jeep, Rogelio climbed out without a word, ambling off toward a row of newly-planted vines. He knelt in the red dirt, fingering several leaves. A moment later a strange rattling rose above the drone of wind, moving above the thicket and up the hill toward them. Ili turned, mesmerized as the rattle became a vibrating din, like a thousand shaken maracas winding through the dense scrub. Rogelio stood and pointed toward the sound, yelling above the drone.

"You hear them, Ili?"

"What are they?" She glanced at the thicket.

"The katydids, they sing to us. I never hear them this early in the day and so loud."

She cupped her hands around her mouth, calling to him over the noise. "They sound magical, like some strange music."

"They remind me of the Mexican gourds my grandmother kept."

"They sound like gourds? Yes, of course. It is as the fortuneteller told us. I wish I could remember what also he said."

"What who said, Ili?"

She shook her head. "Oh, it is nothing, Rogelio."

He turned back to the vines, continuing his inspection. Ili watched him for a while and then stood, leaning her elbows against the roll bar and raising the binoculars to survey the horizon. Suddenly a flock of ducks appeared in her view, hugging the horizon and racing along the tree tops before disappearing all at once.

She lowered the binoculars as a flash of light caught her eye. Beyond the vineyard, a dark sedan sat parked alongside the highway, the windows tinted black as night. Scanning both directions, she found no owner. Then two figures appeared from behind a clutch of trees, moving toward them at a steady pace.

She raised the binoculars again. A wave of fear passed through her as Jorvic and his bald companion hurried toward them. Turning to Rogelio, she struggled to catch her breath, finally finding her voice.

"Rogelio, you must come quickly!"

He looked up as she beckoned him with a frantic wave of her arm. Glancing back, she found the men quickly closing the distance between them. Just as she turned to Rogelio, a pistol shot cracked behind her. Rogelio leapt into the jeep, grabbing her arm and pulling her out in one motion. She grunted as she hit the dirt.

"You forgot to tell me *why* to come quick, senorita!"

"I know of these men. They will kill you and kidnap me. We must get back in the jeep and leave."

"We have nowhere to go. The road, it is no good, a dead end. But I will see what the hombres think of my shotgun."

He crouched behind the jeep, reaching beneath the seat and searching the floorboard. A moment later he sighed and pulled away, leaning his back against the fender.

"I remember now. Vix, he took the shotgun to get it fixed. The stock was broke."

"What will we do, Rogelio?"

"A man must know when to run. Now we run like rabbits. We must go to those trees, the cedar and the mesquite." He pointed to the thick wall of scrub edging the vineyard.

"Won't they find us in there?"

"Vix, he lets me hunt down here. I know where to go. Andale, Ili!"

Crouching near the ground, Rogelio grabbed her hand, pulling her into the dense brush. She stumbled along, tree limbs slapping at her face, able only to watch the ground pass beneath her feet as they wound through the cedar break, careful to avoid the thorns of scattered cactus and mesquite. The bright sunlight faded to a dim glow beneath the green canopy.

After what seemed a long while, Rogelio stopped in a small clearing, cocking his head to listen. Ili crouched next to him, peering through the thicket yet unable to spot any movement. He held up a hand, turning to her and putting a finger to his lips. Beneath the roar of wind she could just make out the sound of footsteps moving over the dry leaves carpeting the forest floor. The sound moved one way then the other, parallel to them but never closer. A moment later, the sound retreated, disappearing behind the rattle of leaf and tree limb. Rogelio leaned toward her, whispering.

"I do not like being a rabbit. I would fight instead. But I think they give up on us now."

"So we can go to the jeep?"

"It is too soon. We must wait and listen for the car to leave. Good thing we scare the katydids and they stop the singing."

"How long do we wait?"

"The young, they always must hurry. It is good to go slow sometime."

He sat, leaning his back against the trunk of a small tree, and then motioned for Ili to do the same. "This is not so bad, eh Ili?"

"It is not so bad, yes."

"See, it is good to sit still."

She leaned her head back, feeling the wind on her face. "You have cared for the vineyard long, Rogelio?"

"When I was a boy, my father worked a vineyard right on the border, near the town of Del Rio. It is a very old vineyard. The priests there, they kept buying wine for the mass when the government would not allow the local people to buy. Most wineries went out of business. They called the damn thing prohibition. My father spit always when he heard that word. I learned the vines from him."

"Vix was lucky to find you."

"No, Ili, I have the luck. After I got hurt, I did not know what to do for work."

"What happened to you?"

"A crazy bull, he gored my horse. When the horse fell, I jumped free but landed on some big rocks and broke my back. I am lucky to walk again. My horse was not so lucky."

"You are twice lucky, then."

"Yes, that is true. The luck, it is with me. I walk and now I have a good job. All that my father taught me of vines I remember again. My work in the vineyard honors him."

"That is a nice thought. I hope a bit of that luck is with us now."

"We lose them, I think." -He nodded, staring into the thicket. "So, what of you, Ili?"

"What of me?"

"Tell me of your Lim."

"He is not my Lim, Rogelio."

"Then he is a young fool. If I was thirty years younger, I would not let you be lonely."

"Rogelio, you embarrass me. I like Lim but I barely know him."

"He is young and you are young. What more do you want?"

"I don't know what I want, Rogelio."

"It will come to you when the time, it is right. Now we must stop talking and listen for the bastards to leave."

They sat still and Ili peered into the mass of crisscrossing limbs, trying to hear any sound beyond wind coursing through treetops. Suddenly, Rogelio tensed and jumped to his feet, peering through the thicket in all directions. Ili hopped up and looked about, straining to find anything amiss.

"What is it, Rogelio?"

"A sound I do not wish to hear."

An instant later, a wisp of smoke snaked through the branches above them, followed by the unmistakable crack of burning wood. Without a word, Rogelio grabbed her hand, diving into the underbrush. He called to her over his shoulder as they rushed along a narrow trail.

"The bastards, they set fire to the cedar! With the wind, it will roast us like pigs. We must reach the lake before it."

Smoke streamed thick about them. Holding tight to Rogelio's hand, Ili tried to shield her face as they rushed along the crowded path, the leafless branches pulling at her clothes, fear rising in her throat. She glanced back, finding a wall of smoke rolling through the thicket behind them. As she stumbled along the trail, anger began to grow in her chest, anger for her fate, for the fate of all women, for the assumption they need to be taken care of, all of it crowding out her fear. She let go of Rogelio's hand, determined to find a sense of control.

Suddenly the trees fell away. Rogelio burst onto a rock-strewn ledge, careening toward the edge, the lake eighty feet below. Just managing to grab his wrist, Ili swung him in a half-circle. He hit the ground inches from the drop-off. She fell back onto the dirt, gasping, at once enveloped by the streaming smoke. A tongue of flame leapt above the tree line.

She scrambled to the cliff edge, trying to stay beneath the smoke as she looked for a way down. Rogelio crawled over to her, peering over the precipice. He coughed and shook his head.

"It is no good, Ili. This ledge, it sticks out too much."

"I see a way down." She pointed toward a small eroded area thirty yards down the cliff. "We must get there before the fire."

Crouching low to the ground, they hurried toward the narrow ditch, the heat hissing in the trees above them. Ili reached the washout first, sliding along the face of an exposed boulder then stair-stepping down the rock wall from stone to stone, ledge to ledge. She turned to Rogelio, finding him still near the top, frozen in place, his eyes wide.

"Rogelio, what is wrong?

"On horseback is high enough. I don't like any taller.

"You must climb down! The fire comes quickly.

He glanced behind him, shielding his face from the heat. She held out her hand, again calling up to him.

"Slide down the big rock and take my hand. There is room enough to stand."

"This world, you think you know it?"

"What?"

"It will slap you down like a damn cockroach."

"Come now, Rogelio!"

A swirling cloud of wind-tossed embers enveloped him. Slapping the coals from his clothes, he took a breath before jumping onto the boulder head first and bumping down the rock face, landing on the narrow ledge next to Ili. He rose, pressing his belly to the cliff.

Ili edged along the wall of stone, the sheer rock keeping her from moving downward more than a few yards in any one direction. The heat and smoke swirled around them in bursts. She could see that the brush above and on either side would soon catch fire. Turning, she found Rogelio hugging the cliff as he inched along behind her. Below him, a scattering of jagged boulders poked above the restless lake like giant teeth. She peered at the cliff face before her, finding nowhere to move.

A sudden stillness descended upon them as the ledge slipped into deep shadow, the crackle of burning wood still sounding above. For an instant she thought she heard Luster's voice calling to her. Fearing some new danger, she looked up. The sky seemed impossibly close, hued an odd gray-green and roiling with clouds. She glanced at Rogelio just as a clap of thunder shook the air, followed by a wall of rain, drenching them in seconds. He squinted upward, yelling over the hiss of rain.

"God, he plays with an old man. First he roasts him then he drowns him. But this storm, I never see it. It comes from nowhere."

"Yes, it is like magic."

Rogelio peered up the cliff face, squinting into the rain. Although the fire still raged above, run-off cascading over the edge drenched the nearby trees.

"The trees here, they will not roast us yet, but we need the big magic to get off this damn rock. Can you move ahead, Ili?"

"I have nowhere to go. Do you see a way?"

"I see fire over me and rocks under me but nothing more. I am like a fly on the wall."

"I will pray for a miracle, then."

"Pray for me too, Ili. I stopped going to mass long ago and God, he has forgotten my name."

## Twelve

A plume of smoke appeared above the horizon, fleeing before the wind in a ragged line. Beyond, silver bands of rain slanted toward the earth. Slowing the truck, Vix leaned over the steering wheel, squinting at the black cloud. Lim followed his gaze as a thin strand of flame leapt over the tree line. An instant later, Vix jammed the accelerator to the floor. The truck lurched forward, the engine straining, slamming Lim against the seatback. He righted himself and turned to Vix.

"What is it?

"That smoke says we've got a wildfire, maybe at the ranch or close by it. I can't tell for sure."

Lim stared at the highway, trying to gather his thoughts as they flew over the blacktop.

"Is that a coincidence, a fire all of a sudden near your place?"

"I think it unlikely. We best make sure Ili is safe before we do anything else."

"But what about your house?"

He shook his head. "A house can be replaced."

As they rounded the broad curve leading to the ranch, the fire came into view across the road from the house. Vix passed the gate, racing on toward the vineyard before spotting the jeep where it sat twenty yards from the smoldering thicket, the fire still raging in the brush beyond. In the distance, the flaming roof of a house jutted above the treetops.

Scanning the vineyard, they found no sign of Ili or Rogelio. Steam floated above the rain-soaked highway. Just ahead, a black sedan sat at the edge of the road, the doors open. Lim jumped toward the dashboard.

"I recognize that car from the kidnappers place."

Vix slowed, angling the truck off the roadway. An instant later, two men appeared from behind a line of trees. Spotting the truck, they jumped into the car, speeding away in a cloud of dust. Lim stared after them, trying to reason out the connection between the men and fire. They had to have set it. Vix started after the car but Lim held up his hand, signaling him to stop. He nodded toward the charred thicket, fear for Ili rising in his throat.

"If those men were after Ili, she and Rogelio must have gone in there. Could anyone survive a fire like that?"

Vix peered at the charred forest. "Rogelio knows these woods better than me. If he went in there, he had to have figured a way out. The lake is on the other side of the break and I believe that's where he would've gone. I know a way there."

He pulled onto the highway then turned on a gravel road paralleling the vineyard, bumping along the washboard path upwind of the fire. Lightning flashed above the flames, the rain having done little to slow their progress.

Rounding a curve, the truck slid to a stop just above the cliff. Lim hopped out of the cab, hurrying to the edge and peering through the smoke. Ili stood perched on a narrow outcropping below the charred thicket, Rogelio next to her. The fire roared above them. Waving Vix over, Lim pointed down the cliff.

"There they are! They've escaped the fire."

"Not for long they haven't. That rain bought some time but those cedars will fry them if they catch a spark."

"There's no way they can climb down from there. We have to do something."

Lim started toward the edge before Vix grabbed his arm, pulling him back toward the truck.

"You won't help if you burn up too. That fire is too hot. We have to try a different way."

Reaching into the truck, Vix pulled out a coil of rope and a half-used spool of bailing wire. Lim followed as he hurried down the slope and away from the fire, toward an arching section of cliff that turned back on itself. Ili and Rogelio stood on the ledge below, across a gap of thirty yards. Tying the rope to the wire, Vix handed Lim the spool.

"If we can get them the rope, Rogelio will know what to do."

"The fire looks close, Vix."

"The wind has changed directions. We best hurry."

"What can I do?"

"My shoulders aren't much good anymore so you'd better throw. Aim good, son. This spool of wire won't hold together for long."

Lim gathered the rope in one hand, swinging the coil in a tight circle. The wire hummed as it gained speed. Taking aim, he released his grip, the spool arcing across the gap and bouncing several yards below Ili's feet. She jumped at the sound, turning toward them in surprise.

"Lim, I knew you would find us!"

He called back. "There's a rope below you."

She looked past her feet. "I see it."

"The fire has turned. You must hurry. Can you reach the rope?"

She shook her head. "I am stuck."

"There's a small ledge below your feet. If you sit where you are now you might be able to reach it."

Holding the rock with both hands, she knelt and slid one foot after the other over the side. She hesitated, looking across the cliff to where Lim waited. Then she slipped off the edge, dropping onto the stone below with a thump while hugging to the cliff. As she grabbed the coil, Lim called out to her.

"Now, throw the rope to Rogelio."

"I am ready, Ili. With a rope, I will get us off this damn rock."

"But how, Rogelio?" She tossed the spool to him.

"We will go to the lake and swim away from this damn fire like fishes."

She turned back to Lim. "But I'm afraid of the water, Lim. I can't swim. I would rather stay here than drown."

133

Vix leaned toward Lim, nodding past where she stood. "The gale is taking that fire all the way down to the shoreline. They don't have much time."

"Will they be alright if they get to the lake?"

"I doubt it. Rogelio is just putting on a show to keep her from panicking. He can't swim a lick either. And with all the brush along the edge, the heat will be intense."

Lim turned to Ili, yelling into the wind. "We'll figure it out when you get there, Ili. But you must get down to the lake now. You have to trust me."

Rogelio secured the rope to a thick stump, stretching the line under his shoulders as he moved down the cliff face to her. Together they threaded a path toward the rock-strewn shore, the rope groaning beneath their weight. Lim watched them, speaking under his breath.

"What do we do now, Vix?"

He shook his head. "I wish I knew."

An instant later a ship's horn blasted behind them. Lim pivoted, spotting a reconditioned tugboat plowing toward the shore, diesel smoke streaming from its smokestack. A figure emerged from the cabin, moved to the bow and began waving to them. Lim peered at the boat.

"There's someone waving at us, Vix."

"I know that boat." Vix squinted at the man. "What the hell? Good God, I believe that's Luster."

The boat slowed and another man in a blue cap and raincoat leaned out the cabin door, a bullhorn in his hand. His voice echoed off the cliff.

"You folks get to those rocks lickety-split and we'll be able to reach you."

-Luster cupped his hands around his mouth as a cloud of sparks swirled from the cliff, disappearing above the lake. He yelled above the gale.

"Ili, you must hurry!"

Following Rogelio, she slid down the remaining slope, scrambling onto the teeth-like boulders edging the shore. The boat backed toward the rocks, the hull shuddering as the lake smashed against the side. Ili hesitated and then jumped onto the deck, tumbling into Luster's grasp. Rogelio followed just as another cloud of spark-filled smoke descended from the cliff, engulfing the boat. Holding his breath, Lim watched for it to reappear. An instant later the boat shot from beneath the cloud in a spray of whitewater, soon vanishing across the lake.

# Thirteen

A tower of black smoke filled the western horizon as Vix pulled his truck up to a blue and white frame house perched on a ledge of sheer rock. The lake lapped the shore fifty feet below. Set on twelve foot piers and fronted with a mast-like flag pole, flat roof and protruding porch, the home resembled nothing more than the conning tower of a great, wooden ship. Fish nets and buoys lay scattered about the yard.

Lim followed Vix up the broad stairway. Sirens echoed in the distance, mixing with the sound of Luster's voice drifting above them. The fearful image of Ili fleeing before the fire dogged his thoughts as Vix knocked on the door. A moment later a ship's bell rang from behind the house, leading them to second deck set high above the lake.

Behind a wooden table, the man they had seen on the boat, still wearing the same raincoat and blue hat, stood studying a tumbler of brown liquid. Luster, Ili and Rogelio sat facing him, glasses in hand. The man drained the glass, puffing out his ruddy cheeks.

"Hot damn, now there's a whisky to put hair on your chest!"

Luster sipped his glass. "I doubt if Ili much cares for that thought."

"Right you are, Luster. We'll say it put roses to your cheeks. How's that for you, Ili?"

"I feel my whole face must be the rose." She put a hand to her mouth.

"That's the idea!"

Noticing Vix and Lim, the man smoothed his bushy mustache and held up the empty tumbler, half-yelling as he spoke.

"Welcome aboard, men! That damn fire burned a dozen homes but the scanner says they have it contained, so you can relax a bit. Get yourself a glass and join us."

Ili jumped from her seat, hurrying to where they stood. She took Vix's hand.

"How will I ever thank you for saving us?"

"You would do the same for me, Ili." Vix patted her arm. "Besides, I believe our captain here did the real saving. He's the one we all should thank."

"Nonsense!" He waved off the comment and refilled his glass. "I haven't had that much fun since I helped the feds haul a plane loaded with pot from the bottom of the lake, two Mexican fellers still in it. The agent said the passenger shot the pilot. Now you'd have to be on drugs or stupid or both to do that."

Ili stepped over to Lim, putting her arms around him for a moment before pulling away. "I knew you would find us, Lim."

"We were almost too late."

"But the rope, you gave it to us in time."

"I don't believe I've ever seen Rogelio move so fast." Vix chuckled, shaking his head.

"No, I don't want to get barbecued like a poor goat." Rogelio drained his glass and stood. "But I tell you if that damn storm didn't come from nowhere, I would be talking to the angels now instead of you."

"It was like magic, Lim." Ili peered into Lim's eyes. "The rain kept the fire away until I saw you."

He nodded. "You were lucky, Ili."

"No, Lim, it was not luck. There is the stillness and I hear Luster calling me. Then the rain, it comes. You tell him, Luster. Tell him what you did."

"Surely you don't believe Luster can control the weather?"

"Then why is he in the boat? How does he know this?"

He glanced at Luster. "I don't know, Ili."

"I'll tell you how, Lim." Luster leaned back against the table. "When I was in El Consuelo I had a feeling something was wrong, nothing certain, just a sense so I decided to return. On my way back, I heard about the wildfire. I knew it was near Vix's place so I hurried back here and asked Nelly for his help."

"I get it. You reasoned that someone caught by the fire might have headed for the lake. By following the smoke you'd know where to find anyone that was trapped."

"That's one way to look at it. But my intuition played a part as well."

"I'd call it your mind reasoning out a logical possibility."

"Reason or intuition, I'm not sure the difference." Luster shrugged. "A feeling that you all were in peril is what compelled me."

Ili waved a finger in Lim's face. "You see, Lim, it *is* a miracle that brought Luster to us."

"Well, Ili, I'm glad for it, whatever it was."

The man in the raincoat handed Vix and Lim half-filled glasses and held out his hand. "Vix, you old polecat, where in the hell have you been hiding?"

"I'm a busy man these days. I got myself mixed up in the vineyard business and there's always something that needs doing."

They shook hands and he faced Lim.

"I was born Horatio Nelson Spencer after a great navy man, an Admiral. That could be the reason I became a harbor pilot. In those days people called me Captain Nelly but now that I'm four hundred miles from the sea I just go by Nelly."

Vix nodded at Lim. "Nelly, this is Lim."

"I know who you are." He took Lim's hand. "I've gotten an earful about you already. I forgot how much Luster likes to hear his own voice. Until we found these two refugees, I was about ready to send him back to El Consuelo."

Ili sat next to Luster. "Yes, Luster, what of this El Consuelo? My sister, did you learn of her? Have you found Mirela?"

"In a way I have. But I'm sorry to say the news is not what I'd hoped for, Ili."

"What do you mean?"

"My friends were able to find Mirela and make contact but she refused to see me."

"I don't understand. You have found her?"

"I know where she is."

"Then we must free her."

"It's not as simple as that, Ili." He pulled at his beard. "She doesn't want to leave."

"Then I will talk to her."

"She refuses to see anyone from outside the compound, even you."

"She will see her own sister."

He shook his head. "She may be willing to see you eventually but not now. You must wait."

"She is my sister. Why must I wait, Luster?"

"When a new member joins this group they agree to avoid contact with the outside world for a period of time. How long it is depends on the circumstances."

"They make her agree to this? I cannot see her in this place?"

"Her time of isolation is almost complete but apparently she chooses to have no visitors."

"How can this be?" She stared at him. "What have they done to her, Luster?"

"It's hard to say but groups like this have been known to brainwash new members."

"No, this must not be!" She slapped the table. "I will go to her anyway. Where is this place, Luster? I will take her back from them."

"It's not that easy, Ili. These people are well-armed and highly suspicious of outsiders. Besides, the time she agreed to lasts only a short while longer. Then we will try again and see what she says. You can wait that long, can't you?"

"I wait but only because I must, Luster. After that, I wait no more."

Nelly held up the half-empty bottle. "It sounds like we got time to burn, ladies and gentlemen, and Nelly just happens to have a pot of his world famous chili ready and waiting for just such an occasion."

"We best be getting back to the house, Nelly." Vix drained his glass and set it on the table.

"At least have a taste before you decide. I use the best beef and cook it all day."

Lim leaned toward Vix, speaking under his breath. "I want more than a taste. I missed breakfast *and* lunch."

"You have a point, Lim. We never did get that burger, did we?"

"Me, I got to have cold beer with my chili." Rogelio patted his belly. "You got any spare cans lying around, Nelly?"

"I like beer with my chili too, Rogelio. This whiskey is just a warm up for dinner. What do you say, Vix?"

He turned to Ili. "It's Ili I'm concerned for. She's had some bad news on top of a hell of a bad day. I'll agree to whatever she wants. Do you want to stay, Ili?"

"You are too kind, Vix." Ili managed a weak smile. "But even on bad days one must eat."

Nelly started toward the kitchen. "Then get your taste buds ready for a treat."

The sun sat low in a cloudless sky as Lim leaned his elbows against the rough wood of the table. In the distance, telltale fingers of smoke lingered among the scorched hills west of the lake. He watched it rise, drifting on the light breeze before merging with the late afternoon haze as if it had never existed.

For a moment he could almost believe the fire had been only a dream, one part of a larger dream that started even before Luster appeared, beginning at the moment he cradled the small revolver in his palm. The black cloud of failure and shame surrounded him again, blotting out all thought, all hope. He stared into the distance, seeing nothing.

Then footsteps sounded behind him, pulling him from his thoughts. Nelly walked past the table, turned and began pacing the deck, tapping his fingers along the rail and mumbling to himself. After a moment he stopped, faced Lim and took a breath.

"I'm not one to hem and haw when I got something to say so here goes. Luster told me you're out of work and you lost your house to the weasels at the bank."

Lim snorted. "He doesn't waste any time in getting around to how pitiful I am, does he?"

"There's no future in feeling sorry for yourself, son. Besides, I didn't need him to tell me. I noticed a lost look about you right off."

"I'm that obvious?"

He waved off the question. "No matter if you are or you aren't, you got to get on with things. Men need to work. That's what I'm here to tell you."

"You're telling me I need to get a job?" Lim squinted at him.

"You're damn right."

"I've been looking for three years with almost nothing to show for it. Where am I going to find a job way out here?"

He slapped the table. "I know just the place."

"You do?"

"I've been talking to Vix about his plans for the vineyard business."

Lim leaned back, realizing his meaning. "You think I should work for Vix?"

"Hell yes, I do."

"Why would he hire me?"

"He's at the point now that he's got more work than he and Rogelio can handle."

Lim shook his head at the thought. "But I don't know anything about grapes."

"Now there's the sort of attitude that just won't do, Lim. You've got to believe you can do whatever needs doing. You're not stupid, are you?"

"Why would you say that?" Lim frowned at him. "I was good at my job."

Nelly slapped his thigh and pointed at him. "There you have it! Go tell Vix he needs to hire you."

"How can you be sure he needs the help?"

"Trust me, Lim. I've been there and know how it is. Besides, Vix isn't as young as he used to be. He works hard but age has a way of catching up with you."

"I just go up to him and ask him to hire me?"

"Hell no!" He waved a hand through the air. "You tell him he has to hire you or his plan for the vineyard will never happen."

"What's his plan?"

Nelly leaned toward him. "You mean you don't know?"

"He never talked about it."

"You mean you never asked. You got to look out for yourself, Lim. Find a spot where you can do something needed, something of value. That's where the jobs are."

"So, what are his plans?"

"He's already got enough vines to make a boatload of wine." Nelly paced as he spoke. "He wants to plant more but he needs to find someone to buy the grapes. That's going to take time he doesn't have. He also needs to research and find the vines that do the best here. He doesn't have time for that either. Don't you see, Lim? He's at the very beginning. That's the perfect time for a young feller with his whole life ahead of him to get involved."

The door behind Lim squeaked open and Nelly looked up, a grin spreading across his face.

142

"Well, if it isn't the man himself. How's that for timing? Come on over here, Vix. Lim has something he wants to say."

Vix rounded the table, looking from Lim to Nelly and back.

"You two look like you're up to something."

"Go ahead, Lim, now's your chance. Ask him."

"Well… uh… Vix, I…" Lim ran a hand across his mouth, trying to find the words.

"Come on, Lim. You know what you want to say so just say it."

Vix glanced at Nelly. "Give him time, Nell. Go ahead, Lim."

"It's just that… well, I… I think you should hire me."

"You think I should hire you to do what? I don't even know what I'm doing."

"But that's the reason you should hire me. I can do the things you don't have time for, like finding buyers for your grapes."

"Well, it's true the folks that said they'd buy the grapes backed out and I haven't gotten around to finding someone else." Vix rubbed his jaw, squinting at him. "What else can you do?"

"How about if I get information to help you decide what to plant next? Nelly said you plan to add more acreage."

Vix frowned at Nelly. "You're always scheming, Nell. I should've known."

"Let him finish telling you, Vix."

Lim stood. "Before you plant, you need to know which grapes are in demand and which grapes are likely to do best here."

Nelly leaned toward Vix. "What do you say?"

"Hold on, Nell. I need to think. When I started the vineyard I just planted what the extension agent said would sell, but lately I've been wondering about how hot it gets here and if some other grape is better suited to the place."

143

"In a business it's usually good to diversify. That way if one thing doesn't work out you have something to fall back on."

Vix pulled on his ear, mulling over the idea. "You're making good sense, Lim. But I can't pay you much, at least not until we get the grapes sold."

"I don't care about that, Vix. You're already giving me a place to stay."

"Alright then, we have a deal. Rogelio knows about taking care of the vines. You'll learn what you can from him before starting in on these other ideas."

As they shook hands, Luster stepped through the door.

"Are you congratulating yourselves on a job well done or getting reacquainted?"

"Hell, Luster, it's way better than that." Nelly slapped his palm on the table. "Vix has hired Lim to help with the vineyard."

"That's excellent news, Lim. But we have some unfinished business."

"We do?"

"I'm planning a return to El Consuelo in a few days. It could get risky so I'd like you come along. Will you go?"

"I told Ili I'd help find her sister. I won't back out on my promise."

Luster looked to Vix. "What do you think?"

"You won't get any argument from me. A girl's future is more important than a field of grapes. If you're expecting trouble, maybe I should go along too."

"Where we're going, fewer are better despite the risk. Besides, I was hoping you'd make sure Ili stays out of harm's way while we're gone."

"Don't tell her that or she'll say I'm the one that needs protecting."

Nelly held up a finger. "Speaking of those gangsters or whatever they are, my law enforcement friends told me the sheriff went after the two men reportedly behind the fire, but the house had been cleared out. Maybe they think they got rid of Ili."

Luster shook his head. "I would like to think so, Nelly. But these types of men only stop when they have what they want or know it's out of reach."

Vix turned to Luster. "Rogelio and I will keep an eye on Ili. You and Lim just concentrate on finding her sister. When will you leave?"

"We'll start for El Consuelo the day after tomorrow."

Vix leaned against the deck railing, smiling at Lim. "So, you have a day. You can start work in the morning."

## Fourteen

Lim stepped onto the wide porch fronting Vix's home and into a patch of sunlight. Before him a broad rectangle of pasture stretched toward the gate, cresting the arc of hill before fading from sight down the slope. Blonde grass gleamed in the hazy light. Drifting above the horizon like smoke from cannon shot, puffs of cloud dotted the morning sky.

Midway down the pasture, Rogelio stood next to a gnarled scrub oak, one hand blocking the sun, the other raised to his mouth. A shrill whistle drifted up the hill. An instant later, half a dozen goats crested the rise, followed by a black and white collie. The dog crept low to the ground, racing beside the flock in short bursts, changing speed and direction with each whistle.

Rogelio turned as the goats passed him and moved toward a small corral, the collie close behind. As they reached the entrance, the flock hesitated, turning in all directions as if ready to bolt. He whistled again and the dog moved one way then the other, molding the goats into a tight circle and hurrying them through the gate.

Closing the latch, he stopped to rub the collie's neck before ambling up the hill, the dog dancing about his feet like a puppy. He looked up as he drew near the house, noticing Lim on the top stair. Blowing out his cheeks, he pulled a bandana from his pocket and wiped his forehead.

"Whew, it's already hot out, Lim. You better get ready to sweat."

"That was some show."

"You never see a sheep dog work before?"

"I couldn't take my eyes off her."

"My Rita, she's young but she can move those goats. I wanted a sheep dog ever since I worked that stinking goat ranch near El Consuelo. Goats, they don't smell too bad if you got only six or eight of them. Even if they did it makes no difference to me. I will put up with a little smell so Rita, she can work. If a sheep dog has no work, she goes loco."

"She seems to like you."

"She is okay with me but Ili, she is her madre. She helped me to pick out Rita."

"It was not so hard. I just chose the sweetest of them."

Lim turned to find Ili standing beside him. "I didn't hear you come out the door."

"That's because I've been here all along, watching Rita and waiting for you to notice me."

"That fire, it nearly cooks us, so I decide I better do what I want before I got no more time left." Rogelio stood at the bottom step, looking up at them. "I can't ride but I can watch Rita and it's the same, almost. Well, I got to get her fed or she'll start to herd me. Then Lim, you and me, we can go to the vineyard."

He limped off. Lim studied Ili's gray eyes, searching for some clue to her feelings, wanting to ask where he stood with her but unsure how to begin. Before he had a chance, she spoke.

"I am so glad to hear of your new job, Lim. You must feel proud to know Vix believes in you."

"I don't know about that. It's not like it's a real job. Depending on how it goes I may never get paid. But I'm grateful he's willing to give me a chance."

"I know you will do well in whatever you do."

He looked out over the pasture. "After being out of work for so long, I'm not so sure."

"I am sure. I know you, Lim. You are a good man."

He turned back to her. "Good enough for you, Ili?"

"Lim…"

"What about us? Can't we finish the conversation we started before the fire?"

"Oh, Lim, you see how it is for me. I have no home, no family, and my sister is lost to some cult far from here. How can I think of being with you or anyone?"

"But this could be your home, Ili."

"No, Lim, it cannot. It's true, I do feel welcome here. Luster, Vix and Rogelio are so good to me. But I have no home as long as Mirela is lost. I can think of nothing beyond her return. When that day comes, then I can make a future, but only then."

"So, I can still hope?"

Before she answered, Rogelio rounded the corner, a broad-brimmed hat in hand, Rita trotting beside him. He looked up at Lim.

"Are you ready to go work? I don't see no hat. On a day like this you got to have yourself a hat. I have one in the jeep if you don't have any."

"That's lucky for me, I guess."

"Then we better go."

Lim pivoted but Ili had disappeared through the door.

The jeep bumped along a gravel road paralleling the vineyard's southwest edge, far from the charred remains of the still smoldering cedar break. Scorched limbs stretched toward the sky, etching the blue horizon, their blackened shapes intimidating even from that distance. Lim struggled to keep his thoughts from what might have happened had he and Vix arrived too late. The vine-draped path ahead narrowed before disappearing from view between walls of green foliage, a cloudless sky rising above. Grape leaves fluttered around them in the light breeze.

Pulling past the vines Rogelio climbed out, motioning Lim to join him at the end of a row. He knelt to inspect a small rose bush, checking under the leaves, fingering the branches, feeling the soil beneath. Lim looked to his left and right, finding the same compact plants at the end of each row. Rogelio leaned back and pointed to his right.

"See the rose bush with no roses?"

"I see it."

"Check if the dirt is wet. The roses, they get water from a drip line that runs down each row. A plugged line is a little problem so I hope that's it. We don't want the big problem on a hot day like this one."

"What's the big problem?"

"The bugs, they bring a sickness that will kill the vines. It is bad luck to talk of it. You go find the hat in the back of the jeep and put it on."

Lim searched the jeep but found nothing so he reached under the seat, pulling out a floppy canvas hat covered with purple dots. He held it up, calling to Rogelio.

"I couldn't find the hat. All I found is this."

"That's the one. Now go check the rose bush so we can move on."

"You want me to wear this?" Lim looked at the hat dangling from his fingers. "I'll look like some old lady."

"You will feel like some old lady if you don't wear it. We will see a hundred degrees or more today."

He yanked on the hat and stumbled across the rocky soil toward the bush in question.

"Why does Vix have roses in the vineyard, anyway?"

"They are like the guard dog. If a sickness comes the roses will tell us before the vines do. We can maybe kill it before many vines go bad."

Lim dropped to his knees, sifting the red soil under the bush through his fingers. Leaning back, he called down the rows of vines.

"It's dry as a desert under here. You must be right about the line."

"I get old but I can still see. My father, he used to tell me I had the eye for the vines. I was young but I spot the sick ones before the other workers."

"Should I clear the line now? This whole row looks like it needs water."

"No, we fix the line later. Let me show you how to care for these vines, make them grow lots of grapes. The staked vines, they can grow a long time, maybe a hundred years or more. That's how old I feel on a hot day like this one."

Rogelio pushed aside a thick mat of leaves, lifting a handful of black grapes. He held them up to the light.

"This is the Syrah grape. The Aussies, they call it Shiraz because down there everything is different, kangaroos, wallabies, emus, so they give the grape a new name but it is the same more or less. When the grape is almost ready to be picked, Vix will test to see if the sugar is right. We must do that soon."

"But we don't have a buyer."

"Yes, this is a big problem. You are going to fix it for us, yes?"

"I hope so."

"But now we must take good care of the vineyard. After the leaves fall off we trim back the vines almost to the big part, the part like a tree trunk. That is so the vines will make more grapes when they grow again, when it is warm again." He pointed up the row. "You see the land, how it goes up the hill pretty good, steep enough to make you sweat when you walk up there?"

"I see it. The vineyard must slope toward the lake."

"That is good for the vines. They like to be thirsty. A vine will die if it gets too much to drink. The ground must be right too, not too thick.

Lim dug the toe of his boot into the dirt. "This soil doesn't look so good. There are stones everywhere."

"No, the stones are good. Vines, they like the limestone. The limestone feeds the vines and helps the ground stay dry the way the grapes need. We must also check the irrigation to be sure the vines stay strong, not too much and not too little."

"That sounds tricky."

"No, I can see you have a good eye, Lim. You will get used to seeing when the irrigation is right just by looking down the row and by feeling the leaves."

"You know a lot about the vines, Rogelio."

"My father, he was a good teacher. Still, there is more to learn always. I will show you what I have learned but I think you will teach me too. Now, we see what you can do with that plugged line."

As Lim worked to clear the piping, a truck appeared at the edge of the vineyard. Rogelio stood, disappearing down the row. Lim paid him little notice. A moment later, footsteps sounded behind him.

"Lim, you and me, today we are lucky. We have a visitor, a lady visitor."

Lim snapped the final section of line together and scrambled to his feet. To his surprise, Blanket stood not three feet away, her blue eyes shining. She stared at him without a word. In spite of himself he did the same, the words he wanted to say lost beneath his racing thoughts, her strawberry-hued face filling his mind. Rogelio looked from one to the other, shaking his head.

"I never see two people go mute at the same time. I better go call the doctor."

Blanket blinked, stumbling back a step. She blinked again and faced Rogelio, pursing her lips.

"I can talk! Vix asked me to come and see his vineyard, so I'm here. Should I just turn around and leave?"

"No, no, you are welcome here." Rogelio held up both hands. "I mean no offense."

"No offense taken, then."

He nodded and gave Lim a quick wink.

"This one, she has some spark, some chispa. No wonder you forget how to talk."

"I just stood up too fast and my mind went cloudy." Lim ran a hand across his face, trying to gather himself.

"Oh, is this what happened?"

"Sure it is. Rogelio, this is Blanket. I was with Vix when he asked her to come out. Blanket knows about vineyards and wine-making. Vix wants to hear her ideas."

"I am glad to hear also." Rogelio took her hand in his. "We need the young people to show us the new ways to care for vines. Wine-making is very old but as I said to Lim, there is more to learn, to make better."

"I hope I can help but I'm still learning too, Rogelio."

"Then we learn together."

"Lim, you show Blanket the vines while I go tell Vix she is here." He started for the jeep. "But first take off that old lady hat. I don't know why you like to wear it."

Lim yanked off the hat. "I don't…"

His voice trailed off as the jeep sputtered to life. Turning to Blanket, he led her to a rise offering a view of the vineyard and the horizon beyond. She bent, taking a leaf in her palm and tracing the veins. Lim stood behind her watching the sunlight play across her honey-colored hair. Letting go of the leaf, she stood and surveyed the rows of vines spreading before them in fingers of green.

"It's beautiful here."

"I'd say so, Blanket."

"I'm glad Vix asked me to come out. Learning the botany of grapes and the chemistry of wine from books is one thing but standing in the middle of a well-kept vineyard is something else altogether. I look out across these vines and think of the thousands of years people have cultivated grapes, the countless ties wine has to religion, culture and geography in countries across the entire world. What could be more fascinating?"

"That's some description. Most people don't give much thought to grapes or wine."

"My dream is to go to California and get a job in a winery."

"You're going to leave?"

"Would you want to work in a feed store your whole life?"

"It might not be so bad if you liked your customers and where you lived. I'm new here but I can see this is a beautiful place."

"I suppose some people consider it nice country." She turned a circle, surveying the horizon. "I've lived here since I was born so I don't much notice. But I refuse to spend my whole life doing something that bores me. Uncle Bunk says I'm not much good with people but I think I could be good at growing grapes and making wine. I want to learn all I can and maybe have my own winery one day. Imagine opening a bottle of wine from Riddell Vineyards. Wouldn't that be something?"

She faced him, her cheeks flushed. He pointed down the row, unable to take his eyes from her.

"You can't stay here and do that?"

She smiled and followed his arm with her gaze. "This is a nice vineyard. But there are so many more wineries on the West Coast. I wouldn't have a bit trouble finding work."

"But with so many there's bound to be more competition."

She faced him, a determined look in her eyes. "I'm not afraid of competition."

"Why not get in on the beginning of the wine-making business here? You know the area, where the best soils should be, who owns the property. You're a step ahead of someone coming from California to start a winery, not to mention all you've already learned about wine."

She squinted at him. "Are you always this nice to people you just met?"

He hesitated, thinking of all the excuses he could make to sidestep her question. Yet he took a breath, letting his thoughts come through just as they were, without care to how he might sound or what she might think.

"You've been good enough to pay us a visit, Blanket. I think I should try to be friendly."

"Is that all? It sounds like you want something."

"I'm going to be working for Vix, helping him develop the vineyard. You and I have a similar interest that way. I thought we might be friends and work together, learn together."

"What do you mean?"

"I've listened to you enough to know I like the way you think."

"You like the way I think?"

"You're smart but you're thoughtful too. One doesn't always go with the other."

"No one has ever told me that before."

"I know saying this when we've only just met may put you off but I want to answer your question as best I can. Does that make sense?"

"I'm not sure."

He looked at her, again hesitating, struggling with the familiar self-doubt. Then he forced the thought from his mind, continuing as before.

"Well, it doesn't hurt that you're good-looking. But I think we have a lot in common, things we could talk about. You like history and geography and so do I. You know about wine and I want to learn."

"You like the way I look?" She squinted at him again.

"I do."

"You mean you think I'm pretty?"

"Of course, Blanket, just like everyone else that meets you."

"I've never really thought of myself that way."

"I can't imagine why not."

"Well, I like the way you think too, Lim Specter." She pulled at her hair, staring at him, and then cocked her head to the side. "But it takes me a while to get to know a person. I don't trust people easy."

"Does that mean we can't be friends?"

"No, it doesn't mean that exactly but…"

They turned at the sound of the jeep bouncing up the gravel road. Vix waved them over as he stepped out.

"Well, Blanket, what do you think? Will I make it in the vineyard business or should Rogelio and I go back to poking cows?"

"You have a beautiful vineyard, Vix. I see what looks like Cabernet Sauvignon down these rows. Have you planted any white grape varietals?"

"No, I just started with what I was told would sell. Why do you ask?"

"In school I learned that a grape called Viognier does well in the hot climate we have here. You might want to consider planting a test plot of an acre or so to see how it does."

Rogelio nodded and spit. "Vix, maybe you want to hire her instead of Lim, I think."

"You think so, Rogelio? It's not too late."

Lim glanced at Blanket. "I was afraid you were going to say that, Vix."

"Rogelio is making good sense, Lim. I'm not sure you can even spell that grape much less find us the root stock. I imagine Blanket can get a hold of some right away. What do you say, Rogelio?"

"I say our Blanket here, she knows more than all us put together."

Lim again glanced at Blanket. "Vix, should I resign now or are you going to fire me?"

She took a step back, looking from one to the other. "Lim, stop playing around! Vix, I know you're not going to fire him... are you?"

"We'll see, Blanket. But we'll have to wait until he gets back from his trip. Lim, Luster asked me to tell you he needs to leave now instead of tomorrow morning."

"Why the change in plans?"

"He said something about needing to see a chemist before you head into hostile territory."

"What on earth for?"

"He didn't say chemist exactly. It was something like that but different. Let's see… maybe he said an alchemist, whatever that is."

"He's going to see an alchemist? That figures. He of all people would actually know one."

155

"You can take the jeep back to the house. I'd like to stay and hear what else Blanket has to say, if she can give us a lift back to the house."

She nodded and then faced Lim, peering into his eyes. "Is the trip dangerous?"

"I'm not sure… maybe."

She reached into her jeans pocket, pulling out a silver button and handing it to him. "It's from my grandmother's wedding dress. She said it brings good luck."

Distill (dis'til) - to extract the essence of; a process of vaporization and subsequent condensation, as for purification or concentration.

# Fifteen

Running from the tilted sun, thin lines of shadow stretched northward across the two-lane road, the autumnal equinox now less than a week away. In spite of the calendar, summer refused to abate. Lim followed the narrow blacktop southwest toward El Consuelo, past long-abandoned homesteads and rusting windmills. Silver pools of heat vibrated above the highway. Luster leaned against the seatback, silent and brooding.

The torn horizon carried no sign of settlement, no rooftops, no chimneys, only the occasional power line disappearing into dense stands of scrub oak and mesquite. Dry creeks and washes wound out of sight, their limestone beds bleached white as bone. Beyond the endless miles of barbed-wire fence, blue-tinted hills reached into the distance like rolling waves.

Further south the landscape grew hardened, the trees stunted, sotol and cactus filling the rock-strewn earth in dust-covered clumps that vibrated before a steady breeze. Flat-topped mesas streaked with landslides slit the horizon. Lim stared at the ruler-straight road, unwavering, mesmerizing, and an image of Blanket's face came to him. He searched her blue eyes for a hint to her feelings but found little he could be certain of.

A moment later Luster sat up, raising his hand as he peered through the windshield. Lim glanced at him, trying to keep an eye on the road. The highway followed a tight curve sloping between stands of scrub oak and juniper. As they rounded a tree line, a group of weathered buildings came into view, their rusted tin roofs dull beneath the cloudless sky. Guinea fowl and chickens scurried across the dusty yard. Luster pointed toward a gravel parking area beneath a sprawling oak and Lim angled the car toward it, pulling to a stop.

"Where are we, Luster?"

"In this part of the world they call it a saloon. We've come to find an old friend, somewhat of a mystic."

"You mean the supposed alchemist is here?" Lim surveyed the unpainted building before them.

"Call him what you like but I need a dose of his wisdom to prepare for what's to come.

"A beer joint isn't the sort of place I'd expect to find a prophet."

"It's the very place I'd expect to find a free-thinker like him. People have relied on beer to lubricate the mind and encourage contemplation for centuries, Lim."

"Then I'd better have several. I need to contemplate what the hell I'm doing here."

They walked toward an open door, metal bottle tops crunching beneath their feet, and into a small room plastered with festival posters and battered license plates. A cast iron stove stacked with beer bottles filled the center of the room. Several men in sweat-stained caps and overalls hunched over a small table scattered with dominoes, taking little notice.

Luster stepped up to the counter. The bartender peered at him, rubbing his jaw and mumbling as his eyebrows danced above his eyes. He opened his mouth as if to speak but then closed it and leaned toward him, a gap-toothed smile spreading across his face.

"Why, I ought to remember a name to go with that face. I reckon all that cheap beer has gone and scrambled my memory. I do recall you used to come in here a lot. But that was a long time ago."

"Yes, a very long time."

"You didn't have no beard then, neither."

"You remember more than you think."

"Wait, I almost got it! Your name is something like Shiny except I never did know anybody with that name. Maybe it's Skinny. I've known a few and hardly any of those fellers was skinny."

"Maybe I go by Thirsty?"

"You're name is Thirsty? That's some name you… wait! I believe you're funning with me. You want something to drink, don't you?"

"Two beers will do."

He reached below the counter, pulling out the bottles and popping off the caps.

"Hold on, now! I got it. Aren't you a friend of Tolly Jobert's?"

Luster paid him and handed Lim a beer. "Right you are."

"I'll bet you're Luster Lester."

"Right again."

The man slapped his palm against the counter. "Dang, I remembered after all!"

"The memory was there all along. You just had to let it come to you."

"That could be. Maybe I still have a few miles left in me after all."

"I don't doubt it, Marlin."

The man started, again leaning across the counter. "You remembered my name!"

He nodded toward Lim. "And this is Lim, my nephew. Marlin has run the place for almost forty years, if memory serves."

"I've done better than that, Lim." He rapped his knuckles on the counter. "I hit forty-one years last April. A young feller like you won't believe it but I don't feel as old as that sounds. In fact, it seems like only a year or two since I opened the place."

Lim glanced around the room. "These buildings look pretty old."

"That they are, Lim. This was once a post office and general store. Across the road is an old drinking hall where the Germans who settled here would dance every Saturday night. They had a brewery near here too. Those folks had their priorities straight, if you ask me. But then the teetotalers came along and nearly ruined the place. The

160

buildings had been closed a long time when I bought them."

"And you've kept the tradition going all these years, Marlin. The place has hardly changed since I first came here."

"So, what brings you out this way again, Luster?"

"I'm looking for Tolly. Does he still have his cabin above the grotto?"

"The old hermit is still up there but you just missed him. He's gone to town and won't be back for a couple of hours. You're welcome to relax here until then if you want. I best get back to work."

Marlin stepped around the counter to check on the domino players as Lim followed Luster through the door and onto a tree-shaded patio. Finding an empty table, they sat amid the dappled sunlight cast by the big tree. Lim leaned back, surveying the scene. Bikers in skullcaps and leather leggings drifted through, their steel-toed boots clicking on the stone walkway. Down the slope, four men in pearl-buttoned western shirts played horseshoes, kicking up a cloud of dust as they moved between the stakes.

Lim turned as a stout man in a Hawaiian shirt and jeans crossed the beer garden, looking to his left and right, beer bottles jingling in his arms. He paused and scanned the tables, spotting Lim and hurrying toward him. Setting down the bottles, he looked both directions again before taking a seat. Luster looked at Lim and shrugged.

"You boys mind if I join you? I'm trying to outrun a cowgirl in heat. I've heard about wild Texas women but she's too much even for me. I'm Billy Fordham of Picayune, Mississippi."

He shook both their hands.

"I'm Luster and this is Lim. We're fellow travelers as well. Please feel free to tell us your dilemma."

He slid them each a bottle of beer before downing his and opening another.

"Well, I have a construction company and we're setting the slabs for those big wind turbines you see popping up everywhere. This place being the only entertainment within a hundred miles, I've been spending a lot of time here drinking beer and chatting up the locals. Then last night this full-bodied woman comes along and the next thing you know we're in the sack setting some kind of record. That was all fine and good but I'm a free spirit, if you know what I mean. I can't get myself tied down to any one thing, especially when we're talking women."

"I take it she has another perspective on the matter."

"You're called Luster, right? How in the hell did you come by that name? You don't mind my asking, do you? That's a name you don't hear every day."

"I was born bald as a cue ball and almost as shiny. My mother was a writer and thought the name had a certain poetry."

"I'm sure glad my parents didn't think that way. When I was born the doctor used forceps and I ended up with two black eyes. They could've named me Coon. I would've had hell growing up in Mississippi with that name."

"Anyway, you're right about that cowgirl. She thinks she owns me now and she's not one to be messed with." He emptied his bottle and opened another. "I don't believe she knows the meaning of the word no. I'll bet she's trained horses so long she expects to treat a man the same and he'll like it. Are all Texas women like that?"

"We do have our share of strong-minded women. Living on the frontier probably required it."

"So, what brings you hombres way out to the badlands? That's how they say it here in Texas, isn't it, Luster?"

"We've come to see a friend. He lives not far from here."

He opened another bottle, sliding it across the table to Lim.

"How do you tolerate this heat? It gets warm back home but I'm close enough to the bay to catch a breeze. It's just plain hot here. And it's so dry nothing much can grow. Don't you feel like you're going to shrivel up and blow away?"

Lim set his empty bottle aside. "You have to be near water to stay cool this time of year, Billy."

"That's just the problem, Lim. Back home there's water everywhere you turn but I haven't been able to find so much as a trickle around here. What they call rivers are more like creeks, and creeks like ditches, and all of them are dry for the most part."

"Maybe that's why we like beer so much, Billy."

"Well hell, I'll drink to that!"

He went on rambling from one thought the next as the afternoon drifted by. Lim lay back on the bench and closed his eyes, the warm day settling around him, pulling from his mind all thought, all concern. A hint of breeze moved past, stirring the hot air, and he felt as if he floated on a calm sea. Lapsing into a dream, an image of Blanket standing at the edge of a cliff came to him, her lips moving without sound or word as a wave of fear crossed her face. An instant later she stumbled back, slipping over the edge.

He awoke with a start. Sitting up, he looked about, his sweat-soaked shirt stuck to his back, the sun now low in the sky. Luster and Billy were nowhere in sight. Footsteps sounded in the gravel behind him and he turned to see Marlin approaching the table, a case of empty beer bottles in his arms. He nodded toward a stand of trees beyond the buildings.

"Luster is at Tolly's place. The path is across a footbridge on the other side of those trees. He said to send you on up as soon as you were awake."

## Sixteen

Lim crossed the wooden bridge, following the trail as it wound up a rock-strewn slope between stands of mountain laurel and persimmon. Broken shards of flint littered the path. Coming on a set of steps carved into the limestone, he paused and peered up the steep bluff, the image of Blanket again coming to him, crowding his thoughts. He blinked and took a breath, grabbing hold of a heavy chain that flanked the stairway and hoisting himself up.

Moments later he mounted the last step. Before him, a ridge top fell away in both directions above the sweeping curve of a river. He followed the narrow crest, the trail winding through gnarled scrub oak and juniper before descending into a broad grotto surrounded by cypress and willow. Angel hair fern sprouted from the shallow cave, dripping spring water into an oval pool that stood undisturbed and clear. A cool breeze drifted past him, the air fragrant with new growth.

At one end of the pool he spotted Luster atop a white boulder, facing a small man with a shock of white hair that reached toward the sky. The man gestured at Luster with both hands, his voice echoing along the circular walls in short bursts. Luster motioned toward Lim, beckoning him over with a wave, never taking his eyes from the man.

Wearing a goatee that reached down his chest, the man turned at Lim's approach, studying him without a word, his eyes darting about as if taking in every detail. Luster raised his eyebrows at Lim and shrugged, waiting for someone to speak. Then the man tapped the white rock with his index finger.

"You ever hear of travertine?"

Lim thought for a moment, trying to recall what he knew of geology.

"It's a type of stone, a stone made of calcite, I think."

"Very good. Travertine is a form of limestone."

"If I remember right, you find it near hot springs."

"The springs don't have to be warm." The man wagged his finger at Lim. "The key is the mineral content. This rock we're sitting on is beautiful example. See how it comes right out of the grotto like a waterfall turned to stone?"

"It's used for building, isn't it?"

"That's an understatement, son. Architects and builders have used travertine for centuries. The Ancient Romans built with it. One of the best-know examples is the Coliseum in Rome. But I like the rock in its natural state. I call this my philosopher's rock because I've had many a good debate right here with our friend Luster. Something about the rock makes us sit and talk for hours. At night it glows of phosphorescence. Sounds magical, doesn't it? Well, it is and there's nothing better, especially if you have a few cold beers on hand."

"Rocks have a lot to say if you'll listen." He pulled a flat stone from his pants pocket. "They tell of history, of weather, of chemistry. That grotto behind me shows what eons of flowing water can do to stone. The striations of limestone higher on the walls tell of the inland sea that once covered this place."

He held out the palm-sized stone. "Run your finger along the top."

Lim traced his forefinger across the stone. An instant later a golden line emerged from the dark surface.

"You see what he's made of, Luster?"

Luster nodded. "I do and I'm not surprised."

"What is it?" Lim peered at the rock."

"This is a touchstone, Lim."

"I've never seen one before. But isn't a touchstone just an ancient method of assaying metals for quality?"

"It's that and more, Lim. This stone measures merit in all things, not just precious metals."

Lim looked at Tolly askance. Luster shook his head.

"He doesn't believe you, Tolly."

"Look around you, Lim." Tolly swung his arm through the air. "Are you telling me you can't believe in the beauty, the magic, of this place?

Lim turned a half-circle, the green cave looming before him, countless springs flowing from its walls. A cloudless twilight danced across the oval pool, casting amber shafts of light along the shoreline.

"I don't know what to believe. But I can't deny this is a beautiful spot."

"Then sit with us while Luster and I make a plan. You and he have a common purpose, Lim. The question is how best to proceed."

Luster sat up and frowned, pulling at his beard. Then he reached behind his back, pulling out a leather-bound book and holding it up to the light. Lim grabbed the book, immediately recognizing it as one he had taken from the kidnappers.

"This is the book by Dimitrie Cantemir. Where did you get it?"

"I found it along the path while Ili tended you. You got out with it after all, just as I knew you would."

"So I did have three books! But why didn't you tell me?"

"I was waiting for the right time, Lim."

"I don't understand."

"Haven't you wondered how I got involved with Ili and her sister?"

"Yes, but I got to a point where it didn't matter. They need our help. That should be enough."

"I agree. Still, there's more to the story and now you need to know it."

Tolly tapped the white rock again, peering at Lim with a grim expression. "Do you believe in good and evil, Lim?"

"No. There's truth and there's what lies outside truth."

"But how do you know what's true?"

"I depend on reason and science to separate fact from fiction. That's how I know."

"But some things lie outside of science. What about right and wrong? How do you know which is which?"

"I reason it out."

"Which direction is that?" Tolly pointed away from the grotto. "Don't think about it, just answer!"

"That's east, I think."

"Are you sure?"

"I believe so."

"How do you know?"

"I just do."

"But how?"

"I don't know how."

"You didn't reason it out?"

"I didn't have time."

"And still you were right. That is east, exactly. You relied on your intuition to tell you."

"Alright, maybe I did. But even geese can tell north from south. Do they use their intuition?"

"You're damn right they do. They use everything at hand, and then some. There's more to understanding than what you can puzzle out, Lim. Some things lie beyond your mind's ability to reason. That's where your intuition comes in."

"I don't know…"

Tolly slapped the stone with his palm. "So, do you believe in right and wrong?"

"I suppose so."

Tolly nodded. "He does believe in something."

Lim squinted at Luster. "What does this have to do with Ili, her sister and the book?"

He took a deep breath, searching for a place to start. "Long ago I did something wrong, something I regret, something I've hoped to make up for ever since. I tried becoming a monk but you know how that ended. So, I wandered the country looking for opportunities to do good, to make the world a better place. That didn't go much better. Then I came here and everything changed."

"Luster was tapped out emotionally and spiritually when he got here." Tolly passed his hand across the rock as if blessing it. "I could see it as soon as I opened the door. So, I gave him something real to focus his mind, something with meaning and purpose."

Lim held up the book. "Does it have something to do with this?"

"It does. I belong to a group that seeks to find and preserve great works from the past, literature, science, history. Civilization is a thin and fragile veneer over chaos and anarchy, Lim. So much has been lost. When invaders burned the ancient Library of Alexandria, an untold amount of knowledge was lost forever. The Dark Ages followed soon after.

"During the American Revolution, the Library of Congress was burned by British troops, and then burned again by accident on Christmas Eve 1851. Vast numbers of irreplaceable works and the ideas they contained were lost to future generations. Our group works to find and replace those books."

"Who is this group?"

"We prefer to remain anonymous. We're just an assortment of people who value ideas and knowledge enough to do what we can to protect and promote them. We were asked to assist in replacing the books Thomas Jefferson sold to the country after the British burned the original Library of Congress, books from his personal library, books that were lost in the second fire. So, when Luster showed up that night I knew I would enlist him in the project."

Luster nodded. "Tolly knows me well enough to figure I couldn't resist such a mission, especially in my demoralized state. Having heard that some of the books thought lost in the fire were actually saved by Helmut Freiburg, a German immigrant, volunteer fireman and booklover, the Library investigated only to discover the books he saved had been stolen from him not long after the fire. But they also found that gangs operating out of Eastern Europe had recently adopted the practice of using rare books to launder money. With a bit of luck, they traced some of the Jefferson books to a gang known to be working out of this area and farther north."

Tolly pointed at the Cantemir. "The Library didn't know for certain what the gang might have but they had a general idea. We decided to send Luster to the gang posing as a priest in search of donated books, books for an orphanage. Having been a monk, I thought he could pass as a man of the cloth."

"Why not just offer to buy the books?"

These gangs aren't in the rare book business, Lim. They're laundering dirty money from drugs, prostitution, gambling and the like, so they keep a low profile. They prefer to find a buyer on the black market and are suspicious of reputable book agents.

"I found that out the hard way."

"The complicating factor in our plan was the gang's other business."

Luster nodded again, pulling at his beard. "When I realized what had happened to Ili and her sister, I knew I had to get them out. I saw the Cantemir book but only guessed that it might be one of the books I was sent to find. Unfortunately, I was only able to escape with Ili and the kidnappers left soon after. I realized if I could find the book I might find her sister as well. That's when I came asking for your help."

"So, we went to Sam to identify the engraving you saw when you found Ili, and then to Orvis to identify the book."

"That's right, Lim. At that point my main concern was helping Ili find her sister, but I hoped to find the book as well and somehow get hold of it. Then it came to me that Orvis' Baudelaire might be a means."

"My close call with disaster was worth it then?"

"Lim, you did the world a real service by helping get the Cantemir back where it belongs. Soon it will be available to everyone instead of only a small group of wealthy book collectors.

"What happens to the book now?"

"Tolly will see it gets to the Library of Congress."

"That's why we came here?"

"In a sense, it was. To be safe, I wanted to hand the book over to him myself. But I also felt a need to see Tolly, to ask his advice."

"What about?" Lim leaned toward him.

"The people who now have Ili's sister are very serious, some might say extreme, in their beliefs. The fact that Mirela refuses to see even her own sister may be a reflection of that seriousness. Or it may have to do with the brainwashing that goes on in some of these groups. If that's the case, I want to be prepared."

Lim turned to Tolly. "You're an expert on religious cults?"

"Not at all, Lim. I've made a point of doing many things to make a living, from carpenter to teacher to artist. Change keeps the mind young and active. New ideas and new ways of thinking are what hold my interest."

Luster nodded. "That sort of outlook was what I needed, Lim."

"My value to Luster was as a sounding board, a way to organize his thoughts. And I believe he's done that."

Luster nodded. "Yes, I feel we're ready to finish your promise to Ili."

"What do you mean my promise? I said I didn't see a choice whether or not to help. That's not exactly a promise."

"Lim, you've promised many times over with your eyes if not your words."

Lim squinted at Luster and stood. "Let's go."

"Not so fast, Lim." Tolly motioned him to stop. "I have a dozen tamales and pot of frijoles up at the house. And Luster still has some preparations to make. Besides, it's time for a swim."

"I didn't bring a swimsuit, Tolly."

"You don't need one here, Lim. This is my place and I say it's clothing optional."

"You're going skinny-dipping?" Lim glanced to either side of the pool.

"Keep your skivvies on if you like but the free way is the best way."

Tolly stood, stripping off his clothes and wading into the clear pool. Luster did the same. Lim blinked, trying to believe what he'd just seen.

"What if someone comes along?"

"Then I'll invite them in. Come on! You've got to experience life, Lim."

Lim pointed up the hill. "Luster, what if that wild cowgirl we heard about shows up?

"She's welcome too. This spring is a miracle, Lim. Come on in and enjoy nature's gift."

Lim looked about before stripping and hurrying into the pool. The cool water took his breath. Surprised to find it both relaxing and bracing, he paddled to the opposite shore and back, joining Tolly and Luster in the warmer shallows. Tolly lifted a handful of water, letting it drain through his fingers.

"The natives considered springs like this sacred, Lim."

"I can see why, especially on a hot day."

"This water filters through limestone, sometimes for hundreds of feet. There are some who believe the springs are healing and transformative."

"What do you mean? Wait, you're supposed to be an alchemist or something, aren't you?"

"I don't consider myself an alchemist, Lim. But I do find it a helpful philosophy, as a way of looking at the world, at life."

171

Lim chuckled. "If I could change lead into gold, life would look better real quick."

"Don't dismiss the idea too quickly. Alchemy influenced many great thinkers, including Aristotle. Isaac Newton's study of it helped forward the progress of chemistry."

"Isn't a philosopher's stone supposed to turn lead to gold?"

"You're looking at it too literally, Lim." Tolly shook his finger at him. "Would you agree that most of us are trying to improve our lot, to transition to a better place?"

"I suppose so."

"That's what alchemy is about, transforming one thing to another, transitioning from one place to another. That's the other reason Luster came here. That's why he has work still to do."

"You mean because we still haven't found Ili's sister?" Lim turned to where Luster sat lost in thought. "Is that it, Luster?"

"There is more, Lim. The most difficult part I must do after we have helped Ili and Mirela as best we can."

"There's something even more difficult? What on earth is it?"

Tolly stood. "Your question will have to wait, Lim. When Luster is ready, you'll get your answer. Now it's time to feed the body instead of the mind. Come see my refuge in the hills."

They followed a rocky path, climbing the steep slope up past the grotto and on to a small meadow of blonde grass. Just beyond, a stone and timber cabin stood surrounded by gnarled post oaks and knots of undergrowth. A deep porch stretched across the front, scattered with roughhewn benches and chairs.

Lim followed Luster and Tolly across the meadow and past a carved pole rising twenty feet into the air and topped with a brass ring. Lim stopped to study the strange sculpture, running his fingers along the painted wood.

Beneath the pole a pattern of limestone blocks standing on end traced an elongated figure-eight through the grass. Tolly stopped next to him.

"How do you like my analemma pole, Lim?"

"What's an analemma, some sort of alchemy voodoo?"

"You're a man of science. You should appreciate my interest in our planet."

"This thing has something to do with the earth?"

Tolly pointed into the sky. "It has to do with our place in the solar system, to be exact."

"It's a totem pole to the sun gods, right?"

Tolly squinted at him. "Lim, were you born cynical or did something make you that way?"

"Alright, Tolly, what's an analemma pole?"

"You know how the sun gets low in the sky during winter and nearly overhead in the summer? Well, the rocks show the sun's movement at the same time of day over a year's time. The stones farthest from the pole mark winter, the ones closest summer."

"But why are they in a figure eight?" Lim stepped between the stones.

"Can't you guess?"

"The stones represent the earth's orbit?"

"Very good, Lim. Now what about the orbit?"

"My brain hurts, Tolly. Just tell me the answer."

"Not so fast." Tolly waved a finger at him. "Does the earth circle the sun?"

"Of course it does."

"But in a circle?"

"Most orbits are elliptical."

"You're getting close…"

"I see it now." Lim followed the path of stones with his gaze. "The figure eight shows that the earth has an elliptical orbit. If the orbit was circular the rocks would end up in a single, straight line."

"I knew it would come to you, Lim. Now, let's eat."

They stepped through the door and into an open room paneled with redwood planks. Maps, star charts and lunar calendars occupied the far wall. Opposite them sat a long table crammed with fossilized shells, bird nests and insect-filled shadowboxes, the kitchen stove just beyond. Steam drifted from a large metal pot.

Lim and Luster sat while Tolly spooned pinto beans and tamales onto their plates. Stepping in front of a wooden barrel, he pulled three mugs of beer from the tap. Holding up each glass, he studied the dark liquid before setting it on the table.

"This ale is made from spring water I collect just up the hill. Drink up, Lim, and taste its magical properties."

"You made this yourself?"

"Like I said, these springs are sacred. This beer will add years to your life."

"You mean if I drink enough I'll feel as old as Luster?"

Tolly ignored him. "In fact, I recommend you stay the night so you can study its magic thoroughly."

"I have to agree." Luster lifted his mug. "Don't discount the power of the natural world to create change, Lim. There's a reason beer has been around for thousands of years. Even the ancient Egyptians considered it a key staple."

"You mean it was one of the four main food groups?"

"Now you're getting the idea."

As they finished their meal, Tolly reached into his pocket, pulling out a triangular blue pendant attached to a leather cord. The carved stone held a series of concentric circles crossed by two perpendicular lines. He laid the pendant on the table, sliding it across to Luster.

"I want you to take this with you."

"You made it yourself?"

He shook his head. "An old friend gave it to me long ago when I was in a difficult period."

174

"What is it, Tolly?" Lim leaned toward the stone.

"It's a talisman."

Luster held it up to the light. "A talisman is meant to protect and assist in a quest, Lim."

"More of your magic, Luster?"

"Lim, there is a magic to symbols even when they're no more than metaphors. They represent what's possible, what we believe and hope for. In that sense I'd say you're right about it being magic. Considering where we're going, I'll take all the help and protection I can find."

## Seventeen

Without speaking, Lim pointed the car southwest into the morning light, Luster having again lapsed into a brooding silence. Flat-topped mesas drifted over the horizon, yielding to rock-strewn hills thick with sheep and Angora goats, their matted coats stained with dirt. Dense stands of scrub oak dotted the landscape. He peered through the windshield at the open country. To the west, fields of blonde grass stretched toward cone-shaped hills, remnants of a long dormant volcano.

The highway climbed until cresting a ridge top that opened onto a level plain. On one side of the two-lane road the land stretched beyond sight. To the other, stone-draped cliffs disappeared from view down a narrow canyon. Far below, a deep valley cut by winding creeks threaded between the lower ridge tops. Spare homesteads appeared and then vanished behind the jagged hills.

Lim glanced at Luster, wondering what thoughts troubled his stoic silence. Did his atonement for past wrongs plague him and, if so, what wrongs? Lim had first guessed that the cause must be his rejection of Sam. But perhaps his betrayal of Orvis ranked higher. Yet it appeared Orvis had returned the favor, in a sense evening the score. Could there be something else, some past regret that refused to die?

Along a tree-lined curve a hand-painted sign came into view, pulling him from his thoughts. Something stirred in the back of his mind. The sign read only "Nino's". Lim turned the name over in his mind, somehow troubled by it. Then he remembered Rogelio's description of a bar with the same name. Yet he had seen nothing, no cars, no building. He slowed the car, repeating the name again, this time aloud. Luster sat up, looking around, his eyes wide.

"What are you doing, Lim?

"I saw a sign. I think it's one Rogelio mentioned but I don't remember why.

"Stop the car.

What?

"Quickly, Lim, stop wherever you can.

The car rattled onto the shoulder in a cloud of dust.

"We must go back.

"It's a bar, isn't it? Rogelio said it's owned by some guy named Nino. I had forgotten until I saw the sign.

"We must talk to him." Luster turned in his seat, craning his neck toward the rear of the car.

"Who?"

"We must speak to Nino."

"But I didn't see any bar, only trees and the sign."

Luster shook off his comment. "The bar isn't meant for the public, Lim. It's frequented by men who operate outside the law, rough men, men who want to keep a low profile."

"Then why go there? We don't need to go looking for trouble."

"He may know the people who have Mirela."

Lim pulled back onto the highway in a wide arc, retracing their route until the small sign again appeared among a clutch of oaks. A dirt road barely visible below the tall grass threaded between the trees. He angled the car past the grove, following the one-lane path along a rusted fence and through an open gate. As they rounded a thicket, an unpainted frame building appeared in the middle of a clearing, motorcycles and pickups crowding the front steps. Lim cut the engine and followed Luster toward a half-open door painted blood red. As they stepped through, he leaned toward Luster.

"Luster, it's not even noon. Do you think this Nino will be here?"

Luster ignored the question as he surveyed the dim space. Mismatched tables crowded the windowless room, the only light cast by a scattering of neon beer signs. Couples hunched over their drinks, talking in low tones. Several men standing at the bar turned, watching in silence as Luster made his way across the room, Lim close behind. They found an empty table and sat. A moment later, one of the men stepped out the door while another sporting a thin goatee approached them. He tapped his finger on the table then pointed at Luster.

"This is a private bar. You can't come in here."

"Luster studied the man before responding. "Are you the owner?"

"What? No, I don't own the place."

"Then you work here?"

"Hell no, I don't work here."

"But this is a private bar?"

"Isn't that what I said?"

"And because it's private only certain people can enter?"

"That's what the word private means, old man."

"So, who decides who can or can't come in?"

"The owner, who in the hell else?"

"And you're not the owner?"

"Are you demented? I already said so."

"If the owner decides who can come in, and you're not the owner, then you can't decide if we're welcome here. Is that not true?"

"You think you're real smart but I'll tell you what's true. What's true is I'm going to toss you and your little friend out that door over there."

As he pointed toward the entrance his companion stepped back through, making his way to the table. The man with the goatee glared at Luster, waving his finger through the air.

"Give me a hand, Milo. These two got to go."

"Maybe they do and maybe they don't, Pug. Which one of you owns that old Renault out there?"

Luster raised a hand. "I'm Luster and this is Lim. Harriet belongs to me."

"Harriet?"

"I named her after a tortoise. She's slow but steady."

"I'm surprised the car runs at all. How long have you had her?"

"Believe it or not, I bought her new."

"That's got to be some kind of record for a French car."

"I'm surprised you noticed her. Few people in this country are familiar with Renaults, although they're still popular in France."

"I had one when I was a kid, the first car I ever owned. I loved that car."

"The goateed man tapped the table again. "Come on, Milo. Let's get rid of these clowns."

"Damn, Pug, have some patience and you might learn something." Milo sighed, shaking his head.

"But why are they here, Milo? Huh? Can you tell me that? Maybe they're with the feds or something."

"Alright, alright, take it easy."

"I won't, not until they say who they are."

"Milo leaned toward Luster. "What brings you fellers way out here?"

"We're here to see Nino. Is he here?"

"He stepped out but will be back soon. Are you a friend of his?"

"Not exactly. I'm a friend of a friend."

"And what would be your friend's name?"

"Rogelio Garza is his name. He lives a long way north of here."

He stood back and smiled. "You're a friend of that old cowboy?"

"He told us to see Nino, that he could help us with a project."

"Hell, Pug, did you hear what he said? That changes everything."

"You should've said you were Rogelio's friend." Pug ran a hand across his face. "Don't tell him what I said."

"No harm done." Luster waved off his concern.

Milo pulled a large wallet on a chain from his back pocket and held it up. A tiny feather dangled from the clasp.

"Rogelio gave me this feather. Some Indian relative of his from Mexico carved it from a deer antler. I never finished school but I like archaeology and hunting arrowheads. He's showed me some good spots to hunt and sometimes brings me Indian stuff when he comes down. You two are welcome here as long as you want. We have to get back to the bar. You can join us if you want."

"Thanks for the offer but we'll just wait for Nino's return and then be on our way."

"Alright, then. Pug will stand you a couple of beers to help pass the time."

They wandered off toward the bar and a short time later a waitress set two beers on the table. Lim lifted his bottle, wiping off the sweat with his palm.

"I'm getting used to having beer for lunch."

"Enjoy it while you can, Lim. Where we're going, you'll find few bars, if any."

"What do you mean?"

"The people down near El Consuelo tend toward firm beliefs, especially in their religion. Some places even outlaw beer."

"You mean like they did during prohibition?"

"Yes, except on a smaller scale."

"That's hard to believe."

"You've spent your life in the city. It's different out here."

"I call it ignorant."

"It can seem backwards, yet there is a certain magic in being so close to natural world. Can't you feel it?"

"Do you really believe in magic, Luster?" Lim peered at him. "We live in the twenty-first century, after all."

"I believe in the magical, Lim, in the wonder all around us that remains beyond our understanding."

"But knowledge brings progress, sometimes even survival. Not all that many years ago people believed diseases like yellow fever came from swamp gas or bad air. An infection from a simple scratch could kill you. Do you want to go back to that?"

"Of course I don't. The magical and the scientific can coexist. Together, they compliment our understanding of life, especially that part of life beyond the physical."

"But Luster, human beings have the ability to describe the entire universe in mathematical equations. We've gone to the moon and back. We can explore Mars without leaving a computer screen. It's science, Luster, measurable, quantifiable, rational science. Where's the magic?"

"The magic is in what science tells us about the beauty and order of the universe. There is poetry in those numbers, within the understanding of what we discover, that goes beyond the knowledge itself."

"Beyond the knowledge?"

"Lim, when you look up at the stars what do you see?"

"I see the past captured in light. I see the physics of gravity, chemistry, atomic fusion and fission, all interacting in a complex web."

"You see a wondrous display of the physical world?"

"I'd say so. It stretches the imagination."

"And when you talk with Ili, what then?"

"I see an amazing person."

"A human being who can think, reason, communicate?"

"That's right."

"Someone who has an inner presence, a unique self that seems to exist in and of itself, that you might call her soul?"

"I suppose so."

"How do you measure that?"

"I don't know."

"But aren't they both wondrous, Ili and the stars?"

"I'd have to say yes."

"Perhaps even to the point of being magical?"

"Possibly…"

"That's the magic I believe, Lim, not something you'd see on stage but the amazing in the everyday. Don't you see it?"

"It's not that I…"

His voice trailed off as his eyes fixed on a point above and beyond Luster's head. Luster turned, following his gaze toward the bar entrance. Framed in the doorway, Jorvic stood staring at them. Without hesitation, he approached the table and Lim rose to face him, taking his bottle by the neck.

"I know who you are now, Jorvic. Keep your hands out of your pockets or you'll get a face full of glass."

"Your temper could get you in trouble, Mr. Specter."

Luster raised his hand. "Set down the bottle, Lim. I'm sure this man only wishes to sit and talk with us."

Lim remained standing. "What do you want, Jorvic?"

"I believe you have something that belongs to my employer."

"If you mean that book of poems, your friend Orvis sold it."

"That book is nothing, Mr. Specter. I mean the Cantemir."

"If you refuse to sit then I will stand." Luster stood. "The Cantemir is back with its rightful owner, the Library of Congress."

"You have sold this book? Then you must pay."

"No, we did not sell the book. We gave it back to the nation, to the place it should have been all along."

"You will have to answer for this crime."

"The only criminal here is you." Lim pushed out his chair, stepping around the table. "I know you set the fire that nearly killed my friends. We're about to call the authorities and let them know where you are. You can do your complaining to them."

He snorted. "The international authorities try to find me and do not. Why should I concern myself with those in a place like this?"

Milo appeared next to Lim, the other men crowding in behind.

"Pug, I believe we have an uninvited guest in our private establishment. What do you think we should do about it?"

"We could tell him to go back the way he came, Milo. We could tell him his sort isn't welcome around here. Or, we could just throw him out the door and teach him not to go snooping around where he doesn't belong."

Luster turned toward the group. "I believe Mr. Jorvic has found what he came for, gentlemen. I'm sure he was just planning to leave."

"Is that so, mister?" Milo leaned across the table.

Jorvic glanced at the group, sneering at Luster before turning toward the exit without a word. As he stepped through the door a stout man with dark hair and a bristling mustache burst in, knocking him into the doorway. Jorvic's eyes flashed but he continued, vanishing into the sunlight beyond. Milo waved over the man.

"Nino, these hombres are here to see you."

The group drifted back to the bar as Nino strode to the table. He motioned for Luster and Lim to sit before taking a chair himself. Lim saw no welcome in his black eyes.

"I have not seen you in here before and you don't look like you belong here. What do you want of me?"

Luster leaned across the table. "Rogelio told us to come see you."

"Rogelio tests my friendship. For what reason did he tell you this?"

"We're looking for a girl. She is with a religious group somewhere near El Consuelo. She refuses to see us but we need someone to take us there so we can try to reason with her."

He squinted at Luster. "How do you know she will not see you?"

"Someone familiar with the group owed me a favor and found out."

"Your friend will not take you to this place?"

"He's of the same religion and refuses. Do you know where it is?"

"I know of the place but they are very serious people who do not like strangers."

"I heard."

"The compound is like a fortress. These people are well-armed and will shoot at trespassers. If they catch you, no one will know what happened to you and no one will try to find out."

"Will you take us or at least tell us how to get there?"

"I like living too much to go myself but I can tell you how to get there if you must go."

Luster nodded. "We must."

## Eighteen

They followed the highway southwest, through fallow fields and past abandoned farmhouses and barns, their roofs sagging or gone altogether, and into a rough land, forgotten, destitute. Near-deserted towns flashed by the windows, pickups and flatbed trucks littering café parking lots and throughways, their back windows reading 'The End Is Come' and 'God Knows'. Lim absently counted church steeples slicing the skyline.

As they drove further south, gauzelike clouds reached across the wide horizon in thin bands. Lim slowed the car, pulling to a stop in a thin patch of shade. Leaning against the dashboard, Luster smoothed out a hand-scrawled map and studied it. He peered through the windshield. Two roads white with dust intersected before them, vanishing into the blinding noonday haze. Dotting the surrounding plain, stunted trees and low scrub stretched toward a line of jagged hills.

Without a word Luster pointed to the right and Lim turned, following the narrow path as it dipped and rose over the barren land. Dust rose and hovered behind them in a broad column, drifting on the light breeze. In the distance a form appeared above the hills, glowing like a pearl. Luster nodded toward it.

"There's the church just as Nino described it."

"It must be huge. We're still a long way off."

"The church sits atop a hill and is surrounded by other buildings, residences mostly but also schools, workshops, barns and the like. The community is completely self-sufficient.

"Will they let us in?"

"It's not likely but I have an idea what to do. You can't see it from here but El Consuelo is located along a river valley a couple of miles from the place. We'll stop there. I hope to gain some insight on how to proceed from talking to the locals."

Scrub yielded to grass as they crested a low rise, the town appearing along a weed-choked stream following a broad swale. Cypress trees punctured the horizon. Lim slowed as several low-slung buildings came into view at a blinking yellow light. He turned onto what appeared to be the main street, driving past the post office and a small whitewashed church set on low piers, its shiplap siding brilliant in the afternoon light.

Luster leaned forward and peered through the window, motioning toward a two-story frame house that had been converted into a café. A deep porch extended across the front. On one side, stone pillars framed a set of stairs leading to the entrance. The porch creaked beneath Lim's feet as he opened the door and followed Luster to a nearby table. A moment later a waitress appeared with a sweating pitcher of ice tea. She handed them menus.

"The special today is chicken fried steak. Otherwise, you can order off the menu. You all want something to drink? It sure is hot out."

Luster nodded toward the pitcher. "Tea would be fine. And I believe I'll have the special."

"And what does a man's man like you want for his lunch, darlin'?" She flashed a lipstick-stained smile at Lim.

"I'll have the same."

"We also have a question." Luster motioned for her to stay.

"What can I do for you, hon'?"

"Is there someone in town that could tell us about the religious group located near here?"

"You must mean those Bread of Life people. What do you all want to know?"

"We'd like to visit the place but we're not sure how to go about it."

"Well, those folks haven't been too friendly even to us that lives here so asking is probably a good idea."

"Our questions won't take much time."

"This is Tuesday and that means the mayor will be in shortly." She ran her fingers along her cheek, checking her watch. "He's also the town barber so he would be your best bet. I'll send him over as soon as he shows up."

They had just finished their meal when a short man in a white, collarless shirt appeared beside the table. He smoothed back the few remaining hairs on his shining head and held out a hand.

"I'm Lamar Shultz and I hear you'd like to talk to the mayor. Or maybe you'd rather talk to the barber. Either way you can call me Lamar. Did you know when I started barbering I had a full head of black hair? Now I'm one step away from a human cue ball."

Luster nodded. "We appreciate you taking the time, whoever does the talking."

"The thing is, barbering brings in even more news that mayoring does." He pulled out a chair and sat. "We've got a special today on beard trimming, if you're interested."

Luster shook his head. "Another time, perhaps. We have important business to see to."

"I understand you want to go visit the Bread of Life compound. You know what's funny about that name? Those folks make their own bread out there for real. They farm it, mill it, bake it, the whole deal. Anyway, to say those folks are private is like saying I've only lost a hair or two. They want to be left alone and don't mind saying so. That's not usual for a small town. Why do you want to go?"

"A girl we know was taken there to be someone's wife. We're unsure whether or not she went under her own power. She may have been coerced to go."

He leaned toward them, speaking under his breath. "I've heard rumors the Rangers are looking into some illegal goings-on out there. The Sheriff says they have weapons but he's mostly closed-mouth about the place. Some say there's child abuse and wife beating and all sorts of bad business but tongues will wag in a small town and you have to be careful what you believe, especially when you're the barber. Of course the mayor has to be careful too but he only has to listen when he wants to."

"Can you give us any advice on what we should do?"

"Maybe I can. Now, let's see. There's a main gate straight from town that you don't want to use. But there's also a side gate. That's the one to try. I can't tell you how to get there but I know who can. If they've got wind of the Rangers they'll be guarding everything pretty heavy-like but if not you might could slide on in without too much trouble. They require silent meditation in their rooms every afternoon at four so the gate tenders may be away."

Lim leaned his elbows on the table. "You know a lot about them, Lamar."

"That's just because I barber some fellers that make deliveries out there. The man that can tell you how to find that side gate is named Early Stevens. He lives not far from there. Early is not the easiest man in the world to get along with but he'll talk to you. I'll give him a call here in a minute to let him know you're coming. Now, whatever you do don't stare at him. And don't ask what happened to him either. He won't tolerate staring or pity."

"Why would we stare at him?"

"Well, that's the thing, Lim. He lost an arm and a leg working a power line back when he was a lineman so he uses a wheelchair to get around. But don't underestimate him. Early is a crack shot and as tough a man as I've ever known. He lives way out by himself and takes care of his five hundred acre goat ranch mostly on his own."

"He does that from a wheelchair?"

"He can do a lot more, besides. I'll tell you how to get there shortly. But as mayor I have to ask how you liked your lunch. This café is new and I want people to support it. Getting support for anything around here is a tough sell. We've had three cafes close in the last year."

"That's a lot for a town this size."

"I just can't understand why these people don't care about their own town." He shook his head, glancing around the room. "They refuse support anything new. About the only thing most of these people *would* support is a good hanging."

Lim sat up. "Did you say hanging?"

"Well, in truth it was a lynching."

"Someone got lynched here?"

"A bank robber dressed up as Santa Claus robbed several banks in the area and finally got caught. Then he made the mistake of trying to escape jail. He didn't make it but he did kill a jailer who was also a deputy, a popular one too. After all that, the town decided enough was enough and strung him up. They even did a play about it. But that was eighty years ago so we're not likely to have another hanging anytime soon."

Lim swallowed, glancing at Luster. "We thought lunch was good, mayor."

"Well, I know you have someplace to go. If you leave now you should be able to get to that gate in time."

They drove through the town, past unused grain silos and shuttered feed stores, their metal walls streaked with rust. On either side of the road, brick-paved side streets held churches of all sorts, some in abandoned warehouses, others in former banks. Signs reading 'Cowboy Camp Church', 'Calvary Evangelical Fellowship' and 'Disciples of Yahweh' lined the curbs.

The spare trees fell away as the town passed from view, the land once again losing color, fading to a dingy white. Above the highway a group of low peaks cut the horizon, the blue-gray Anacacho Mountains rippling beyond. Then the scrub-covered bulk of Boiling Peak rose before them, a thick ledge of gray limestone slicing the slope in two.

Lim turned off the highway toward a red metal gate hung with a large tractor tire, also painted red. Welded script across the top of the gate read 'Get Out'. He angled the bumper against the tire, pushing the gate open long enough for the small car to slip through. The gate closed behind them with a metallic thud.

Following the washboard road, they wound through dense breaks of juniper and over shallow washes, blinding white beneath the mid-afternoon sun. Herds of multicolored goats scattered before the car. As they crested a slight rise, Lim spotted a low-slung cabin almost hidden by a grove of live oaks. A screened-in porch dark with rust stretched the length of the house. Past the rooftop, he could make out a steep bluff of limestone rising above the trees.

After pulling to a stop, they sat for a moment wondering if anyone was home. A moment later the screen door swung open and a man wheeled through using his only leg to pull and his remaining arm to push a low-slung chair. A leather scabbard bolted to one side carried a Winchester rifle. The man stopped just beyond the doorway, squinting at them, his red face and hair shining in the spattered sunlight. With a wave of his arm he motioned them out. Luster climbed from the car, followed by Lim.

"You boys don't look illiterate."

"What do you mean?" Lim glanced at Luster.

The man smoothed his red goatee. "Do you think the words on that gate mean to just come on in whoever you are?"

"I'm Lim and this is Luster. Didn't Lamar phone that we were coming?"

"Hell no, he didn't. I got rid of my worthless phone a month ago. I've decided to go off the grid. The damn government wants to take me for everything I'm worth. Well, I say to hell with them."

"But the phone company isn't part of the government."

"They might as well be the way they nickel and dime you for every little thing. The feds will probably take away my disability check next. You just watch. After four tours in 'Nam, this is how I'm treated. That's why I'm cutting all ties."

"But doesn't your disability check come from the government?"

He squinted at Lim. "Did you come here to argue?"

Luster put a hand on Lim's shoulder. "No, Mr. Stevens, we're here to ask for your help."

"Mr. Stevens was my father. I go by Early. What did you say your name was again?"

"I'm Luster Lester and this is my nephew, Lim."

"Why do you keep saying that?" Lim glared at Luster. "Not now, Lim."

"We're not related, Luster."

"We're here to talk with Early."

"But when will…"

Early wheeled toward them. "You girls want me to leave while you have your little spat?"

"Our apologies, Early." Luster raised his hand. "We've been on our search for some time now and it's wearing on us. We're here because we need to see someone at the Bread of Life compound, a girl who we think was taken there against her will."

"I'm not surprised." He spit into the dust. "I don't trust those moonbeams any more than the damn government. I know for a fact Bread of Life is involved with human trafficking, probably with the Mexicans but this close to the border there's no telling who it could be, Russians, Ukrainians, Columbians or even the damn Chinese. Whoever they're dealing with, the Breadheads are armed to the gills and would just as soon shoot you as look at you. That's why I carry a pistol on the seat of my pickup and old Duke stays with me wherever I go."

He patted the rifle stock. Lim leaned toward him. "You named your rifle after John Wayne?"

"Who in the hell else would I name it after?"

"Good point. So, will you help us, Early?"

"Getting to talk with someone on the inside won't be easy, son. Those nut balls are as nervous as a bull in a dress."

"Lamar said we might have a chance if we go to the side entrance. They have silent meditation every day at four so it might be unwatched. He said you could tell us how to get there."

"That would be the way to go. I've got an old pistol that's not worth a damn but still works. You want to take it along?"

"No thanks, I'd probably hurt myself." Lim shook his head, thinking again of the black revolver.

"Well then, come in and have a drink before you go."

"Do we have time?"

"Sure you do. The entrance is just down the road. Besides, where you're going a dose of liquid courage might do a young feller some good."

They followed him through the screened porch and into an empty room filled with black and white photographs of bird's nests, crow feathers, cactus leaves and fossilized shells, all in the palm of someone's hand. The far end of the room opened onto a wide kitchen. Wheeling to the counter, he took three glasses from the cabinet before moving to a metal door set in the middle of the far wall. He slid it open and turned to Lim, nodding him into the room. Rough-hewn limestone walls stretched along both sides of the windowless space. In the middle of the room a stainless steel tank stood among a web of pipes. Early motioned Luster through the door.

"I hope you boys like vodka."

"Is that a still?" Lim peered at the metal contraption.

"Like I said, I'm off the grid. So, I'm making my own liquor now. Draw us out three glasses and see what you think. I'll bet you never tasted vodka like this before."

As Lim stepped up to the still, he surveyed the dim chamber. The room appeared carved out of sheer rock. Early switched on the lights.

"Looks like a cave, wouldn't you say?"

"You built your house on top of a cave?"

"Not exactly, son. I blasted this out. Notice how nice and cool it is. Beyond that far wall I have eight hundred feet of buried pipe. I pump air in one side and it cools to a nice seventy-one degrees by the time it comes out of the other side. Between the underground space and the air cooler, I can keep the house comfortable year round without using hardly any electricity, so little in fact that I get what I need from a wind turbine up on top of the bluff. It's always windy as hell up next to Boiling Peak."

"You really are off the grid."

"I sure as hell am. Now quit your gawking and fill up those glasses. I can see Luster drooling from here."

Luster sat at a low table near the door and Early pulled up next to him. Lim handed them each a glass. Taking a sip, Luster leaned back and blew out his cheeks.

"Early, you're an artist."

Lim took a sip, surprised at the cool burn and rich flavor. "I thought vodka wasn't supposed to taste like anything."

"You're thinking of the cheap stuff, Lim. The best part of making my own is I get to give it some real flavor. But water is the key. I have a well nearly six hundred feet deep. Rain filters through all that limestone before reaching the aquifer. There's no better water on the face of the earth or under it."

"You have some unusual photographs." Lim nodded toward the front of the house. "Where did you get them?"

"You mean those up in the front room? That's just something I do myself. I can't say why.

"You took those?"

"I'm no photographer. I just get these ideas and I have to see them through or they'll pester me to no end. I know it sounds crazy."

"You're quite the Renaissance man, Early." Luster leaned his elbows on the table.

"I don't know about that. But when something big happens to you, it changes you, the way you see the world, the way you choose to live. You can't go back to what you were so you find what new you can be."

Lim looked at Early for a moment, sensing something behind his words, something important but just out of reach. Luster tapped the table with his glass, peering at Early.

"You must mean your accident."

"How come you boys haven't asked me what happened to my arm and leg?"

Luster shook his head. "Lamar told us not to ask, that you wouldn't like it."

"Lamar knows about half what he thinks he does. I suppose he told you himself?"

"He did."

"I don't mind the asking but I won't tolerate pity."

"You look like you're doing alright to me, Early." Lim lifted his glass, tilting it toward him. "Here's to finding who we can be."

They drained their glasses and Luster stood. "We thank you for your hospitality, Early Stevens, but we must be on our way."

The car shuddered as they climbed to the top of a broad plateau, the church tower and façade coming into view. Dust-covered plants vibrated before a stiff wind, the road ahead nearly lost in the barren plain. Lim slowed the car. A short distance ahead, a metal gate appeared between two ends of a twelve foot wire fence stretching beyond sight in both directions. Nearby, a three-sided guard shack stood empty.

Shifting into reverse, he backtracked to a cedar break a hundred yards from the gate, angling behind the thicket and cutting the engine. Then he hurried to follow Luster, already halfway to the entrance. As they neared the gate a girl in a blue dress stepped from behind the shack. She eyed them as Luster walked to where she stood.

"Hello. My name is Luster and this is Lim. I hope we didn't startle you."

She shook her head, saying nothing.

"We didn't realize anyone was here. Are you waiting for someone?"

She glanced to her left and right. "Is there someone coming?"

Luster shook his head. "Not that I'm aware of."

"You didn't tell anyone I'm here?"

"No."

"You're sure?"

"I'm sure."

She took a breath, a hand on her cheek. "Oh, Jesus, you scared me."

"If you're not waiting then why are you here?"

"I should be in my room but I had an argument with my parents. They won't let me have a boyfriend. So, I snuck out. You won't tell will you?"

"No, we won't tell."

"I'm so relieved."

Luster searched her face. "Would you be willing to do something for us?"

"It depends. What is it?"

Lim stepped next to him. "We're looking for a girl named Mirela."

"I know her." She nodded. "She hasn't been here very long but she seems nice."

"We'd like to talk to her."

"Is that all?"

"That's all."

"Why do you want to talk to her?" She eyed Lim.

"It's personal. You know what that's like, don't you?"

"I get it. She's your girlfriend, right?"

He shook his head. "Not exactly. Her sister and I are... you know."

"You need to talk with Mirela about her sister?"

"Something like that."

"That's good. Sisters know what to do. I always wished for a sister but all I got was stupid brothers."

"Do you know where Mirela is?"

"She's close by. Wait here. I'll be back soon."

She turned and hurried up the road, disappearing over the hilltop. Luster pulled out the talisman Tolly had given him, lifting the leather cord over his head and draping it around his neck. Lim watched as he held the blue stone to the light.

"Feeling underdressed, Luster?"

"I'm hoping for good fortune."

"It's just a rock, probably low-grade agate."

"This pendant helps keep my hope alive, Lim. Hope is a powerful force."

"You don't actually believe it brings you luck. The stone is just an object, a piece of rock."

"This rock is also a symbol. Symbols have real power. Don't underestimate them."

"I'd rather rely on the real thing."

"You mean reality?"

"I mean something I know is real.

Luster pointed to a nearby tree. "What do you see there?"

"Here we go again." Lim sighed. "I see a tree. What do you see?"

"But what we call a tree is just our way of explaining the world we can't see. It's a metaphor."

Lim walked to the tree and tapped it with his finger. "It feels real to me. Am I just imagining it?"

"In a way you are. The tree you just touched is mostly space held together by a web of energy. What we think of as solid is really a metaphor for a vibrating mass of atoms. And atoms are just another metaphor for energy waves and particles we can't see and don't understand."

"Where are you going with this, Luster?"

"Don't you see the magic in that, Lim? We're surrounded by moving, living energy. We're even made of it ourselves. That tree is no more than a complex interplay of attracting and repelling forces but it feels solid. Isn't that amazing?"

He tapped the tree again. "Well, when you put it that way it does sound incredible."

"Particles of energy, if that's how you want to think of them, pass through us at all times yet we're completely unaware. It inspires awe to think of it."

"But what does that have to do with your talisman?"

"It has everything to do with it. There is much beyond our perception, beyond our understanding. Just because we can't see something doesn't mean it's not possible. The talisman reminds us of what can be, not what is. The stone is about belief in the possible, about the power of hope."

"The tree I can see is amazing enough for me."

"I couldn't agree more. Along with the knowledge and understanding it brings, science also carries a sense of awe and respect for the unknown."

"Luster, I can't believe my ears." Lim squinted at him, shaking his head. "We finally agree on something."

The girl reappeared and trotted down to meet them. Bending over, she spoke between breaths.

"She can't leave now… but she has to stand watch here tonight."

"She's guarding this gate tonight?" Lim stared at her. "How often does she do that?"

"The women watch the gates when all the men are required to be at a big meeting, only once every three months."

"Are you telling me we've shown up on the one night in three months she has guard duty? How can that be?"

"You're pretty lucky, I guess."

"I don't believe it."

She snapped her fingers. "You're luckier than you think. They rotate from the front gate to this gate so she won't be back here for six months."

Lim turned to Luster. "Don't even say a word about that rock around your neck."

"I had no intention to." Luster held up his hands.

The girl leaned toward Luster, whispering. "Is he just excited to be talking to his girlfriend's sister?"

"That's probably it." Luster nodded. "What time will she be here?"

"Her shift starts right around sunset. Be sure to stay out of sight. You never know who might come along. I have to get back before they discover I'm gone."

She pivoted, disappearing up the hill.

## Nineteen

They walked back into the café, now mostly empty, and sat at a corner table next to a jukebox loaded with old vinyl records. Black and white photos of the town in better times littered the walls. Determined to keep an eye out for Jorvic, Lim angled his chair toward the door. He glanced at his watch, figuring they had a couple of hours before Mirela would arrive at the gate.

Two women stepped through the door and he again thought of Blanket, wisps of sun-streaked hair blowing about her face, the vineyard stretching past her. He wondered what it would feel like to wake up each morning knowing how he would spend the day. Luster stood, craning his neck before catching the waitress's eye and waving her over. He nodded toward the front counter.

"Lim, I see cans of beer in that cooler if I'm not mistaken."

"I thought you said they don't allow that around here."

"Perhaps I was wrong. Let's find out."

The waitress ambled over to the table. She eyed Lim up and down before speaking. "Well, you all decided you just couldn't stay away, huh darlin'?"

"Ah… well, is there any chance we can get a beer?"

"Do you got a nickel, hon'?"

He stared at her. "A nickel?"

"In order to drink here you have to join our private club."

"If I join your club I can buy a beer?"

"That's right. And you can thank your new friend the mayor for getting the law changed. He pushed for it to pass so this poor, pitiful town could survive. Me and Stanley, the owner, wouldn't still be here if it wasn't for the beer sales."

"What does it cost to join?"

"A nickel and a kiss."

"What?" He sat up and peered at her.

"Minus the kiss."

"Well, I…"

"I'm only joshing with you, hon'… well, sort of joshing anyway." She shook her head. "You all want two beers?"

Lim nodded and watched her walk across the room.

"You're looking a little red in the face, Lim."

"Sometimes I don't know what to make of women, Luster."

"There's an age-old problem if there ever was one."

She returned, leaning toward Lim and smiling as she set the beers on the table. Just as she turned to leave, the door opened and Vix walked through. Lim sprang to his feet.

"Vix, what are you doing here? Is something wrong? Where's Ili?"

"Slow down there, Lim." Vix clasped his shoulder. "Ili's still out in the truck. She wanted to freshen up a bit after the trip. It's a dusty drive down here, you know."

"But why are you here?"

"I didn't have a choice. Ili said she'd hitchhike if I didn't bring her. I got stubborn about it but when she headed for the highway I knew I was beat. She's a determined woman, I'll give her that."

Luster pulled out a chair, motioning for him to sit.

"I'm surprised you found us, Vix."

"I'd heard enough from Rogelio to guess the whereabouts of El Consuelo. Plus, that little French car tends to stand out in this part of the world."

"Harriet does make an impression."

"Have you made contact with the girl?"

He nodded. "We're set to meet her tonight."

"Ili will want to go."

Lim sat opposite him. "It's too risky, Vix."

"Then you best be the one to tell her, Lim. She won't like it."

Lim heard the door open then felt the touch of Ili's hand on his shoulder.

"Don't be mad at me, Lim. I had to come."

"I just want you to be safe, Ili." He looked up into her gray eyes. "We don't know what to expect from these people."

"And I want you to be safe as well. So, we stay together. Besides, when it comes to my sister's safety, I will not be afraid. Now, aren't you going to offer me a drink?"

"Let me take care of it." Vix stood and moved toward the front counter.

"So, you have seen Mirela?" Ili sat across from Luster.

"Not yet, Ili, but tonight."

"She is safe?"

"I don't know."

"But I will see her, yes?" She squinted at him, her eyes dark.

"You can come along but I want you to wait in the car and let us make sure it's safe. Will you agree to that?"

"As long as I see Mirela, I can wait."


An orange haze filled the western sky as Lim again pulled the car between the trees, beyond sight of the compound gate. A restless wind passed through the junipers, their clicking branches the only sound. He glanced at Ili in the rearview mirror, her face beautiful but showing little emotion. She did not stir as they climbed out of the car. Vix leaned his arms against the roof, scanning the fading light before looking from Lim to Luster.

"You want me to go with you so Lim can stay here with Ili?"

"The girl expects to see Lim. You'd better stay here."

"I wish I'd brought my shotgun. In my hurry to corral Ili, I forgot all about it."

"This group is well-armed, Vix. I doubt one shotgun would be much help. There's a stick behind the seat I use to prop up the hood, in case you see a rattlesnake."

"With my luck I'll see a skunk instead."

"We'll be back once we make contact with the girl."

They rounded the trees, making their way toward the gate in the half-light, a moonless night rolling toward them out of the east. A single star crested the horizon. Rising above the gate, wall-like, monolithic, the church façade shone beneath the dim glow of dusk. Lim scanned the fence line, seeing no one about. Then a figure stepped from the guard shack. As she approached, he strained to see her face. She hurried toward them in the gathering darkness, motioning them behind a cluster of trees. Lim leaned towards her.

"Are you Ili's sister?"

She nodded. "I am Mirela."

Lim studied her face, not unlike Ili's yet more exotic, more striking in some indefinable way. A bandage covered her left hand. He pointed toward Luster.

"This is Luster and I'm Lim."

She squinted at Luster, confusion in her eyes. "I have seen you before, someplace I cannot remember."

"I was at the house where you and Ili were held."

A wave of recognition crossed her face. "Yes, I remember now. You are a priest. Did you take Ili away to a church or some other place?"

"That's why we're here, Mirela. I was able to help Ili escape. And now we've come for you."

"What of Ili?" She turned to Lim. "My young friend, Susanna, said you know of her. Please tell me."

"Mirela, do you want to leave this place?"

"I don't know." She stood back, frowning at him.

Lim squinted at her. "Either you want to leave or you don't."

"How would I know this?"

"It's a simple question."

"No. It is not simple."

Luster raised his hand. "Give her time, Lim. Just tell us about yourself, your past, Mirela."

"Why I do tell you this?"

"It may help you to see what you should do now."

"There is little to tell." She peered into Luster's eyes. "I was born in a small town in Romania. I did not talk until I was very old, maybe four or five. And I could not read. Ili helped me to hide my problem but my father, he found out. My mother told him it was because Ili is older and she does everything, read, talk, for me. But I had the word blindness. What do you call it?"

"You had dyslexia?"

"Yes, I could not read and so did poorly in school. My father would beat me because he thought I was lazy. Then when I was eight my mother, she died of tuberculosis, just like that. I didn't understand. I felt I had done something wrong, that if I did better in school she would be alive. I did not want to live anymore. My father he was off gambling. But Ili, she helped me."

"Ili is very important to you?"

"It is true, when I was a child Ili was important to me. No person was more so. But…"

"But Ili can't go in there, Mirela." Lim shook his head, pointing toward the gate. "She can't even visit you. If you want to see her you have to leave."

"Let her talk, Lim." Luster searched Mirela's face, sensing something wrong.

"No, he is right to say this to me. Being here in this place, it changes you, confuses your mind. But one thing is clear to me. I have no other place I can go, no person who cares for me."

"Ili cares for you."

"Does she?" She took a step back, glancing toward the gate. "I would not be here if not for her."

"What do you mean?"

203

"She stole from the gang. That is why they kidnapped me."

"But they kidnapped both of you."

"No, she followed when they took me. Then they caught her."

"I don't understand, Mirela." Luster pulled at his beard. "I thought both of you were kidnapped because your father owed money."

"My father owed money to the bank. He borrowed to pay off the gang. All people with a business must pay. But he had lost too much gambling so he had to borrow. When he died Ili said the money, it belongs to us. So she stole from the gang to get our money back."

"How did she manage it?"

"She got a job in the casino keeping the books. She took only a little at a time. She almost got away but the mob, they discovered what she did. They said if she didn't pay back the money, I would have to earn it back."

Lim turned toward the car, trying to understand what he'd heard, thinking of Ili waiting not a hundred yards away. He turned back to Mirela, searching her face."

"If Ili doesn't care about you, why would she ask us to find you?"

"She asked you to do this?"

"What would you say to her if she was here?"

"What would I say to her? Is Ili here?"

"Do you want to see her, Mirela?" Luster held out his hand.

She hesitated then took his hand in hers. Lim followed as they walked past the tree line and around the thicket. Mirela stopped, dropping Luster's hand as the car came into view. Vix stood nearby. Mirela turned to Luster.

"Where is Ili? Do you lie to me?"

"No, Mirela, she is here."

The car door opened and Ili climbed out. Mirela stared at her in disbelief.

"Ili, is it you?"

"Mirela, can I come to you?"

She motioned her to wait. "I never thought I would see you again, Ili."

"Did you want to, Mirela?"

"You let them take me."

"I only wanted what belonged to us."

"They took me because of you. I thought I would die, Ili."

Ili put a hand to her mouth. "I never meant for you to get hurt, Miri."

"They beat me but I would not be a whore. They did other things, things unspeakable. When I would not do as they wished, they sold me instead of kill me."

Ili lowered her head, her voice just above a whisper. "Forgive me, Mirela."

"It was horrible, Ili." She stared into the distance.

"Mirela, please…"

"Are you truly here, Ili?" Mirela looked up at her and, after a moment, held out her hand. "Do you come for me?"

Ili rounded the car door, running to where she stood, wrapping her arms around her as Lim stood by. Then she stepped back, holding her sister at arm's length, noticing her bandaged hand.

"What happened to your hand, Miri?"

"I would not do as the gangsters wished even when they did this."

Ili grabbed her arm, holding her hand to the light. "Oh my God, Miri. Your finger, it is gone."

"They do this and still I would not sell myself for them."

Ili stepped away from her and turned to Luster, her eyes glistening. "Luster, what have I done?"

Lim started toward her but stopped as Mirela took hold of her. An instant later, footsteps sounded behind him. He pivoted as two men, rifles at their sides, rounded the trees, one in a black cap, the other holding a flashlight. They stopped and raised their guns, surveying the group with the light. Lim glanced at the car as he backed toward Mirela and Ili. Then one of the men called to Mirela.

"What are you doing with these people? You're supposed to be guarding the gate. You know visitors are not allowed here."

"This is Mirela's sister." Lim stepped next to Ili. "She has come to see her."

"She has a sister? We were told she has no family. What about it, Mirela? Is this your sister?"

Mirela waved her bandaged hand in the air. "Please put your guns away. They make me too nervous to think."

The men lowered their rifles. She nodded to them.

"It's true, this is my sister Ileana."

"You said you had no family."

"I felt I had no family left. But I was wrong."

"Why is she here?" The man with the flashlight pointed it at Ili.

"She is here because of me."

"What does she want?"

She turned to Ili. "What do you want, Ili?"

"You don't belong here, Mirela." Ili took her hand. "Come with me."

The man in the cap shook his head. "You're wrong about that. Your sister chose to come here."

"What do you mean?" Lim squinted into the light.

"We paid her way so she could marry one of our men."

Lim laughed out loud. "You think she's a mail order bride?"

"The man we paid said women in Eastern Europe line up for the chance to come here. It's done all the time. There was nothing illegal about it."

"What did this man look like?"

"He was thin and pale, with dark hair."

Lim snorted. "And he has a scar down his face?"

"Do you know him?"

"He's no marriage broker. You were duped. He's part of the gang that kidnapped Mirela."

"What are you saying?"

"The man is a hired killer. He works for a gang dealing in laundered money and forced prostitution."

"He doesn't arrange marriages?"

"Not even close. He cuts off people's fingers. Didn't you wonder about her hand?"

"She said there was an accident on the boat. Mirela why didn't you tell us?"

She lowered her head. "I was ashamed, ashamed for my family, ashamed for myself."

"We've talked enough." Lim stepped in front of her. "Ili was right. Mirela doesn't belong here. We're going to leave now."

"She can't just leave." The man in the cap raised his rifle.

"Why not?"

"How we live here is private and we intend to keep it that way. She knows too much. Besides, we paid a bundle for her."

Lim turned as the crunch of gravel sounded nearby. An instant later Early's face appeared above the car hood, his Winchester rifle trained on the two men. He spit and smiled at Lim.

"Well, howdy-do, Lim. I believe we got ourselves a genuine standoff here."

He nodded at Vix. "Say, aren't you Van Zandt Lester from way up near the clear fork of the Brazos? The same Van Zandt Lester that won the El Consuelo Turkey Shoot three years in a row?"

"I can't deny it." Vix nodded. "Do I know you?"

"The name is Early Stevens. That was close to thirty years ago and I'm an arm and a leg lighter than I was then so I doubt you remember me. But I remember you. I would've won those shoots if it wasn't for you."

207

Vix peered at him. "Why sure, I remember you now. I only beat you by a hair."

"You still know how to shoot?"

"When I need to I do."

"Then come over here and take my pistol." Early nodded to his side.

Vix stepped behind the car and lifted the gun from the wheelchair before switching on the headlights. He looked up at the men, waving the pistol through the air as he spoke.

"You men need to know we mean you no harm. Now just set your rifles down and we'll leave them there for you to pick up later."

The man shook his head. "Why should we?"

"We got cover and you got no cover." Early chuckled and spit again. "I've seen my partner shoot. He'd drop you before you got off a single shot. Is that enough reason for you?"

"What I said still holds." Vix pointed the pistol to the sky. "We don't want trouble. We just want to leave."

The man in the cap shook his head. "God led us to this place in order to establish his kingdom on earth, to propagate, seek justice and restore his true word to the world. We can't let people desecrate the sanctity of our mission by coming and going as they please."

Luster stepped between the car and the men, knowing he had stepped into the line of fire.

"You say your god a just god?"

They both nodded.

"And you believe in your right to observe your religion as you please?"

"There are few things more important to our group. That's why we moved way out here, why we live the way we do."

"I think I speak for us all when I say we respect that right. You only want the freedom to live as you see fit. Is that not the case?"

"What you say is true enough."

"Yet you want to deny Mirela and Ili that same right?"

"Why, no we don't want that. Women have their place and men have their place but we believe freedom is for all."

"But you say she can't leave. How is that not denying her the same freedom you claim for yourselves?"

"We paid for her to come here."

"You paid assuming she had made a decision of her own free will. You know now that was not the case. Does your god believe in such injustice?"

The men shook their heads. "God is just and merciful."

"Then let us leave in peace."

They glanced at each other, hesitating a moment before disappearing behind the trees. Lim took a breath and turned to Ili but she was already halfway to the car, her arm around Mirela.

Part II


"Hope is the thing with feathers
That perches in the soul
And sings the tune without the words
And never stops at all."

-Emily Dickinson


"… every hour of the light and dark is a miracle,
Every cubic inch of space is a miracle"

-Walt Whitman

# Twenty

Lim stood upright, surveying the rows of vines as he brushed the reddish dirt from his hands. The vineyard spread out below him, stretching down the long slope toward the lake. Wind-ripped water glittered beyond the burned-out trees. In the weeks since Mirela's return, he had come to feel at home here. Torn strips of cloud drifted overhead like cartoon sailboats. He again thought of his mother, imagining her last moments, how the water might have pulled at her, its grip gradual, relentless, until she vanished beneath the waves.

The sound of wheels against gravel pulled him from his thought and he turned, spotting Luster's green car as it bumped along the vineyard path. Vix's truck followed at a distance, Ili behind the wheel. They pulled to where Vix stood, not twenty yards away, and Ili climbed out. She looked Vix in the face and smiled as she handed him the keys, scarcely glancing at Lim before she turned and walked away.

Watching the car disappear over the crest of the hill, he felt the ache of her disinterest lodged in his throat. He swallowed, again kneeling in the red dirt, trying to focus on the vine while Vix stood by without a word. Lim took a breath and looked up, waiting for him to speak. Vix scanned the vineyard before facing him.

"What do you hear from Blanket these days?"

"Nothing much." Lim shrugged, turning back to the vine.

"I haven't seen her around here in a while. Is Bunk working her too hard?"

"I don't know."

"You don't know or you haven't bothered to find out?"

He shook his head. "I don't know."

He again looked up. Vix squinted at him.

"Well, why the hell not? The last time she was out here it looked to me like you two had taken a shine to each other. Was I wrong about that?"

"No, I guess not."

"But you haven't seen her since?"

"I've been busy is all."

"So, you're saying you plan to see her?"

"I suppose sooner or later I will."

"That sounds like no to me."

Lim stood and faced him. "Ili won't even look at me, Vix. I don't know what I've done wrong to make her treat me that way."

"I doubt you've done anything wrong, son." Vix's voice softened.

"Then why does she act like I don't exist?"

"You know as well as I do what she's been through."

"What does that have to do with me? I didn't cause it."

"A woman can seem cruel when she's made up her mind."

"What do you mean?"

"Put yourself in her place, Lim." Vix paused, searching for the right words. "You finally find your sister, knowing it's your fault she was kidnapped in the first place. Now what do you do?"

"I don't know."

"I'll tell you what you do. You get on with your life."

"I thought once she found Mirela, things would be different, that she and I could…"

Vix waved his finger at him. "You have to move on, Lim."

"But why can't I be part of her new life? I've asked her. Why won't she give me an answer?"

"I believe she already has."

"How do you mean?"

"Her answer is in what's bothering you right now."

"Maybe it's not too late." Lim looked up the hill to where he'd last seen her. "Maybe I can make her see it would work."

Vix scanned the horizon. "Last time Bunk and me were at the Dog House, all he did was complain about some young feller name of Watty Wells hanging around the store at all hours."

"What's he doing there, looking for a job?"

"How's Blanket doing these days, Lim?" Vix faced him again, peering into his eyes.

Lim took a step back. "You're saying he and Blanket have a thing going?"

"Do you want to wait around pining over Ili or find out for yourself?"

Lim stepped onto the broad porch, hoping to find Ili alone, still wanting a chance to talk yet worried what she might say. Instead, he found Luster sitting at the far end, his feet on the rail, a notebook in his hand. He said nothing as Lim surveyed the meadow down to the gate, wondering where she might be. Giving up his search, Lim ambled to where he sat scribbling into the small book. After a moment Luster spoke, never taking his eyes from the page.

"Ever wonder how much a cloud weighs, Lim?"

Lim felt in no mood for more of Luster's riddles. "Now why would I wonder that?"

"The natural world is endlessly fascinating, Lim. The more I learn, the more I sense the presence of a higher power, God if you like."

"You don't believe in God. You're some sort of pagan."

"Where on earth did you get that idea?"

"You're always talking about magic and alchemy, and you carry around that pendant Tolly gave you, that talisman."

"That talisman did a fine job. Mirela is back and no one got hurt."

"If you believe in all that magic, how can you believe in God?"

"Look around you, Lim. The universe is awe-inspiring, from photons and electrons to neutron stars and black holes. The fabric of the cosmos is the stuff we're made of. How can you imagine that and not feel a higher presence? After all, we can't see into atoms or to the edge of space. Our understanding of the world is based on belief, belief in theories, belief in evidence. That's where some of the magic I believe in resides."

Lim sighed and pointed toward the horizon. "Okay, Mister Scientist, how much does that cloud over there weigh?"

"An average cumulus cloud weighs about as much as eighty elephants."

Lim thought for a moment, figuring the amount in his head. "Eighty elephants would weigh over two hundred tons. I don't believe it."

"Would you say water is one of the heavier things you come into contact with, say compared with aluminum or wood?"

"I guess so. A bucket of water is pretty heavy."

"That cloud is made of water in the form of water droplets, millions of them."

"Did you figure that up in your little book?"

"No, just now I was measuring the cloud."

"You can't measure something floating thousands of feet in the air."

"It's simple geometry, Lim. Do you remember how to compute the area of a triangle? Well, it's similar except you're going for volume."

"Alright, I give."

"I just figure it by…"

-The door opened and Ili looked out, hesitating as she spotted Lim. Then she turned to Luster.

"Mirela wants to talk with you. She is in the kitchen."

"We'll finish our lesson later." Luster stood and looked from her to Lim. "Are you two still avoiding each other?"

"I am not avoiding Lim." Ili stepped onto the porch. Lim shook his head. "Same here."

"I'm glad to hear it. I'll go see what Mirela wants."

Luster disappeared through the door. Lim watched as Ili moved to the rail, avoiding his gaze. She finally turned to him.

"Lim, I am sorry but…"

"Wait!" He held up his hand. "I have to ask you. Did you ever really care, Ili? Or were you just playing me along so I'd do what you wanted."

"I don't know what you mean." She took a step back.

"Ili, you lied to me, to us. You claimed you were kidnapped because of your father when it was because of you, because of what you did."

"I see no difference. The gang had no right to make him pay only for having a business. That money belonged to us. I decided I would find a way to get it back."

"But Mirela paid for your decision."

"You do not need to remind me of this." She glared at him.

"Why didn't you tell the truth? I still would have helped you."

"You don't understand what it was like for us, Lim. We had nothing, barely enough to get by. I refused to live like that. I did what I had to."

"Does that include using me?"

She stared into his eyes, refusing to answer.

"Did you ever have feelings for me, Ili?"

She shook her head, sighing. "Lim, I did not mean to hurt you."

"I know. You did what you had to."

Life is not so simple, Lim. But it does not matter now."

"What do you mean?"

"Mirela found our aunt, my father's sister, in New York. We leave tonight to go live with her. She has sent us the tickets."

"You're going tonight? You were going to leave without telling me?"

"We only just learned this. That is why Mirela wanted to see Luster."

Lim stared at her, speechless, unbelieving, the anger and hurt blotting all words from his thoughts. He turned away from her, moving down the stairs and out the gate, her voice fading as she called out to him. Minutes later he stood in the vineyard. A stiff breeze coursed through the vines and on toward the lake, its windswept surface fractured by the low sun.

Sitting at the top of the slope, he watched thin lines of cloud trail over the horizon before vanishing into the coming night. The silver speck of a jetliner appeared low in the sky and he imagined Ili on her way to a new life, new friends, new loves. Then footsteps sounded behind him. For an instant he found himself wishing the steps were hers but knew otherwise, realizing his folly even before Luster spoke.

"It's quite a ways down here even for a young person."

"I needed to walk."

"I didn't so I drove Harriet."

Lim turned to him. "Will you let me borrow her? I'd like to be away when Ili leaves for the airport."

"Of course you can, Lim. But are you sure that's what you want? Saying goodbye to her might not be a bad idea."

He shook his head. "I'm sure, or as sure as I am about anything."

"You'll see this in a different light some day." Luster sat next to him. "Ili is a beautiful woman, there's no denying it. But you met her at a peculiar point in your life."

"My life is still peculiar."

216

"Ili came along when you were most vulnerable to suggestion, Lim. In her you saw who you wanted to see, not who she is in truth."

"Who is she in truth, then?"

"Ili is a survivor. She's had to be."

"Does that mean she might lie and manipulate to get what she wanted?"

"It might."

"It sounds like you're making excuses for her."

"No, Lim, I'm trying to understand her. You have your family here. She has finally found hers and wants to be with them. It just worked out that way. Is that so wrong?"

"I don't know but I'm tired of things *not* working out."

"We can't control what happens to us but we can control how we respond to it. And how we respond makes us who we are."

Lim sighed. "Can I take the car now?"

Luster reached into his pocket and held out his hand. In his wrinkled palm, the blue pendant lay next to the keys.

"You still have that thing?"

"I still have work to do, Lim. I hope the talisman will help me finish my task."

"But you found Mirela."

He shook his head. "There is something more. You know there are people here that care for you, don't you, Lim?"

"Ili will be leaving soon." Lim took the keys from him and stood. "I should get moving."

"Where will you go?"

"I don't care as long as it's away from here."

Vitriol (ˈvitrēəl) - cruel and bitter criticism; sulfuric acid.

## Twenty-one

The lights of town rose before him in a yellow glow, silhouetting the dark horizon, reflecting off low clouds that raced overhead. Lim again followed the tree-lined avenue toward the town center. Beyond the sidewalks, the tidy houses now stood dark against the gold hues of shuttered windows, blurred figures passing in and out of view behind them, ephemeral, ghostlike. An image of his mother again passed through his mind and he puzzled over why her memory would reappear after so many years.

He turned beside the town square, rounding the well-lit courthouse before passing a movie theater crowded with cars and pickups. Couples standing near the entrance waited for the doors to open. For a moment, he felt the ache of Ili's rejection rise in his throat. Turning again past the old post office, he pulled to a stop in the shadows of a towering pecan tree. Across the boulevard, a bar and restaurant crowded with people filled the lower floor a two-story building. Light spilled from the broad windows. He climbed out, making his way across the street and through the heavy wooden door, determined to forget Ili if he could.

Passing through the main restaurant, he walked into a small bar near the back of the building and stepped to the counter, ordering two beers and downing the first one in moments. He sat and surveyed the crowded room. Waitresses hurried back and forth between the kitchen and the main dining room carrying trays stacked with glasses and plates. Men in pressed shirts and ties hunched over tables, talking in low tones.

He decided he liked the feel of the place just as Blanket walked through the door, a blonde-haired man beside her. Lim turned to the bar, hoping to avoid her notice. He leaned against the counter, studying the empty bottle in front of him and listening to the musical lilt of her voice, unable to make out the words. A moment later the blonde-haired man walked past the bar and disappeared around the corner. Then Lim felt a hand on his shoulder and Blanket's strawberry-hued face appeared next to him.

"Lim, I thought that was you."

"Hello, Blanket." He glanced at her, unable to face her.

"What are you doing here? Is Vix with you?"

"No, I'm here by myself. I noticed you're with someone."

"You saw me come in? Why didn't you say something?"

"I don't want to bother you when you're on a date."

"You wouldn't bother me… ever. Besides, it's not like that."

He turned to her. "How is it, then?"

"He's asked me out so many times I finally said yes, that's how."

"Congratulations."

Blanket sighed, shaking her head in frustration. "You don't understand, Lim."

"Who is he?"

"His name is Watty Wells."

"What's wrong with him?"

"There's nothing *wrong* with him. He's nice enough. It's just…"

"No, don't tell me, Blanket." He held up his hand. "You just need to live your own life now. You need to find yourself. Isn't that right?"

"I don't understand."

"I know how it is with women."

"I don't what you're talking about, Lim."

"You can't be bothered with anything that might tie you down. You have to follow your dream. That's the truth, isn't it?"

"What's wrong with you?"

"Are you afraid to admit it?"

She stepped away from him, her voice rising. "Why are you talking to me like this?"

"Well, are you?"

"That's all you can say? I thought you were my friend, Lim. I thought maybe you and I... forget it."

She turned to leave then hesitated near the doorway. Lim sat staring into his beer, angry and ashamed of himself. A moment later he looked up. Seeing her still in the room, he hopped off the stool and went to her, taking her arm and turning her back towards him. She faced him, gently pulling his hand free and leaning toward him, speaking just above a whisper.

"You don't have to grab me, Lim. Just say so if you want to talk for real."

"I don't know what's gotten into me, Blanket. I'm usually not like this."

"I know you're not."

"I didn't mean what I said."

"I can see that, Lim."

"It's not about you, Blanket." He ran a hand over his face.

"Tell me what it is about, then."

She led him to a corner table and took a chair across from him. "My life is a mess, Blanket. It has been for a while. I don't know what I'm doing half the time."

"Join the club, Lim. Is that why you didn't call after you got back from down south?"

"I wanted to. It's just, I don't know..."

"Vix told me about that other girl, the one you helped out."

"He did?" Lim felt the blood rush to his face.

"He likes to come in the store and talk to me about you."

"Why on earth does he do that?" He peered into her eyes.

"He cares about you, Lim. He wants what's best for you. He says it helps to get a young person's perspective on things. That's why."

"What else did he say?"

"He said your Uncle Luster is sometimes in his own world and..."

"He's not my... never mind."

"And you need someone with their feet on the ground to help you see what's what."

He squinted at her. "I can handle my own life."

"I know you can. He means someone to support you, not tell you what to do. We all need that, don't you think?"

"I suppose."

She leaned toward him. "My feet are on the ground, Lim."

He looked into her blue, depthless eyes, wishing he could say what he felt at that moment but knowing he had no time, knowing she would have to leave any moment. As if reading his mind, she stood without another word and disappeared into the restaurant. A moment later, Watty Wells walked past him and through the doorway.

Lim stood at the bathroom mirror, combing and then re-combing his hair. His stubborn cowlick refused to lie flat. Having finally summoned the nerve to call Blanket, he had watched as the clock slowed to a crawl, the time seeming to drag on without end. He checked his watch and grabbed the keys to Harriet, hurrying toward the door.

Vix and Rogelio stood near the stairs as he stepped onto the porch and into a gusting wind. A flurry of leaves cascaded off the roof. At the slap of the screen door, Rogelio turned and whistled through his teeth. Vix leaned his back against the rail. Lim looked from one to the other.

"What?"

Vix cast a glance at Rogelio. "Looks like someone is going out on the town."

"Vix, I never did see Lim so clean." Rogelio chuckled, shaking his head. "That Blanket, she is good for him, I think."

Vix nodded. "You got plans or you just playing dress up?"

"Blanket's got tickets to a benefit dance over in Bunger."

"What does it benefit?"

"They're raising funds for the volunteer firefighters."

"They've had a rough year, that's for certain."

Rogelio reached in his pocket and handed Lim a twenty dollar bill. "Now I've seen that wildfire up close, I got to do my part."

"Take what you need and some extra for dinner." Vix handed him his wallet. "It's on me. Did she ask you or vice versa?"

"After I made a fool of myself at the restaurant, I went to see her. We sort of thought it up together."

"I reckon young women these days aren't the sort to just wait around for something to happen. Now Lim, I don't hardly ever give out advice but I'm going to this time if you'll allow it. I won't take long."

Lim nodded. "I'd like to hear, Vix."

"Make her your friend, Lim." He placed a hand on Lim's shoulder, looking into his eyes. "Don't worry about anything but that. Romance is all fine and good but friendship lasts longer. Elna and I were best friends almost from the start and we stayed that way all throughout. I never forgot how lucky I was to have a friend like her. Do you understand what I'm saying, son?"

"I think so."

"Alright then, I'm done with preaching. Is this dance of yours over at the barn?

"I believe that's what they call the place."

"I went to plenty of dances there as a young man. Do you want to take the truck instead of that French rust-trap of Luster's?"

"Don't let him hear you say that. But I'd appreciate the use of your truck."

"The keys are in it. Ya'll have fun."

"Speaking of Luster, where is he?"

"He's off on one of his sojourns." Vix nodded toward the gate.

"He's taking a walk now, in the dark?"

"That's not the half of it. He's taken to staying in his room. He has a pile of books in there and hardly shows himself except when he goes on his treks. I haven't been able to get two words out of him in days."

"That doesn't sound like Luster. He loves the sound of his own voice. What do you think is wrong with him?"

"He's tormented by something but what it is I can't say. In any case, he's a cause for worry but not your worry, Lim, not tonight."

"Maybe I should go find him."

"No, you go on and have yourself a good time." He pushed Lim toward the steps. "Tomorrow I'll see if I can get him to help finish staking up this year's vines."

"That's a good idea. He'll do better if he has something to occupy his time."

"Now you don't go near that damn tequila, Lim." Rogelio pointed at him. "A little beer is okay but that worm juice will make you loco. You don't want to be loco when you are with a pretty chica like Blanket."

Sunset stretched across the sky as Lim pulled the truck into the feed store parking lot, angling beneath a cottonwood tree before setting the brake and climbing out. Overhead, the broad leaves rattled in the restless wind. As he closed the door a whistle sounded to his right. He peered into the shadows, just able to make out the dim figure of a man standing next to the building. An instant later Orvis stepped into the light. He looked both directions before hurrying to Lim.

"I thought you'd never get here. Bunk said you were on your way about an hour ago."

"What are you doing here, Orvis?"

"I need your help."

"You can ask me for help after what you did? You know how close Ili came to dying in that fire?"

"But she didn't and I thank the gods for that."

"Clavo Ortiz, the cook for the kidnappers, wasn't so lucky." Lim leaned toward him, peering into his face. "You had something to do with that too, no doubt."

Orvis stepped back. "Cyril told me he's going to be alright. Besides, I know what I did, Lim. That's why I'm here."

"What do you mean?"

"I want to explain so you can tell Luster."

Lim shook his head. "Go tell him yourself."

"I can't, Lim. I can't face him. I want you to tell him for me. Will you do it?"

"Why should I trust you, Orvis? This could be just one more in a long list of betrayals."

"Damn, this is going to be tougher than I thought." Orvis paced a circle.

"I'm glad to hear it."

"But you'll help?"

"Give me one good reason I should help you. On second thought, don't. I have somewhere to go.

Lim took a step before Orvis grabbed his arm.

"Lim, you don't know the whole story. Just listen before you make up your mind."

He glanced at his watch. "Make it quick, Orvis."

He took off his glasses, cleaning them on his shirttail and looking about as if searching for what he wanted to say.

"My son got involved with the gang not long after they moved into the area. I don't know the details but his difficulties had something to do with a deal that went bad and he couldn't pay what he owed them. He came to me

225

fearing for his life. When I learned of the Cantemir book I saw my chance and offered to pay off my son's debt and provide some useful information in exchange for their promise to leave him alone."

"You told them about our plan to free Ili's sister."

"They know how to intimidate and said they would have no problem putting you off your search."

"Some friend you are, Orvis." Lim shook his head, disgusted by the thought."

"They said no one would get hurt, or at least not badly."

"And you believed them?"

"You got out okay. When I told them you had gone to Vix's, I didn't know about Clavo."

"How does the book figure into it?"

"Alright, I've gone this far so I might as well go all the way." Orvis glanced around as if someone might be listening. "In exchange for the information I also wanted the Cantemir."

"You didn't know it was missing?"

"Of course they didn't say so until after I told them where you'd gone. My plan was to buy it from them for next to nothing."

"So you could make a big profit."

"No, I wasn't going to let anyone know what I had, at least for awhile. I thought I could use the book to track down others like it, more books from Jefferson's lost library."

He snorted. "You traded us for a book?"

"You don't understand, Lim. The Cantemir was the chance of a lifetime for a bookseller. I would've shot to the top of the bookselling world. But more importantly, I would have had a jump on finding any others out there. That's huge."

"Is that supposed to make what you did okay?"

"No, no, of course it isn't. I was blinded by the book, by what it could mean, by what it could bring me."

"You mean you got greedy."

"Yes, yes, I got greedy and I'm sorry for what it caused. That's what I want you to tell Luster. Tell him I didn't mean for it to go the way it did. I was greedy, yes. I wanted my son safe, yes. I was still angry at Luster, yes. But I didn't mean for any real harm to come to you all."

"I don't buy it, Orvis. There has to be something else. What did Luster do to you?"

"He forged a book and nearly ruined my business, remember?"

"There's more, I know there is. What is it, Orvis? Tell me if you want my help."

His face went pale and he paced about, mumbling to himself. Then he stopped and took a breath, facing Lim.

"Sam left me for him."

"You and Sam…?"Lim squinted at him.

"We were lovers before Luster came along. We remained friends of a sort but I never forgave Luster for it. Then when I realized what I'd done, involving those thugs, I knew I'd gone too far. I was wrong, very wrong, and I regret it."

"Talk is cheap."

"I'm doing something now, aren't I? This is a start. And if there's a way, I want to make up for what I did. Will you tell him?"

"I'll think about it, Orvis. I have to go now."

"I suppose I'll have to settle for that." He sighed, looking at the ground. "One more question, Lim. What happened to the Cantemir?"

"You don't know?"

He shook his head, a desperate gleam in his eyes. "I can't stop thinking about it."

"Then I'll leave it for Luster to tell, if you're ever brave enough to ask."

Lim turned and walked into the store.

## Twenty-two

The dashboard lights danced across Blanket's sun-streaked hair as Lim followed the narrow blacktop south from town, past hay-filled barns and riding stables closing for the night. Sunset faded along the dark horizon, casting the fire-ravaged hills in silhouette, hiding the blackened landscape until morning. He glanced at her reflection in the windshield, wishing he could again study the depth of her blue eyes.

A moment later, a red metal building appeared out of the blackness, light spilling from the broad doors. In the shadows, men stood alongside pickups and flatbed trucks, leaning against the side rails and sipping from plastic cups and cans of beer. The low hum of their voices drifted on the brisk wind. Lim pulled past them, cutting the engine and facing Blanket.

"Back at the store I meant to tell you how good you look tonight. I thought it but I didn't say it. I'm saying it now."

She blushed. "You did seem sort of quiet. Is anything wrong?"

"I just saw someone I didn't expect to, that's all."

"Was this person a man or a woman?" She squinted at him.

"He's someone out of Luster's past."

"Good. I don't want any woman from your past showing up unexpectedly."

They stepped out of the night into an open room scattered with wooden tables and benches. High in the corners, bird nests hung from metal rafters, beardlike, stirring before the breeze. A band milled around a makeshift stage. Lim bought two beers and several raffle tickets before following Blanket to a table. Before he had a chance to sit, the music started and she grabbed his hand, pulling him onto the dance floor. Beneath the dim lights, he gazed into her face.

Time seemed to stop while they circled the floor, lost in the music. Finally, Lim stepped from the crowd and took her hand, leading her back to the table. They sat beneath the ceiling fan trying to cool off when an old man in a white, pearl-buttoned shirt appeared in front of them. He stuck his hands in the back pockets of his jeans and bent toward them.

"You're in third place in the dance contest, you know."

Blanket glanced at Lim before leaning across the table. "Only in third?"

"Well, you've got to dance some more if you want to win." The man winked at her.

At that Blanket stood, again grabbing Lim's hand and pulling him into the rotating crowd. The shuffle of boots on concrete melded with the whine of steel guitar as she leaned into him, resting her cheek on his shoulder. Neon light cast the dancers around them in hues of red and blue. Lim pressed his hand into Blanket's back, feeling her meld to him.

He looked out over the crowd and through the open door into the warm night, the cloudless sky beyond spattered with stars, and a feeling came over him he scarcely remembered, a feeling from a time before his parents had gone, when the world was a place he belonged, a place he felt at home. A tremor passed through him, of sadness mixed with hope. As if reading his mind, Blanket raised her head and peered into his eyes. Then she kissed him before pulling close again and pressing her cheek to his.

The music ended and they returned to the table without a word, sitting close in spite of the heat. The crowd spun beneath the sparkling lights. A moment later the old man again appeared before them and winked at Blanket, smiling as he held up two fingers.

"Don't stop now. You're in second place. But you best force fluids in this heat."

He set two sweating bottles of beer on the table and walked away. Just as Lim lifted the bottle his phone sounded above the music. He stood, pulling it from his pocket and glancing at his watch, the time well past midnight. Vix's voice echoed in his ear.

"Lim, I'm sorry to interrupt your night but we need your help."

"What is it?"

"We've got a wind coming, a big one. They're predicting in excess of fifty miles an hour by morning. Without stakes to protect them, those young vines will be torn to pieces."

Lim peered into Blanket's face. Taking his hand, she rose to meet him.

"I'm on my way, Vix. Blanket is coming with me."

Lim bent before the jeep headlights, taking a slender vine and tying it to a nearby stake. A swirling wind pulled at his sweat-stained shirt. In the next row, Blanket hammered stakes alongside the rangy plants. Lim watched her highlighted form for a moment, wondering if she regretted coming along. As if sensing his thought, she turned and smiled before stepping to the next vine.

A hundred yards away, Vix and Rogelio moved along the rows in similar fashion. Turning into the heavy wind, Lim let it pass against his face. He stood and stepped toward the next vine as footsteps sounded behind him. An instant later, Luster emerged from the shadows. He clasped Lim's shoulder, peering into this face, calling above the wind.

"I'm here to assist."

"Where have you been? We tried to find you."

"I've been searching for something."

"Well, I hope you found it because we need your help staking these vines. A big wind will be here by morning."

"Yes, yes, I know of the windstorm. Don't be surprised if we have a haboob instead."

"A what?"

"Haboob is the Arabic name for a dust storm."

"Where'd you get that idea, Luster? No one said anything about a dust storm."

"It's just a feeling, Lim."

"I might've known. But if your intuition is right, it's all the more reason to work fast. Start tying these up."

He handed Luster a pair of pliers.

"Shouldn't I help Blanket?"

"She wants to do it on her own. I'll go check on her."

Lim walked to where Blanket bent over a pile of stakes, laying his hand on her shoulder. She faced him, her hair swirling about her face in a golden cloud, her eyes shining before the headlight glare.

"What is it, Lim?"

"I'm sorry the night had to turn out like this, Blanket."

"Don't be sorry, Lim." She shook her head, pulling the hair from her eyes. "I loved dancing but right now I'd rather be here. Vix needs our help and I mean to do my part. We must save these vines and we need to hurry, isn't that right?"

"That's right."

She waved a finger at him. "Then stop talking so we can get back to work."


Lim opened his eyes, straining to listen. He could just make out a low roar, as if a freight train moved somewhere in the distance. Filtering through the porch windows, a viscous light spilled across the living room floor, casting the walls in a yellow glow. He threw aside the covers and sat up on the couch, feeling a night of staking vines in his stiff back as he looked about the room. No one else seemed to be awake. Cocking his head, he listened again. The sound outside seemed to be nearing.

He left the couch and walked down the hall to the front bedroom. Peeking in, he found Blanket still asleep. He backed down the hall, slipping out the front door and down the stairs. Near the end of the house, Luster stood staring into the west.

Lim stepped beside him, following his gaze toward a morning sky featureless and without definition. He blinked, trying to focus on the yellow haze. In the dim light a form began to take shape above the horizon, dark and ill-defined yet reaching far into the air. Within moments a dense wall of dust emerged from the haze, roiling toward them like a brown avalanche, obliterating the horizon as it went. He turned to Luster.

"That dust storm is coming fast! What do we do?"

"Luster, are you listening?" Luster stood as if in a trance. Lim grabbed his arm, turning him. "We have to do something."

He faced Lim, shaking his head. "'God shall make the rain of thy land powder and dust: from heaven shall it come down upon thee, until thou be destroyed'."

"What on earth are you talking about?" Lim peered into his face.

"It's from the Bible, Lim, the book of Deuteronomy."

"What's happened to you, Luster? Are you sick?"

"In a way I am, sick in my soul." He nodded. "I've avoided the most important part of my quest and betrayed you in the process."

"Luster, listen to me." Lim waved a hand before him. "We have to act now. Go inside and wake Vix and Blanket. I'm going to find Rogelio."

Lim pointed him toward the porch and hurried toward Rogelio's cabin. In the corral beyond, three horses paced tight circles, snorting and kicking the air. He banged on Rogelio's door and stepped back as the lights flashed on. A moment later, Rogelio appeared in the doorway, staring through the screen at him. He blinked and pointed over Lim's head.

232

"I see the daylight but why do you wake me when I'm working all the night? Rogelio, he is not young like you."

Lim waved him out the door.

"Come quick, Rogelio. There's a dust storm and it's coming fast."

He pulled on a shirt and followed Lim into the yard, the dark wall of dust towering overhead.

"Mother Mary, it is the black witch, la tormenta de polvo. The horses, Lim, we must cover their eyes."

"Can't we put them in the stable?"

"We are working on the stable and there is no room. The blankets are by the door. Bring them quick."

A gust of wind coursed between the buildings, mixing with the roar of the storm as Lim hurried across the yard. He threw the blankets over his shoulder and returned to where Rogelio stood just inside the corral gate, tying the last of the horses to the fence. Lim handed him a blanket and he draped it across a sorrel's back, drawing it forward and over its head like a hood before tying it in place. He motioned Lim to cover the other two while he hobbled the others, hoping to keep them from bolting.

By the time Lim had covered the third horse, clouds of dust raced about them in a swirling cloud. Lim peered over the fence, realizing he could no longer see the house. An instant later a gust sprayed them with grit. Caught between the horses, Rogelio dropped to his knees. He bent to the ground, trying to wipe the grit from his eyes. Lim pulled off his shirt, wrapping it around his face and grabbing hold of Rogelio. Lifting him up, he guided him through the gate.

They inched along the corral fence, buffeted by the gale as Lim squinted into the storm, searching for sign of the house. Deciding he must take the chance, he took hold of Rogelio and stepped away from the corral. They leaned into the fierce wind, blindly staggering over the rock-strewn ground.

Lim peered into the darkness, finding nothing to guide his path. Fearing he had taken a wrong turn, he glanced over his shoulder, wondering if he should turn back. Then Luster appeared out of the cloud like an apparition, waving them toward the porch. Lim stumbled toward him. As they neared, Vix appeared alongside the house, swinging a storm shutter over a window and latching it shut. Lim yelled to Luster above the roar of wind.

"Where's Blanket?"

Luster moved to him, taking Rogelio's arm and turning toward the porch. He pointed toward the far end of the house.

"She went looking for you."

"Are you sure?"

Luster nodded. "She was going to the bunkhouse."

"But that's the wrong way."

Luster shrugged. "She said she was worried and meant find you."

## Twenty-three

Lim turned into the wind, holding the porch rail as he stumbled past the stairs and around the corner. Squinting through the storm, he could find no sign of Blanket. He pushed off the porch and leaned into the gale, the storm's full force nearly lifting him from the ground. Moving from point to point, he angled back toward Rogelio's cabin, hoping Blanket would have followed the same path. Trees appeared out of the dust, groaning before the wind but offering some small shelter.

Crouching in the shadow of a thick oak, he again peered into the storm. An instant later a crack sounded above him as a black limb came crashing to the ground. He pressed himself to the trunk. The wind shifted and for an instant Blanket's form appeared against the stable, kneeling in the dry grass and hugging a short stretch of wall.

He stood and lurched forward, careening before the wind as the dark mass of the building again appeared out of the storm. Aiming toward where he last saw her, he stumbled across the space, landing at her feet. She lifted her head at the sound.

"Lim, it's you! I was afraid something had happened."

"Are you alright?"

She nodded. "I'm just dirty is all."

"Come with me." He grabbed her hand.

They hurried along the wall, pushing through the stable door and slamming it shut as a rush of wind swirled in behind them. Lim stood next to her in a narrow passage between the outer wall and a line of stalls in various states of disrepair. Boxes of nails and lumber lay scattered about the room. Blanket moved into the passageway, taking his hand and leading him to a bench propped next to a small table. She motioned him to sit before sliding next to him.

"I guess we should wait out the storm here."

"It's too risky out there." He nodded. "A tree limb nearly fell on me."

"Uncle Bunk is going to have a fit that I'm not at the store. I'm supposed to open up today."

"I don't think there'll be too many shoppers this morning, Blanket."

"He never lets me slide on anything, Lim. After daddy died, Bunk felt obliged to make up for me not having a father around."

"What happened to him?"

"You mean my daddy? He got killed in a tractor accident. We had a farm back then. After the accident mama had to get a job and raise me on her own. Uncle Bunk never did have much confidence in her as a mother so I guess he went a little overboard."

"She probably did the best she could."

"That's a nice thing to say, Lim." She studied his face. "I think she did alright. Raising a child by yourself isn't easy."

"I guess not.

"What about your folks, Lim? Do they live around here?"

"No, they're both gone."

"Both of them? I'm so sorry, Lim. What were they like? What do you remember about them?"

He turned to her, surprised she asked something other than what had happened to them.

"I don't remember much but I think my father was quiet and serious but friendly in his own way."

"He sounds like you."

"Do you think so? I've never thought of myself as much like him. He used to say I took after Luster."

"What else?"

"He loved music even though he was tone deaf." He chuckled. "You wouldn't want to be in the same room if he started singing."

"What about your mother?"

"She was an artist."

"What sort of artist?"

236

"A painter and a good one too, according to Luster."

"Your mother and Luster were close?"

"Growing up, Luster was always around. For a long time I thought he was my uncle."

"I don't understand. Aren't both Vix and Luster your uncles?"

"No, Vix is Luster's uncle. At least, I think he is."

"But at the store Vix introduced you as his nephew."

"It must be a family tradition. Luster does the same thing. I've tried to get him to stop but he won't listen. It annoys the hell out of me."

"Don't be angry with him, Lim. I think it's sweet. Some people don't have any family. Be glad Luster and Vix think of you as part of theirs. Speaking of family, do you have any kids?"

Lim felt himself blush at the thought. "What?"

"Children, do you have any?"

"No, Blanket, I don't have any kids."

"Have you ever been married?"

"No, I never have."

"How about a girlfriend? Do you have one of those back where you came from?"

"You don't mind saying what's on your mind once you get to know a person, do you?"

"Well, do you?"

"Once, I did."

"Once you did but not anymore?"

"No, I don't have a girlfriend."

"Do you ever think about going back?"

"There's nothing for me there. My life is here now."

He surprised himself saying it. She peered into his eyes for a moment."

"So, you have reason enough to stay?"

"I'm not sure, Blanket, but I hope so."

"You hope but you don't know?"

"Hope is worth something."

"Not as much as what you know for certain."

"What do you know for certain, then?"

"I know I have reason enough."

She leaned and kissed him on the lips. Then the building groaned and she pulled back.

"Did you hear that?"

"No, I didn't hear anything."

She kissed him again, this time harder, then pulled away and looked about the room.

"But listen, Lim."

He cocked his head. "I don't hear a thing, Blanket."

"That's just it. What happened to the wind?"

He stood and peered at the cracked wooden walls, taking her hand in his.

"We'd better go find out."

As they stepped out the door an orange haze still hung on the light breeze. The stable walls and fence carried a heavy coating of reddish dust. Sand drifts filling window sills spilled out onto the ground. Lim could feel the grit beneath his shoes as he led Blanket across the yard and toward the house.

They climbed the back porch stairs, pushing through the door into the kitchen where Vix and Rogelio sat in the dark drinking coffee. Glass from a broken window littered the floor around them. Vix held up a hand.

"Watch your step, Blanket. We had a tree limb come through the side window. If I'd been thinking clear I would have closed the storm shutters before the storm instead of in the middle of it. I still have grit in my teeth. In any event, I'm glad to see you two are alright. Pour them up some of your good coffee, Rogelio."

"Do you like it dark like this?" Lim looked about the room.

"Of course not, Lim. The storm took the power out. At least we've got gas. Ya'll have some coffee."

"No thank you, Vix." Blanket shook her head. "I'd better get going."

Vix frowned at Lim. "Now what did you do to make Blanket want to leave so soon, try to kiss her?"

They stood together red-faced until Blanket pointed toward the door.

"No... it's just that... I mean... I've got to get to the store."

She headed for the kitchen door then stopped and faced Lim. "The German Market is this evening at St. Mary's. Will you go with me? The Archbishop is coming to bless the market."

"The Archbishop will be there? That sounds important."

"I don't know about that but I love the market and try to go every year. Bunk wants me to deliver an order nearby but I'm free afterwards. Will you meet me there?"

"I've never seen an Archbishop before."

"There's a lot more to it than that, Lim."

Vix slapped the table. "Lim, a pretty woman just asked you out on a date and all you want to do is talk about the Pope? What's wrong with you, son?"

Rogelio pointed a finger in the air. "Lim, he talks much when he gets the nerves."

Blanket looked around the table and back to Lim. "You know you're outnumbered, don't you?"

He nodded. "Yes, Blanket, I'll meet you there."

Sublimate ('səblə‚māt) - to divert or modify (an instinctual impulse) into a culturally higher or socially more acceptable activity; a solid deposit of a substance that has sublimed.

.

## Twenty-four

Lim swept the last of the dirt from the stairs, returning the broom to its place inside the house. A moment later, footsteps sounded on the porch. He peered through the screen door, spotting Luster climbing the steps before making his way to a chair at the end of the porch. He sat, staring into the fading daylight.

Lim stepped back through the door, walking down the porch and sitting next to him. After a moment, Luster turned and peered into his face as if noticing him for the first time. Then he turned back to the dim horizon. Lim studied his profile before speaking.

"You looked tired, tired and troubled by something. Have you been off on one of your walks?"

Luster nodded.

"Why do you walk, Luster? It's clear you're not doing it for the exercise."

"Lim, I believe you're finally beginning to listen to your intuition. I walk because I'm trying to work something out, something that seems to have no answer. Walking helps me think."

"What did you mean earlier when you said the windstorm was a punishment, that you had betrayed me?"

"Did I say that?"

"You did, right before the storm hit."

"I hope to tell you someday, but not now."

"You worry me, Luster. Is there anything I can do for you?"

"Perhaps there is. Vix tells me you're going to St. Mary's for the German Market."

"Blanket and I are meeting there."

"Will you give me a ride?"

"You don't want to drive Harriet?"

"Understand that I have no intention of intruding on your time with Blanket." He held up a hand. "Harriet is having some work done. And perhaps I'll get to see a bit of

241

the market while I'm there. The real reason for my trip is to see someone, not there but nearby. I won't need a ride back."

They followed the northbound highway, passing out of the wooded valleys and again climbing onto the rock-strewn plain, scrub-filled and broken by low cliffs, hollowed out, empty. The sky spread above the torn horizon in a cloudless swath of blue. All at once the land softened as they crested a broad rise, the plain transformed into rolling hills scattered with dairy farms and feed mills, their silos pricking the air like church steeples. Fields thick with grass streamed past the windows.

As the highway topped a low hill, a town came into view in the center of what had once been a massive buffalo wallow. The scattered buildings marking Wilder lined the crossing of two roads, a single yellow light blinking over the intersection. Above the town, St. Mary's stood atop the crest of a steep rise, its red brick tower framed by the dome of sky. Lim peered at the façade. In the sharp light of day the church seemed grander than he remembered, tall and stately.

He tried to force the memory of Clavo's ash-colored face from his thoughts as he pulled Vix's truck into the church parking lot. Up the hill, crowds of people milled between rows of tents that stretched past the pavement and onto the lawn. At the far end of the church grounds, a band played polkas, while cojunto music drifted from a stage nearby. The sound of accordions blended in the warm evening like smoke from two fires.

They climbed from the truck, walking past a vendor in lederhosen selling knackwurst and potato pancakes. A booth next door offered fajitas and guacamole. Lim approached a table filled with small planks of painted wood, some with a likeness of a saint or the Virgin Mary, others with scenes of everyday farm life. Lifting an arch-shaped panel of a blue-robed Mary, he held it up to the light just as Blanket rounded the table. She took the painting from his hand and faced Luster.

"Luster, I've been looking all over for Lim. Do you suppose he's out searching for me too?

"Well, Blanket, I can't say but I'm sure you've not left his mind even for an instant.

"How can you be so sure? Maybe he's off somewhere eating sauerbraten and sausage. Or maybe he's had the sudden urge to do some early Christmas shopping."

Lim sighed and plucked the panel from her hand. "We just got here, Blanket. And, yes, I was looking for you. I figured you could be in any of these tents so I started with this one."

"Are you sure it's not because you want to buy me a retablo? Aren't they beautiful, Lim? I have to say, you picked a nice one. Her robe matches my eyes. That's why you picked it, isn't it?"

"Ah… sure, that's right, Blanket. What is a retablo, anyway?"

"I think it's a sort of religious folk art from Mexico."

"But isn't this a German Market?"

"Well, lots of folks have moved up here from Mexico so the market has a bit of German and a bit of Spanish. I love it. The people that live here like having it that way too. It's one reason St. Mary's is such a great church."

"Is a retablo supposed to mean anything?"

"You mean something religious? I think so but I'm not sure how."

Luster held up a finger. "Retablos were originally altar paintings. Over time the smaller versions came to be devotional images aiding in prayer or honoring patron saints. They can also symbolize protection and healing."

Lim raised his hand. "Okay, professor, enough of your lesson."

He turned back to the table, paying for two of the small paintings and giving one to Blanket. She took his arm, giving him a quick kiss. The other retablo he handed to Luster. He stared at Lim with a puzzled look.

"I figure you can use the help."

"I didn't think you believed in such things, Lim."

"Since I've finally realized how little I understand, I figure it can't hurt. Now, don't you have someplace you need to be?"

"I suppose I do. But thank you for your well wishes."

Just as he turned to leave, a bell sounded and the crowd began moving from the walkway. Twenty yards away, two priests in red robes stood holding banners above their heads. Blanket grabbed Lim's hand, talking over her shoulder as she pulled him toward the tent opening.

"Lim, the Archbishop is coming."

Luster joined them near the walkway, whispering to Blanket as the procession began.

"I take it we're about to see the blessing of the market. Have you witnessed this before, Blanket?"

"I've been to the market many times but I've never been able to be here for the blessing. There's Father Weiss next to a priest I don't recognize."

The procession moved along the tents and concession booths in a winding line. Behind the flag-bearers, the soft voices of a children's choir drifted through the air. The choir passed and the Archbishop suddenly emerged from the crowd, his white robe and hat glittering beneath the fading light of dusk. He held a silver ball in one hand.

Pausing before Luster, he raised his arm and gave the container a light shake. A sprinkling of drops fell across Luster's face and he stumbled back, startled by the blessing. The Archbishop nodded, continuing on his way. Luster turned to Lim, his eyes wide.

"I've been blessed, Lim."

He nodded, trying to stifle a laugh. "You of all people need it, Luster."

"Yes, and I now know what I must do."

"Who are you going to see?"

"Didn't I tell you? I'm meeting Orvis by the church steps. He's driving over to pick me up."

"Why would you want to have anything to do with him after what he did?"

"He said he had something to tell me. I best be going."

Lim grabbed his arm. "Luster, hold on a minute."

"I mustn't keep him waiting. What is it?"

"Luster, I have a confession." Lim rubbed his jaw, searching for what he wanted to say. "Orvis came to me and told me why he betrayed us like he did. He wanted me to tell you because he said he couldn't face you."

"So, you decided it would be best if he had to tell me himself?"

"Not exactly. I decided the son of a bitch didn't deserve a break."

"But Lim, didn't you see what just happened?"

"You got blessed."

"We all seek the blessing of forgiveness, Lim, even you. Now you are ready."

"Ready for what, Luster?"

"I must go."

He turned and disappeared into the crowd. Lim looked after him, wondering what he could have meant. Then Blanket took his hand, pulling him from his thoughts. They wandered the market, past tables filled with tin crosses and portraits of patron saints, and along booths selling all manner of food and drink. Lim bought a plate of sauerkraut and bratwurst and they sat at a long table, listening to cojunto music and sipping dark beer.

As another song began, he turned to Blanket, studying her profile. A familiar sense of dread filled him, as if after a long journey he had finally arrived at his destination but soon must leave. His past seemed to recede into time, taking its proper place but leaving the future uncertain, threatening. Sensing his gaze Blanket faced him and leaned into his ear.

"Will you go somewhere with me?"

245

He peered into her depthless eyes and nodded. "Wherever you say."

"I want my favorite dessert and I know where to get it if we're not too late. We should hurry."

Grabbing his hand, they ran to the truck and soon were winding through the darkness, the narrow road before them a mere strip of black disappearing into the night. Trees passed in and out of the headlights, restless before the wind.

In the distance, the white face and black hands of the courthouse clock tower again loomed into view, reminding Lim of Sam but also of Ili. For an instant he wondered where she might be. Then he glanced at Blanket, grateful to be sitting next to her on a warm fall night. He turned along the square as she pointed down the block to a frame house painted a crisp yellow. Light from the large windows spilled into the street.

"See the little house near the corner? That's The Breadbox, my favorite restaurant. The building was once a parsonage for the church across the street but they needed the space so they sold the house. The new owners moved it here, restored it and made it an eatery. They're good people, Lim. It's beautiful, isn't it?"

He nodded as he pulled to the curb.

"I hope they cook as well as they restore."

"That's why I wanted to bring you here, Lim. Their pecan pie and carrot cake is beyond belief. But I also wanted to share this place, one of my favorites, with you."

They stepped through the door into a bright, open hallway between two rooms, one a dining room, the other a gallery filled with paintings. The hardwood floor, polished to a high sheen, creaked beneath their feet as they crossed the dining room and found a table overlooking the lighted courtyard. They ordered both pie and cake, trading bites of each, and had just finished when a man wearing an apron and bifocals approached the table. He looked over his glasses at Blanket.

246

"Well, Blanket, your hand looks much better today. How does it feel?

She smiled at him, nodding across the table at Lim.

"Tim, this is Lim. Tim is one of the owners, Lim."

He looked from Blanket to Lim and back.

"Tim and Lim, Lim and Tim, I'm confused already. Welcome to the Breadbox, Lim. Blanket is showing you her favorite spots, is she?"

Lim raised his eyebrows in surprise. "That's a good guess."

"Are you kidding?" He waved off the comment. "All she ever talks about is bringing you here. I'm so relieved it's over so we can get back to having a normal conversation."

Blanket held up her hand. "By the way, my mashed finger is fine but thanks for asking."

"I'm glad to hear it. Even a macho girl like you can't work that big feed store with an injured appendage. Well, I have pies in the oven so I must be off. Come see us again, Lim… or is it Tim? See what you've done?"

He disappeared into the kitchen. A moment later the front door swung open with a bang and three men strode in, their boots thumping on the wooden floor. Blanket glanced up at the sound, a look of dread crossing her face. She took Lim's hand.

"Let's go, Lim. Let's go now. We can leave through the courtyard door. It's just behind me."

"What's the rush, Blanket?" He frowned at her. "I like this place. I'm glad you brought me here."

"I know but it's a nice night." She hunched over the table, facing him askance and nodding out the window. "Let's go see it. We'll come back again sometime."

Lim squinted at her, about to speak, when a voice sounded behind him. "Well, if it isn't the original wet blanket herself."

"You're funny, Watty Wells." She looked past Lim, disgust in her eyes.

"What sort of parent names their kid Blanket?"

Lim started to turn and she squeezed his hand, giving her head a slight shake.

"Go play with your friends, Watty."

Watty looked around the room, his voice just under a yell. "Can anyone give me a reason? I mean, why not name the brat something like Sheet or Towel?"

"Not that you've noticed, Watty, but we're trying to have a conversation here."

"Oh, really? Who're you out screwing tonight?"

Lim jumped from his chair and pivoted, facing the blonde-haired man he had seen with Blanket the night Ili left. The anger he thought long passed returned, welling up, filling his throat with bitterness. Lim moved toward him, his hands clinched, uncaring of what was to come next. Seeing the look in his eyes, Watty took a step back just as Blanket rounded the table, placing a hand on Lim's shoulder. She leaned toward him and whispered to the side of his face.

"No, Lim. You're better than this, better than people like him. I know how you feel about me. I can see it in your eyes just like you can in mine. You don't have to prove it.

She looked up at Watty. "You've had your fun. You should leave now."

He glanced at Lim and shook his head. "We came here for pie and we're going to have pie."

Lim stood still, statue-like, trying to corral his racing thoughts, feeling his anger barely under control. Watty squinted back as if daring him to make a move. An instant later, Tim appeared in the hallway, a huge metal spatula in his hand. He opened the door and pointed the flat end into the night.

"There is no pie, no cake, no ice cream and no party for people who forget how to be behave. Unless you want to find out what it feels like to be a pancake, you will leave our home this minute."

248

Watty started to speak but Tim swung the shining blade around, pointing it at him.

"Yes, yes, you may say this restaurant is open to the public, and it is, but it's also like home to us and our customers. We don't tolerate rudeness at home and neither should you. Now, leave us in peace."

Watty glared at Lim before stomping out the door without another word, followed by the others. Tim watched from the porch as their car disappeared around the corner. Then he turned to where Lim and Blanket stood together, motioning them to sit as he again vanished into the kitchen. A moment later, he appeared at the table with a bottle of cognac, pouring three glasses and sliding one in front of Lim.

"I'm so sorry you had to hear all that, especially on your first visit. This isn't much compensation but I hope it will make the memory of tonight a bit sweeter someday."

Lim lifted the glass with a shaking hand, still struggling to control his emotions. Ili, his house, his job, all he had lost flashed through his mind. He glanced at Blanket, downing the glass in one swallow, determined to keep his focus on the moment, on what he had gained. The warmth of the brandy moved through him and he took a breath, setting the glass on the table. Tim tilted the bottle into it again without hesitation.

"I'm sorry you don't care for this brand, Lim."

"I don't know what came over me." He took another breath. "I wanted to hurt him. I really wanted to."

Tim swirled the amber liquid in his glass before taking a sip. "Don't be too hard on yourself. Neanderthals like that bring out the animal in all of us. No one is immune from that part of themselves, Lim. Now, you two forget about those unfortunates and go out and enjoy this beautiful night."

# Twenty-five

Lim followed Blanket's direction to a bluff southwest of town, angling the truck to the edge before cutting the engine. Light from the courthouse tower rose dome-like into the warm night, casting the trees below them in gold filigree. Beyond, a crescent moon sat perched on the horizon. The pitched squeal of tires briefly drifted on the darkness, marking the still silence.

Blanket slid across the seat and leaned into Lim, kissing him without hesitation. He put his arms around her, pulling her to him, and as she moved to kiss him again, his hand slipped from her shoulder to her breast. She flinched, hesitating for an instant then pushing closer, her breath quickening. Lim melded to her, feeling her warmth, the softness of her hair, the heat of her skin.

A distant ringing pushed itself into his thoughts, harsh, repetitive, relentless. He tried to ignore it but Blanket pulled away from him, her hand against his chest, her eyes locking onto his. She looked around the cab for a moment as if unsure where she was. Then she blinked and sat up.

"That's your phone, Lim."

"Don't listen to it." He pulled her toward him.

"I can't do that." She pushed back. "It might be something important."

"But, Blanket..."

She shook her head. "I can't just sit here and act like I don't hear it."

"They can leave a message."

"It's late, Lim. It must be important for someone to call this time of night. You need to see who it is."

He sat up and stared at her for a moment. "You're probably right."

She smiled. "Things will go better if you just keep thinking that way."

He pulled his phone from beneath the seat. A moment later Vix's voice crackled in his ear.

"Lim, there's something wrong. It's Luster."

"How do you mean? Is he sick?"

"No, it's nothing like that."

"What then?"

"I just got a strange call from him."

"What did he say?"

"That's just it. All I heard was 'bookstore - tell Lim', and then the line went dead."

"Maybe there's a problem with his phone."

"Trust me on this, son. Something has happened. He didn't sound right."

"He did say he was meeting Orvis tonight. Do you think he was at the bookstore when he called?"

"I think it's likely. I want you to go there as quick as you can. Is Blanket still with you?"

He glanced at her, half-wishing he had let the phone ring. "She is."

"You'd best not take her with you. I have a bad feeling about this."


Lim dropped Blanket off at The Breadbox and headed north through the black night, trying to work out the meaning of Luster's call. Dim lights of distant ranches flickered among rough hills and canyons barely visible beneath the starlight. As he rounded a tight curve, the town appeared at once, the scattered buildings of downtown dim beneath the courthouse glow.

Pulling alongside the bookstore, he angled the truck in front of the entrance and climbed out. Light from the broad window stretched across the sidewalk. He pounded his fist on the door without answer then looked inside, seeing little of interest. Standing before the building, he tried to think what else he might do.

He had just turned back to the door when a light tapping sounded from inside the store. He jumped to the

251

window, peering past the book display into the room. Just beyond the entrance to the back shelves he spotted the toe of a shoe. The shoe shifted once and then again.

Lim leapt to the door, slamming it with his shoulder. Feeling no give he scanned the sidewalk, finding a pear-sized stone and hurling it through the window without hesitation. The glass disintegrated into the store. He jumped through and past the broken display. Just beyond the doorway, Luster sat propped against a shelf, his breathing ragged, his shirt soaked with blood. Lim bent to him, touching his shoulder. Luster opened his eyes, managing a weak smile.

"I knew you would come."

Lim pulled a handkerchief from his pocket, pressing it against Luster's chest while scanning the rows for Orvis. As he called an ambulance, Luster tugged at his shirt sleeve.

"I must tell you some things. Lean close so you can hear."

Lim bent toward him. "You don't need to talk. Help is on the way."

Luster waved him off. "Orvis saved me, Lim. You must know that."

"Where is he?"

"He's dead I'm afraid, near the office. Go check on him."

-Lim hurried to a small office to the left of the entrance. Orvis lay just inside the doorway in a pool of blood, a small revolver in his hand. Lim checked for a pulse, finding nothing. He rushed back to where Luster sat, his eyes closed, his face gray. He leaned close, fearing he would find no breath.

"Don't die on me, Luster. Not now, not after being gone for so long. Please don't die."

Luster stirred and opened his eyes, his breath coarse and shallow.

"Was he...?"

Lim nodded. "Who did this, Luster?"

He stared into the distance, speaking between breaths.

"Jorvic was waiting for us just inside the front door. He was after the Cantemir book. Thinking I had lied, he was convinced Orvis had it. The two of us showing up unexpectedly surprised him and he came at me but Orvis stepped in his path. When I tried to intervene, we both went down."

"How did you end up here?

"In the confusion, I was able to get up and away, but slowly. Jorvic left Orvis for dead but he wasn't. He grabbed the pistol he kept by the cash register and shot him as he returned to finish me."

"Jorvic is still here?"

Luster nodded toward a row of shelves as a trio of sirens came to life in the distance. An instant later, flashing lights filled the room.

"The last I saw of him, he was headed toward the back door."

Lim stood, leaning past the shelf and peering into the dim room. Suddenly, Jorvic appeared in the light of the rear doorway and paused, his arm covered in blood. He glared at Lim, his face defiant, before vanishing into the night. Then Luster's hoarse whisper sounded behind him.

"Stay with me, Lim. This may be our last chance to speak."

"Don't say that, Luster." Lim turned and knelt. "Help is almost here."

"But I must…"

Lim interrupted him. "Save your strength, Luster."

"But I have something important to say before they get here, something even more important than what you know."

"What could be more important?"

Luster leaned toward Lim, his breath labored. "Your mother is alive."

253

Lim drew back, staring at him. "What are you saying, Luster?"

"She lives not far from here, Lim. I've told Vix. He can tell you where. The rest you must discover for yourself."

His eyes rolled back in his head and he slumped against the shelf, his chest still.

"Luster! No, please... Luster!"

A hand threw Lim aside as paramedics rushed into the room. He fell back against the wall, unable to move, stunned at what he'd seen, what he'd heard. Someone near the back door called out an all clear but the meaning escaped him, his mind unwilling to move beyond Luster's words.

## Twenty-six

Lim awoke with a start and sat up, for a moment believing he was back in the bookstore, the ambulance lights still flashing around him. Sunlight sliced through the bedroom windows, cutting the floor in jagged lines. He squinted through the curtains at the shadows beyond the porch, the sun clearly high in the sky, and guessed it must be close to noon. Having stayed at the hospital until the early morning hours, he had returned home too exhausted even to undress.

He leaned back against the headboard, gazing into a day too bright, too full of expectation, his throat filling with the pain of Luster's death, the memory of the previous night coming back to him in waves, past belief, beyond understanding. Looking about the room, he wondered if even now he could trust what he knew. How could Orvis be alive when Luster was not? Did Jorvic escape or was he lying dead in some backroom hideout? Could his mother really be living nearby? If so, what was there to count on, to be certain of?

The aroma of coffee drifted into the room. Rolling off the bed, he wandered out the door and toward the kitchen, wishing Blanket was with him. She could him help clear his mind. As he stepped through the doorway, he looked up to find her standing before him, a plate of bacon in her hand. He blinked, unsure if he still wandered inside some dream. She studied him a moment before nodding toward the table.

"You're not awake yet. Coffee will help."

Lim stared at her. "What are you…?"

"Go on and sit. You need to have something to eat."

"You heard what happened?" He eased into a chair, his shoulder still sore.

She set two cups of coffee on the table and sat across from him, laying her hand on his.

"Bunk told me and I'm so sorry, Lim. That's why I'm here. He said to come over and fix you something before I go to work."

He ran a hand across his face. "I'm sorry our evening got interrupted... yet again."

"What are you saying, Lim? You just lost your uncle. We'll have plenty of other nights together."

"Will we, Blanket?"

"Of course we will." -She frowned at him. "Why would you say such a thing?"

"I don't know. Life is so unpredictable. I feel like I can't be sure of anything."

"Seeing what you did last night will do that to a person. It's only natural, Lim."

"I just can't believe he's gone, Blanket. None of it seems real."

"We all have trouble believing what's happened, Lim."

"It's not just what happened, it's what Luster told me."

He sat staring into space, lost in thought. Blanket rapped the table with her fingers.

"Well... what did he tell you, Lim?"

He peered into her eyes. "My mother is alive, Blanket."

She leaned back, puzzled by what she'd heard. "She didn't drown when you were a child?"

"Everyone thought she did but she's living somewhere not far from here. At least that's what Luster told me before he..."

He looked away, unable to finish. She lifted a hand, touching his cheek.

"You poor man. No wonder you look like a lost soul. What else do you know?"

"He said Vix could tell me where she is."

"Vix returned from the hospital a little while ago. He's out back with Rogelio and Cyril. After you eat something you can go ask him about her."

"I just can't believe Luster is gone and she's alive, Blanket. I feel like I'm dreaming."

"I don't doubt it, Lim."

"After all these years, she just turns up."

"I know it must be a lot to take in."

"I need your help, Blanket." Leaning across the table, he searched her face. "I can't get my thoughts sorted out. I don't know what I should do."

She took both his hands in hers, peering into his eyes.

"You go and see her, Lim."

He drove a wide street flanked by abandoned storefronts and dilapidated brick buildings, their windows boarded with warping plywood, and past the church he had spotted above the slim horizon miles before. The broad steeple pierced the pale sky like a blood-red stake. Beyond the church, a two-story building matching Vix's description sat atop a steep rise.

Following a gravel road up the hill, he passed rows of frame houses now gray with neglect. Across the street, a three-story building that once housed a parochial school stood empty, its open doorway and windows gaping, death-like. Discarded mattresses littered the overgrown yards, their sides split, the white stuffing spilling onto the ground. Hoping his destination would prove less bleak, Lim kept his eyes to the road.

He parked before a sign reading 'Hospital' and climbed out of the truck, walking beneath a stone archway and into a square courtyard filled with flowering plants and trees. A tiered fountain rose in the middle. Thin streams of water trickled into the pool below, the splashes echoing off the surrounding walls like distant bells. Above him, a blue and yellow balcony overlooked the garden from all four sides.

He surveyed the lower floor, noticing a red-bearded man in one corner, his head bandaged from jaw to crown. The man stared at him, a panicked look in his eyes, before disappearing into a narrow hallway. In the opposite corner, Lim spotted a door marked 'Office' just as a man in a white coat and glasses stepped out. Seeing him, the man ambled across the garden, his hands behind his back. He stopped before Lim and nodded, leaning back on his heels.

"May I help you?"

"My name is Lim Specter. I've come to see my mother."

The man removed his glasses, cleaning them with the corner of his coat. "Ah, yes, Mr. Specter. I am Mathias Schultheis, head physician for Saint Wilhelm's. We have been expecting you, your mother and I."

"What sort of a hospital is this, Dr. Schultheis?"

He peered over the top of his glasses. "You mean you don't know?"

"All I know is my mother, who I thought was dead, is alive and here."

"Your mother came to us many years ago, nineteen if I'm not mistaken. She is our oldest resident and somewhat of an institution."

"But why is she here? What's wrong with her?"

"Come with me, Mr. Specter."

He pivoted and began walking across the garden at a brisk pace. Lim hurried to catch up as he passed beneath an archway and up a winding set of stairs to the second floor hallway. At the end of the hall, they came to a large room filled with stools, easels and small tables scattered with brushes and tubes of paint. The air reeked of linseed oil and turpentine. Facing the front of the room, each easel carried a half-finished painting.

In the far corner a slight woman, her gray hair piled atop her head, stood before a large canvas. She appeared to be alone. Brush in hand, she moved across the painting in graceful motion. Lim stood in the doorway and watched her for a moment before facing the doctor, whispering as he nodded toward the corner.

"Am I supposed to believe that's my mother?"

"Mr. Specter, I see you are a skeptic."

Lim glanced into the room. "You would be too if you'd lived my life."

"Perhaps that is true. Nevertheless, your mother is there if you wish to see her."

"I have some questions first, but I feel strange talking about her as if she isn't here."

"When she paints, her concentration is such that she is completely unaware of her surroundings. We will have to work to get her attention away from her art and to your questions."

Lim glanced into the room before continuing. "What's wrong with her, Dr. Schultheis?"

He shrugged. "That depends on your perspective."

"She's not in bed, she's not in a wheelchair, she's not hooked up to a machine. I'll ask again, what sort of hospital is this?"

"Saint Wilhelm's is a mental health sanatorium."

"Are you saying my mother is crazy?" Lim took a step back, staring at him for a moment."

"I would never use such words to describe her. She is an amazing person and a gifted artist."

"Why is she here, then?"

"That is a difficult question, Mr. Specter. I could tell you she has a psychiatric condition. Call it schizophrenia, if you like, but that would fail to answer what brought her here. I am afraid only she can tell you that."

"You don't know?"

"I know that she came here after your father committed suicide and she had a breakdown of sorts. I also know she sent you to boarding school because she could no longer properly care for you."

"How did she get here?"

"Your Uncle Luster brought her to us."

"You mean Luster arranged this? That's hard to believe."

"Still, it is true."

"How did he pay for it?"

"He has handled the sales of your mother's paintings since she came here. Her art easily pays for her stay. She has an international reputation, you know. Her paintings command a great deal."

"If that's true, why doesn't she leave?"

"It is a fact that, unlike some of our residents, your mother was not an involuntary commitment. She has always been free to leave. Although I must admit I would have great concern if she chose to do so."

"She's here by choice? Why would she want that?"

"Some people are unable to face the world as it is, Mr. Specter. Beyond that, as I said, only she can answer. Now, come see her. You must stay for only a moment this first visit. Seeing you after all this time will be a bit overwhelming for her. But I do hope you will come again."

The doctor threaded through the easels to where she stood, Lim close behind. She seemed unaware of their presence as she dabbed paint on a portrait of a young woman. Lim stared at the luminous painting, the woman's face both beautiful and haunting. He stepped next to his mother as the doctor took her by the shoulders, turning her toward them little by little. She kept her gaze on the painting as long as she could manage before facing them, her eyes cast toward the floor.

Lim bent and peered at her, at first unable to find his mother in the unkempt gray hair, the pale face etched with lines. Then she looked up and he knew that instant he was looking into his mother's eyes. They had changed little. She looked at him askance, studying him a moment before facing the doctor.

"Is it really him, Dr. Schultheis? Is it my Lim?"

"Yes, Mary, it is him."

"Not the other one, the one that frightens me?"

"This is your son, Mary. Remember, I told you this might happen. He has come to see you. Now, I am going to leave but I'll be right outside."

The doctor nodded to them both and stepped away, disappearing through the door. She reached out, touching Lim's forearm with her fingertips.

"You are real, aren't you? Sometimes I'm not sure when a thing is real and when it isn't. Dr. Schultheis says it happens when I get too involved in my work."

"I'm real, mother. I'm here with you." Lim pulled up a stool, sitting opposite her.

"You used to call me mom, Lim. Please call me mom. Where have you been for so long?"

"I only just learned you were here."

"You just found out?"

"Luster told me."

"Yes, of course, now I remember." She put a hand to her forehead. "How silly of me. I would never let Luster tell anyone. Did he come with you?"

"Mom, there's something I need to…" He stopped himself.

"He came to me, Lim, and said he *had* to tell you, that your welfare depended on it."

"Why would he say that?"

"Because he loves you, Lim. He's always watched out for you."

"What do you mean? He ran off a long time ago."

"That doesn't matter. He's been watching over the both of us for years."

"How could he do that when he left like he did?"

"Luster is a magician, Lim."

"Please don't say that."

"Look what he did for me." She motioned about the room.

"He's just a person, a person like you and me."

"Well, I don't know about that but I'm glad he had you come see me. I don't know why it took you so long."

"You don't know why it took so long? I thought you had died, mom. We all did."

"Why would you think such a thing?"

"Don't you remember? You went out sailing and just disappeared."

She turned away. "Yes, well, I'm sure I must have had a reason to..."

"I was only a kid." He stood.

"I'm sure I..."

"How could you leave like that?"

She glanced at him, her face contorted. "Don't be angry with me, Lim."

The doctor appeared next to him, placing a hand on his shoulder.

"Perhaps we should continue this conversation later."

Lim peered at his mother, seeing the pain in her face.

"Yes, of course. It's time I should go."

She looked up at him, her face brightening. "Oh, yes, please do come back to see me, Lim."

"Well, I..."

"You will come again soon, won't you? Please promise you will."

He nodded, managing a weak smile. "I promise."

"You're such a handsome young man. I can still see my little Lim, but..."

The doctor nodded to him before taking her hand.

"I believe it's time for supper, Mary."

Lim watched them disappear into the hall, his mind filled with questions as he moved toward the door.

## Twenty-seven

Thin lines of shadow reached across the road as Lim drove from the small cemetery, soon moving into the open landscape beyond the town. Broken hills stretched before him, bluish beneath the clear light of afternoon. He stared out the windshield at the jagged horizon, ruminating on Luster's final moments, his complex yet circumscribed life sad but somehow inspiring. Questions about his past came at him from all sides.

Pulling up to the house, he cut the engine, the events of the past week still churning through his memory. All that happened had come into sharp relief after the funeral, memories he could now almost face in the full light of day. He climbed out of the truck as Vix stepped onto the porch. He peered at him from the top step.

"You've been to the gravesite?"

He nodded.

"I don't believe Luster would mind if you took a break from visiting, son."

"I was in town anyway, so I thought…"

He left the thought unfinished. Vix eyed him.

"Well, I have something I want to ask you."

"What is it?"

"Rogelio is moving out. Nelly offered him a good price on a cabin he owns down by the lake. Rogelio always wanted a place of his own and this house fits the bill. So, I thought you might like to move into the bunkhouse once he's out. You would be close to work and you wouldn't have to worry about an old man cramping your style."

Lim waved off the comment. "You don't cramp my style, Vix."

"A man needs his privacy now and then, especially when there's a pretty woman like Blanket in the picture. Am I wrong about that?"

"Well, no…"

"You'll take it, then?"

"I'll pay to rent it. That is, as soon as I make some money."

Vix shook his head. "Nonsense, we're partners and you need your own place. The rest will work itself out in time."

"But you could rent it out to someone else."

He pointed a finger at Lim. "Are you telling me you and Blanket don't need some time alone?"

"No, I just…"

"Then consider it settled. I don't want to hear any more argument."

"You won't get any argument from me, Vix. I appreciate the offer."

"I'm going to sit right here and watch the day unwind." Vix moved to a bench. "Have a seat. I have something else to say."

Lim mounted the stairs, sitting opposite him.

"Have you been to see your mother?"

"I went earlier this week."

"How did you find her?"

"Her memory isn't so good but she recognizes me. She was painting."

"Luster always said that's a good sign."

"I still haven't told her about him, Vix." Lim ran a hand through his hair. "I don't know how."

"Don't rush yourself, Lim. It'll come to you in time."

Lim nodded. "How much do you know?"

"I believe he told me most of the story. I've known about your mother for years."

"Why didn't he tell me about her sooner?

Vix faced him. "He wanted to, Lim. He knew it was hard on you."

"All that time, I thought she was dead."

"You have to understand, it was not his decision to make. Besides, he loved your mother and wasn't likely to betray her no matter the reason."

"He loved her that much?"

264

"He brought her to the house more than once before she met your father. I figured for sure they'd tie the knot. I believe she led him to think so too, maybe even believed it herself. But it wasn't to be. They were out on the porch when she told him she was getting married. He took it well, better than I would have. After she drove off, he stood there staring out at the road for an hour or more.

"I could've ended up with Luster as my father." Lim leaned back in his chair, imagining the scene.

"It's funny you should say that. You came along so soon he even wondered it himself."

"He thought he might be my father?"

"The timing was that close. That's why he always insisted on having you call him uncle."

"I gave him hell about that."

"There's something else you need to know, Lim." Vix leaned toward him. "I'm figuring he didn't tell you."

"What is it?"

"After your mother went into the hospital, he had a breakdown of his own."

"He told me. He became some sort of offbeat, pleasure-seeking monk."

"That's not the whole story. There was a time when he barely knew his own name. I thought for sure he was going to end up like your father."

"Luster, kill himself?" Lim stared at him, startled at the idea. "That's hard to imagine."

"He was living at the house then. He seemed not himself, in his own world and not able to do much of anything. I let it go for awhile but when he started talking I knew for sure something was wrong, bad wrong. His mind was broken as a dropped egg. We got him to a headshrinker straightaway but had to keep a close eye on him for a good while."

"He was that bad?"

"He was smart as a whip, you know. I've seen him read a whole book in a night and tell you every detail the

265

next morning. But he was a real concern for a time. Eventually, he snapped out of it and returned to his old self."

"He didn't tell me, Vix." Lim sat back, struggling to bring this new image of Luster into focus.

"I'm not surprised. If there's anyone he wanted to think well of him, it's you."

"You could've fooled me."

"That was just his way, Lim. He's responsible for your name, you know."

He snorted. "I should've guessed."

"When you were born, he said you were like a poem in the flesh. But he suggested limerick because he didn't want you to take yourself too seriously."

"There was never much chance of that."

"Luster may have been a little on the odd side but don't ever doubt that he loved you like a son."

"I never looked at him that way, Vix."

"It's time you did. And it's time you remember it matters."

"I'd like to understand Luster and all that's happened but there's so much I don't know."

Vix studied him for a moment.

"Lim, I'm going to tell you a story as best I can remember it. Then you can know what questions you might have."

Lim sat up as Vix took a breath, his face grim.

"Luster fell in love with your mother the moment he met her, long before your father came along, and he never stopped being in love with her. But then she met your father and they got married and a little while later you were born. Life was good for a time but your father had a depression that worsened year by year. Eventually, he got to be almost unreachable, even to your mother.

"Then one summer night Luster went for a visit and found your mother in her bedroom, wet-eyed and distraught. She told him your father had left that night without a word. She seemed so upset he couldn't help but try to comfort her. Before he realized what he'd done they were in bed."

Lim peered at him. "Luster slept with my mother after she was married?"

"It only happened the one time but it was their undoing. After that night, he stayed around to be close to her but she was changed, strange and distant. Then when your father died, she felt responsible even though he had long struggled with the depression. Luster couldn't help but feel the same guilt. He believed his love for your mother, even though acted on only that once, had played a part in your father's death; that his feelings for her had somehow added to your father's sadness.

"Soon after that your mother started on a downward path, unable to maintain a normal life for you even though she tried her best. One day her mind just went and she drove to the lake. She had no memory of what had happened when Luster found her wandering the shoreline with thirty pounds of rocks in her clothes, the sailboat nowhere in sight."

"She was going to kill herself too?"

"It seems so if Luster hadn't come along in time. She knew of the hospital and asked him to take her there and promise he would never tell anyone. Since she had no family left other than you, a child, he saw no choice but to do as she wished. He believed it would be for a short while only. But as time passed he could see she would not get better anytime soon.

"He arranged for you to go to boarding school and paid for it with his savings. But after awhile the money began running out, both your mother's and Luster's. He was nearly out of ideas when he realized he might be able to sell her paintings. That's when he met Sam. They got on right away and pretty soon he fell in love with her.

"He still loved your mother, of course, but by that time he had faced up to how serious her condition was.

267

With Sam's help he began to market the paintings to major dealers. Sales were slow at first and the money was nearly gone. So he forged the book, got caught and went on the run, breaking Sam's heart in the process.

"Fortunately, the agent he had engaged to represent your mother started to sell more and more paintings. The proceeds went into a trust that paid for your schooling and you mother's care. Luster kept an eye on things from a distance, afraid any more involvement would somehow ruin it. He felt he had done too much damage to the people he loved. I think he truly believed he had to remove himself from the world before he did any more harm.

"Then everything changed when he was able to free Ili. He knew he had to do the same for Mirela. Something had been telling him to seek you out and all of a sudden he had a reason. He needed your help. I believe you know the rest. He hoped, with time, you'd find a way to forgive him for the mistakes he had made."

Lim sat back, staring at nothing, trying to understand all he had heard. Seeing his struggle, Vix clasped his shoulder.

"It's a lot to take in, I know. But I believe Luster would want you to hear it."

Lim turned to him. "I hated him for a time, Vix, both him and my parents. I know it sounds cold but it's the truth."

"That's only natural, Lim. You relied on them and they let you down." Vix squinted at him. "How about now?"

"He just left, Vix. I was only a kid and he left me. I had no one."

"He had to go away, Lim. He didn't have much choice in the matter. You know that."

"But he could've stayed in touch."

"He said you sent back his letters."

"He should've tried harder. I was just a kid."

"He went to the school but you refused to see him."

268

"Like I said, I hated him. Now I know I had good reason."

Vix sighed and stood. "I've said what I had to say. I reckon now you'll have to find your own answers, Lim."

"But how do I, Vix? How can I forgive him when my own life is such a failure?"

"The past is gone, Lim. You can't change it. I can't change it. We just go forward, try to let go of what's done and find our way day by day."

## Twenty-eight

A breeze swirled through the vines, carrying a slight hint of autumn in its damp chill, the rustle of leaves, grass gone to seed. Lim breathed in the clear air before leaning into the bed of the truck and pulling out a thick roll of irrigation hose. He let it drop at the end of a row. A few rows down, Rogelio stood holding a half dozen stakes as Vix bent to mark out the section of new vines they would plant before spring.

Vix paused and stood, looking up the hill toward the house, the porch and stairs just visible over the low rise. Following his gaze, Lim watched as Blanket mounted the top stair and stepped to the door, her sun-streaked hair shining in the midday light. He wondered what had brought her there and considered calling out to her but knew at that distance she would never hear him.

An instant later another figure appeared, moving through the gate and across the broad pasture separating the house from the road. Lim squinted at the man, a wave of fear passing through him, and then pivoted, scanning highway south of the vineyard. A black sedan sat parked along the roadside, partially hidden behind a thicket of scrub. He turned back to the house, watching as Blanket moved along the porch, peering into the windows. Vix appeared beside him, Rogelio close behind. Lim pointed up the hill.

"Vix, it's Jorvic."

"It is the bastard that tried to burn me?" Rogelio dropped the stakes. "Give me the keys and I will go kill him."

Rogelio started for the truck. Lim grabbed his arm. "No, Rogelio, honk the horn. We have to warn her."

Vix shook his head. "There's no time. Hand me my rifle."

Lim shifted his gaze to the house. Blanket was tapping on one of the porch windows, unaware of Jorvic's approach. Rogelio reached into the cab, pulling out a scarred, bolt-action hunting rifle and a handful of shells. He handed them to Vix before glancing at Lim, his voice just above a whisper.

"The house, we are too far I think, Vix."

Jorvic stepped onto the bottom stair as Vix slipped a shell into the chamber and leaned against the side of the truck.

"I'll just have to make do, then."

He squeezed the trigger and the barrel jumped above the truck rail, the report moving down the highway in a roll of echoes. An instant later, the porch light exploded above Jorvic's head, showering him with glass. He fell to the floor then scrambled down the steps, disappearing down the hill.

Vix swiveled, pointing the rifle toward the black sedan. Two more blasts echoed down the valley in quick succession, the car lurching as the passenger side tires blew out. He lifted his phone from his shirt pocket, handing it to Rogelio.

"Call the sheriff while I make sure our friend doesn't turn back toward the house after he realizes what I did to his car."

Without hesitating Lim hopped into the truck, speeding along the vineyard and across the highway toward the house. He slid to a stop, jumping from the cab and rushing up the stairs to where Blanket crouched at the end of the porch. She looked up at him, her eyes wide.

"Lim, get down! Someone is shooting at the house."

He bent to her, taking her hand and pulling her up.

"It's alright, Blanket. I believe Vix is finished with target practice."

"Vix did that?" She squinted at him. "Why would he shoot at his own house? And who was that poor man I saw running off? He must be scared out of his wits."

In the distance, sirens blared to life.

"I hope so. He's the man who stabbed Luster."

"The man who… what was he doing here?"

"He probably wanted to complete the job by getting rid of his only witness."

"Lordy, Lim, and I just happened to come along. What would he have done?"

"Let's not think about it, Blanket. He's finished now."

"Oh, mercy, I'm feeling a little lightheaded."

Blanket grabbed the rail, slumping onto the top step. Lim sat next to her as the sheriff's cruiser and two highway patrol cars raced past.

"You should rest a moment. It's not every day you get shot at."

The jeep rolled to a stop in front of the porch and Vix climbed out, Rogelio following close behind, talking with every step.

"You can admit to your old friend if you missed, and I know you had to, Vix."

Vix ignored him. "I never did like that light."

"Nobody can shoot a damn rifle that far and hit what they aim at."

"I'm glad to be rid of it. I'll have to ask Blanket to help me pick out a new one."

As they approached the steps, Rogelio waved his finger at Lim.

"Tell him, Lim. Vix, he claims he meant to shoot that damn light instead of the damn firebug. I tell him he missed but he won't admit to it."

"Well, he did win the turkey shoot in El Consuelo three times."

"That don't mean nothing." Rogelio shook his head. "Nobody down there can shoot worth a damn."

Vix waved off the comment. "I was lucky the wind is as light as it is today. If a breeze had come up I might have hit that black-haired feller and then where would I be? I'll tell you where. I'd be spending the next six months filling out papers and answering questions. I'm too busy for that. We have a vineyard to tend to. Isn't that right, Blanket?"

She looked up, blinking at him. "What?"

"I'm sorry I surprised you like I did." He leaned toward her. "I didn't have much choice if I wanted to keep that man away from you. Still, I reckon a rifle shot out of nowhere will rattle anyone's senses. We'll take our argument inside so you and Lim can have some time to yourselves."

They sat together as white puffs of cloud drifted above the horizon, their shadows casting the hills in a patchwork of indigo and violet. Without a word, Blanket took Lim's hand in hers, cradling it in her lap. Then she took a breath and faced him.

"Don't worry, Lim, I'm alright. I just needed a moment to collect myself."

"That's understandable."

She peered into his eyes. "I'm not some helpless female, you know."

"I know you can take care of yourself, Blanket. I've always admired that about you."

"Are you just saying so to make me feel better?"

"No, it's the truth."

"I can be there for you if you need me, Lim."

"I know you can, Blanket."

"Good, and don't you forget it." She stood, pulling him to his feet. "But next time I come visit, I'm going to make sure there aren't any killers lurking about."

"Let's hope you won't have to. What brought you out here, anyway?"

"What brought me…? Oh, yes, I have something to show you, something important."

"Where is it? Show it to me now."

"I can't show it to you just like that. We need to set a time for me to show you."

"Why not now?"

"It's not something you can carry around. It's something big."

"Something big and mysterious, I'd say."

A chill breeze wafted through the windows as Lim ambled across the living room floor. The air smelled of autumn. He squinted through the screen door, the horizon a thin veil of blue against the morning sky. Down the slope, Rita moved Rogelio's small herd of goats toward the practice pen as he stood by watching. In the crisp air, strands of sunlight danced among the live oaks, flecking the grass with gold.

He paused at the door. Down the porch, Vix leaned forward in the rocking chair, resting his foot on the porch rail and inspecting his big toe. A boot and sock sat on the floor next to him. Twisting the top off a small jar, he held it up to the light before dipping his finger into the green paste and smearing it across his toenail. He eased back in the chair with a sigh. Lim stifled a laugh as he stepped through the door.

"So, when did you start painting your toenails, Vix?"

"Not that I have to explain myself, but this here is medicine."

"To tell the truth, it's not your color."

"You wouldn't make fun if it was your toe that was giving you fits." Vix set the bottled aside. "I dropped a roll of wire on it and I can hardly walk."

"That is some nasty looking medicine, if medicine is what it is."

"That shows what you know. This remedy of Cyril's makes walking almost tolerable."

"Cyril's been out to visit?"

"If you weren't off with Blanket all the time you might've seen her."

"She's come by more than once?"

"Let's see, she brought out some soup, and then she came by to talk over planting some lavender next to the vineyard."

"She sure is friendly. I wonder what else she has planned for you."

Vix stood, grabbing the boot and sock before making his way toward the door.

"You best mind your own business."

He disappeared inside. A moment later, Sam's car pulled up to the house, Orvis in the passenger seat. Sam climbed out, walking around to the passenger door and waiting for Orvis to take her hand. Instead he waved her off, pulling himself up and stepping past her, a silver-tipped cane at his side. As Lim watched them he wondered at the strange attachment to Orvis he now felt, his anger over the betrayal having given way to gratitude for trying to save Luster. Was forgiveness of all things possible? Shaking his head at the thought, he let it go and walked down the steps to meet them.

"What brings you out this way?"

As Orvis neared the house Sam grabbed his elbow. "Let me help."

"I'm not an invalid, Sam. I can walk."

"You're just trying to show off for Lim."

Lim peered at him. "He doesn't look a day over ninety."

"Don't encourage her, Lim. We men are supposed to stick together."

"I can't help but worry, Orvis." Sam released her grip. "We nearly lost you..."

"Yes, well, I'm not going anywhere, Sam."

"Good, now tell Lim why you're here."

He reached into his pocket and pulled out an envelope, handing it to Lim.

"This is meant for you. I'm not sure why they delivered it to me."

Lim studied the address. "Maybe because all that's here are my name and the name of the town."

Orvis nodded at the letter. "Aren't you going to open it? My curiosity is killing me."

Lim tore open the seal and pulled out a single sheet of paper, taking a moment to read it.

"It's from my ex-neighbor, Carson Philbank. He says the charges against me were dropped and my ex-boss is in jail."

He stared at the paper then stuffed it in his pocket. Sam leaned toward him.

"That's good news, isn't it, Lim?"

"I suppose so. I was just thinking how long ago it all seems."

"Time does change things, just as it changes us. Speaking of change, Orvis has some news of his own. I'm going to go see what Vix is up to."

Lim squinted at him. "You're not going on a quest for the Jefferson library, are you?"

"That would've been tempting once but nearly dying has changed my priorities. I've decided to spend my time reading books instead of selling them."

"What on earth are you talking about, Orvis?"

"My son is taking over the bookstore. After all that happened, I've lost my taste for it."

Lim stepped back, a look of surprise on his face. "Now I'm the one starting to worry."

"The agreement suits us both. He has legitimate work and I get a percentage of the sales for doing nothing. After ten years, he owns it free and clear.

"No book deals with foreign mobs?"

"Not unless they're done from prison."

"I assume it includes Sam."

"Yes, that she would take me back is a miracle, true enough."

Lim shook his head, eyeing him. "You're starting to sound like Luster."

A smile crossed his lips. "Miracles exist if you're open to them, Lim."

"So he liked to say."

"Then you see them too?"

"I suppose so, if I think about it. My mother is alive. Ili found her sister. You should be dead but here you stand. There is something of the miraculous in all that."

Orvis nodded. "Much has changed, Lim, for good or ill."

Vix swung open the door and leaned out. "Rogelio has got a mess of migas on the stove. You two want some breakfast?"

Lim shook his head. "I have somewhere to go."

Gold (gōld) - a yellow precious metal, the chemical element of atomic number 79; something regarded as having great value or goodness.

## Twenty-nine

Lim watched the hills drift past his window, his thoughts turning to Luster. He had said he came back because he needed his help but Lim wondered if the opposite was true. What would have become of him if not for Luster showing up when he did? He had to admit there was a bit of magic in his timing.

Blanket reached across the seat, taking his hand in hers and pulling him from his thoughts as they passed the entrance to a large cattle ranch, the metal sign above the gate reading 'The Hills of Ivan'. Crossing a narrow bridge, the river below running a muddy brown, they paralleled a tree-studded ridge overlooking a broad valley, the two-lane road carving a long semicircle between the hills.

Past the ridge, the land opened out onto a sloping field bisected by a low stone wall. The pasture stretched uphill to the base of a limestone cliff where a white frame house stood surrounded by live oaks. Blanket angled the truck through the gate, bumping toward the house in cloud of red dust.

She set the brake and climbed out, surveying the field as if she'd never seen it before. Lim watched her turn a slow circle, the sunlight glinting off her hair, and wondered why she might bring him to this place. He looked beyond her to the wide slope scattered with stones, and then to the neglected house, the peeling paint, the missing shingles. Weeds grew thick beneath the massive trees. Behind the house, an unpainted barn sat within feet of the bluff, the weathered wood dark against the white limestone.

Having completed the circle, Blanket reached out and took his hand, leading him up the steps and onto the porch. The worn flooring creaked beneath their feet. She leaned against the rail, again gazing out over the broad sloping pasture and to the ragged horizon beyond. A flock of egrets, brilliant white against the cloudless sky, raced over the treetops before disappearing from view. She spoke, still facing the field.

"How do you like this view, Lim? It's beautiful, isn't it? On a clear day you can see all the way to the lake through that gap in the hills."

He peered at the horizon. "If I'm not mistaken, they call that Gunsight Pass."

"So, what do you think?" She faced him, her eyes smiling.

"What do I think of what?"

She swept her arm above the rail. "The trees, the field, the house, how do you like it?"

"The pasture has a nice look, climbing up to the bluff like it does. And these are some big trees."

"And what about the house?" She faced the house.

"The house... well, the house is quaint in a shabby sort of way."

"This house is not shabby, Lim." She frowned at him. "There's nothing wrong that a little paint won't fix."

"The roof has seen better days."

"Okay, the house needs paint *and* shingles. But you can imagine what it could be, can't you?"

He closed his eyes. "If I try real hard I can. I see... I see... lots of work."

"Oh, Lim, aren't you the least bit curious why I brought you here?"

"Alright, Blanket, I give. Why are we here?"

"This farm belonged to my grandfather and he willed it to my mother." She turned a circle, her eyes shining. "After my daddy died, mama and I would sometimes come out here for the weekend. But then she married a rich guy from Las Vegas and we never visited anymore. She just let it go to pot. I guess she's too busy gambling or whatever it is rich people do to care about it anymore. So, Bunk talked her into giving it to me."

Lim looked up and down the porch. "This house belongs to you?"

"Not just the house but the whole property." She pointed down the broad slope. "Think of it, Lim. That big field is perfect for a vineyard."

"Wait a second, Blanket." He took a step back. "Are you telling me you want to start a vineyard here?"

"We have a sloping field, well-drained and full of limestone, and access to groundwater. There's even a spring back behind the barn. To top it off, the field has a stone wall just like the ones in France."

"Blanket, planting a vineyard is a big risk. A million things can go wrong."

"Don't be such a worrier, Lim. I had the soil tested and it's about as good as you're going to find."

"But vines aren't cheap."

"I've done the math and it's doable. Bunk has agreed to loan the startup money. Everything has come together just so. It's a miracle, isn't it?"

He leaned against the rail and nodded. "That's just what I'd call it, Blanket, a miracle."

"You see now? Luster was right."

"Oh, no, you're not going to start with the magic and miraculous, are you?"

"Miracles do happen, Lim. You're standing in the middle of one."

He turned, peering down the long slope before reaching into his pocket and pulling out the silver button she had given him.

"If you're going to start a vineyard, you'll need some luck."

She stepped next to him. "Start it with me, Lim."

"What are you saying, Blanket?" He searched her face.

"Well, we have to consider the future. We could try some heat-tolerant varieties, get out ahead of the pack in finding what works best here. We don't have to plant what everyone else is…"

281

He interrupted. "I mean… what about me and you? What are you saying about us, our future?"

She studied him for a moment. "I'm saying there's nothing I like more than being with you, Lim Specter. I'm saying that when I look toward the future, I like seeing you in it, here in this place. But let's not say anymore than that just now. I don't want to scare you off. This is a chance to start something new, Lim, our chance. Let's do it together."

"Blanket, I…"

"Shhh…"

She cupped her hands around his face.

"I believe this is the best view of all."